123 篇商務會話
10 大情景單元
10 大職場貼士
3000+ 個運用技巧

# 自學商務英語

## 實況溝通 123 篇

明朗兒　編著

# 前言 Foreword

做白領吃四方飯，難免要有幾句英語會話傍身。職場就如弱肉強食的森林，競爭者漫山遍野，惟有能說會道、實事求是才是勝出的不二法門。如果接聽英語來電都要人代勞，他朝難保自己也會被人取代！最簡單的惡補方法，就是看書聽講！

本書為各位白領新手及精英而設，分十章共百多個商務會話情景，包括面試、電話、開會、推銷、議價、談判等等，包羅萬有，自學必備。

各情景都有特定的說話對象，概分四類：

1. 一般（平輩、同級）
2. 對上（下級對上級）
3. 對下（上級對下級）
4. 對外（面對生意夥伴或顧客）

此外，部分話題更附同義句、反義句、近義句、例句應用、商務貼士，方便讀者觸類旁通。

本書錄音由駐港外籍英語老師朗讀，語音文件根據頁碼命名和分段。譬如第 31 頁的語音文件，檔案名稱為 031.mp3，並以標明。

**使用說明**

同 同義示例
反 反義示例
類 類似示例
例句應用
商務貼士

# 目錄

## Chapter 3 內部會議



## Chapter 4 工作權益

# 目錄 Contents

## Chapter 5 聊天與流言



## Chapter 6 商務招待

## Chapter 7 商務往來



## Chapter 8 營銷宣傳

# 目錄

## Chapter 9 危機應對



## Chapter 10 商務談判

# Chapter 1

# 應徵求職

# 面試通知（對外）

010.mp3

| | |
|---|---|
| 您早，我是瑪莉，活力公司的行政助理。 | Good morning. This is Mary, administrative assistant calling from Dynamic Co. Ltd. |
| 我們想邀請你來面試，是關於編輯職位的面試。 | We'd like to invite you for a job interview regarding the editor position. |
| 我們收到你的履歷。<br>我們有興趣認識你多一些。 | We've received your resume.<br>We're interested in knowing more about you. |
| 請你讓我們認識你可以嗎？ | Would you please let us know about you? |
| 請問可否介紹你自己？ | Can you please introduce yourself? |
| 我剛好看到你的履歷。 | I got the chance to look at your resume. |
| 如你的履歷所述，你曾在旅行社工作。<br>你能夠告訴我關於你在旅遊界的工作經驗嗎？ | As described in your resume, you have worked in a travel agency.<br>Could you tell me about your work experience in the travel industry? |
| 聽起來你有處理顧客特別要求的經驗。 | It sounds you're experienced in handling customers' special requests.<br>藉着電話面試，作初步篩選。 |
| 我想下週見你。<br>你下週有空嗎？ | I'd like to meet you next week.<br>Are you available next week? |

| | |
|---|---|
| 謝謝你的時間。 | Thank you for your time. |
| 你看來是正確人選。 | You seem to be a right person for us. |
| 你好像是我們正尋找那類人。 | You're likely the type of person we're looking for. |
| 我想跟你預約面試。 | I'd like to set up an interview with you. |
| 你可以在五月十五日九點半來到我們的辦公室嗎？ | Could you come to our office at 9:30 on May 15th? |
| 你知道我們的位置嗎？ | Do you know our location? |
| 接近太子港鐵站。 | It is close to the Prince Edward MTR station. |
| 面試前會有筆試。 | There'll be a written test before the interviews. |

There'll be a...... before the interview.
面試前，會有……
There'll be an aptitude test before the interview.
面試前，會有習性測驗。
There'll be an online test before the interview.
面試前；會有在線測驗。

| | |
|---|---|
| 很快再見。 | See you soon. |
| 下週見。 | See you next week. |

Experience 經驗
Resume 履歷
Written test 筆試
Aptitude test 習性測驗

# D 應通知（對上）

012.mp3

| | |
|---|---|
| 對，我是。 | Yes, speaking. |
| 啊，我蠻好，你好嗎？ | Oh hi, great, how are you? |
| 我不錯耶。 | I'm pretty good.<br>雖然來電者素未謀面，也可以盡量表現親切。 |
| 星期五我有空。 | Friday sounds good to me.<br>同 Friday is good to me. |
| 謝謝你讓我介紹自己。 | Thank you for letting me to introduce myself. |
| 我已當了市場主任 3 年。 | I've been a marketing officer for 3 years. |
| 對，正如我的履歷描述，我在 5 年前修讀一個文憑課程。 | Right, as stated in my resume, I took a diploma course 5 years. |
| 我知道這樣聽起來很直接，但我只想省下你的時間。 | I know I sound straight forward. But I just want to save your time. |
| 這份工作的薪酬範圍是多少？ | What is the salary range for the job? |
| 請問你是否有機會詳細看完我的履歷？ | Did you have a chance to read through my resume completely? |
| 我的履歷裏面有甚麼東西令你想打電話找我？ | What on my resume made you want to call me?<br>直接在電話面試時問一些問題，因為有些大公司根本沒有看過應徵者的履歷，便一次過大量邀請應徵者，可能只是安排 10 分鐘的面試，只為了符合人事部的要求；所以，如果對方根本沒有看過你的履歷，或答不上為甚麼會挑選你，那麼，你可考慮是否接受面試的安排了。 |

013.mp3

| | |
|---|---|
| 我樂意告訴你關於我的細節。 | It's my pleasure to tell you more about myself in detail. |
| 當然，我非常樂於當面見你。 | Sure, I'm more than happy to meet you in person. |
| 跟你會面真好。 | That's very nice meeting you. |
| 很高興能探索在你公司工作的機會。 | That's great to explore the job opportunity in your company. |
| 好的，我在三月十日有空。 | Yes, I'm available on March 10. |
| 請問我可以有你的電話嗎？以防萬一。 | May I have your number please? Just in case. |
| 我可以確定一次你辦公室的地址嗎？ | Can I confirm the address of your office? |
| 附近有地鐵站嗎？ | Is it near a subway station? |
| 如何乘巴士到你的辦公室？ | How can I get to your office by bus? |
| 你們位處哪個主要路口？ | Where is the main intersection you are located? |
| 那將會是甚麼面試模式？ | What kind of the interview format would it be? |
| 謝謝你的來電，到時見。 | Thank you very much for your call. See you soon. |

MTR station 港鐵站
Main intersection 主要路口
Interview format 面試模式

# 主持面試（對下）

014.mp3

| | |
|---|---|
| 您早，我是南施，市務部副經理。 | Good morning, I'm Nancy, deputy manager of marketing. |
| 你今天好嗎？ | How are you doing today? |
| 我很好，謝謝。 | I'm great, thank you. |
| 讓我來介紹自己。 | Let me introduce myself. |
| 請坐。 | Please take a seat. |
| 今天真美麗。 | It's so beautiful today. |
| 天氣愈來愈暖。 | The weather is getting warm. |
| | 在正式進行面試前，先寒暄破冰。 |
| 正如你所知，我們在找最適合這空缺的人。 | As you know, we're looking for the best person for this position. |
| 我想了解你。 | I'd like to know about you. |
| 請介紹你自己。 | Tell me about yourself. |
| | Tell me a little more about......<br>告訴我一點多關於……<br>Tell me a little more about your experience.<br>告訴我一點多關於你的經驗。<br>Tell me a little more about your achievement.<br>告訴我一點多關於你的成就。<br>Tell me a little more about your participation in volunteer activities.<br>告訴我一點多關於你參與義工活動方面。 |
| 請把你最近的工作經驗告訴我。 | Please tell about your recent work experience. |
| 你期望一份需要公幹的工作嗎？ | Do you expect a job involving travel? |

015.mp3

| | |
|---|---|
| 你介意到國外工作嗎？ | **Would you mind working abroad?**<br>不要把 abroad 跟 aboard 混淆，aboard 的意思是上船、車或飛機。<br>同 Would you mind working in other countries?<br>Would you mind work trips in other countries? |
| 你介意告訴我們，你現在掙多少塊？ | **Would you mind telling us how much you are currently earning?**<br>同 Would you mind telling us how much you are now earning? |
| 關於輪班工作，你覺得如何？ | **How do you feel about shift work?**<br>How do you feel about......<br>關於……你覺得如何？<br>How do you feel about flexible work hours?<br>關於彈性工作時間你覺得如何？<br>How do you feel about night shift?<br>關於夜更工作，你覺得如何？<br>How do you feel about overtime work?<br>關於超時工作，你覺得如何？ |
| 你對薪金期望有多少？ | **What are your salary expectations?**<br>Expectation 是名詞，它的動詞是 expect，見下句。 |
| 你可否告訴我，你期望有多少薪金？ | **Could you please tell me what you would be expecting for a salary?**<br>除了薪金，也會問及員工福利或津貼。例句：<br>Can you tell me what you are looking for in compensation package?<br>Can you tell me what you are looking for in fringe benefit?<br>（你可否告訴我你想有甚麼福利？） |
| 你跟同事相處得怎麼樣？ | **How did you get along with co-workers?**<br>類 你跟同事如何好好合作？<br>How did you work well with co-workers? |
| 你適合團隊工作嗎？ | **Are you a team player?** |

# 離職原因（對下）

016.mp3

| | |
|---|---|
| 你前一份工作是甚麼？ | What was your last job?<br>同 What was your previous job? |
| 你現時職位是甚麼？ | What is your current position?<br>同 What is your present position? |
| 為甚麼你辭掉舊工作？ | Why did you leave your last job? |
| 你從前職中學了甚麼重要的東西？ | What was the important thing you've learned from the previous job? |
| 你曾否被辭退工作？ | Have you ever gotten fired from a job? |
| 你曾否因為在工作上犯錯而失去工作？ | Have you ever lost a job because of some problems you had on the job? |
| 之前你在哪裏工作？ | Where did you work before?<br>類 What did you do before?<br>你之前做甚麼的？ |
| 你現時的工作幹了多久？ | How long have you worked at your present job? |
| 為甚麼你想辭掉現時的工作？ | Why do you want to leave your current job? |
| 你覺得前一份工作有哪方面令你最不愉快？為甚麼？ | What about your last job did you enjoy the least? Why? |

| | |
|---|---|
| 你會怎樣形容你之前的上司？ | How would you describe your previous supervisor?<br>How would you describe your......?<br>你會怎樣形容你……？<br>How would you describe your previous manager?<br>你會怎樣形容你之前的經理？<br>How would you describe your direct boss?<br>你會怎樣形容你的直屬上司？<br>How would you describe your team leader?<br>你會怎樣形容你那組的領導人？ |
| 你之前的上司會怎樣形容你？ | How would your last employer describe you? |
| 你沒有工作多久？ | How long have you been out of work? |
| 自從你離職後，你做甚麼？ | What did you do since you've lost the previous job?<br>同 What did you do since you've quit the previous job?<br>自從你離職後，你做甚麼？ |
| 前一份工作職位有哪方面令你最不愉快？ | Which aspects of the job did you not enjoy in your last position? |

current/present position 現時職位　previous/last job 前職
direct boss 直屬上司

# 工作經驗（對下）

018.mp3

| | |
|---|---|
| 告訴我關於你過往在這方面的工作經驗。 | Tell me about your previous experience in this kind of work. |
| 我想知道你處理海外訂單方面有多少經驗。 | I'd like to know how experienced you are in handling orders from overseas. |
| 列舉你做得較好的兩、三樣事情。 | Describe two or three things that you have done well. |
| 你的經驗跟這項職位有甚麼關係？ | How do your experience relate to this position?<br>How do your...... relate to this position?<br>你的……跟這項職位有甚麼關係？<br>How do your working skills relate to this position?<br>你的工作技能跟這項職位有甚麼關係？<br>How do your language skills relate to this position?<br>你的語言技巧跟這項職位有甚麼關係？ |
| 你工作時曾經使用過哪類軟件？ | What kind of software have you worked with? |
| 你之前用過這軟件嗎？ | Have you used this software before? |
| 你學習新技能有多快？ | How fast do you learn new skills?<br>類 How long does it usually take you to learn new skills? 通常你需要多久才把新技能上手？ |
| 你參與蠻多義工活動。你可否告訴我為甚麼你那麼投入？ | You've participated in quite a lot of volunteer activities. Can you tell me why you got involved in these? |

Language skills 語言技巧　　Volunteer activities 義工活動

# 處境問題（對下）

019.mp3

| | |
|---|---|
| 如果上司派任務給你但不給任何指示，你該如何準時完成？ | If your supervisor assigns you a task without any instructions, how would you finish it on time? |
| 若你急需做一個決定，但碰巧上司不在，那麼你會怎樣做呢？ | If you have to make a decision when your supervisor is away, what would you do then? |
| 如果你的意見跟主管相左會如何？ | What if your opinions are different from your supervisor's? |
| 你的主管有否説過你應該跟他的方法？你怎樣回應？ | Did your supervisor ever say that you should follow his way? How did you respond? |
| 你可否描述一個處於工作壓力下的情況，你又怎樣處理？ | Can you describe a situation when you were working under pressure and how you handled it?<br>類 Please describe a difficult situation you handled well.<br>請形容你處理得不錯的困難局面。 |
| 如果上司在通知你後的短時間內要你完成一項任務，你會怎樣處理這個情況？ | How would you deal with the situation that your supervisor requires you to get a task done with a very short notice? |
| 當你知道自己沒有犯錯，你會怎樣處理憤怒的顧客？ | How would you deal with an angry client while you know that it's not your fault? |

020.mp3

| | |
|---|---|
| 給我一個例子，顯示出你可以同時處理多項任務。 | Give an example from your work that shows that you can handle multitasking.<br>Give an example from your work that shows......<br>給我一個例子，顯示出……<br>Give an example from your work that shows you are a quick learner.<br>給我一個例子，顯示出你很快把新事物學上手。<br>Give an example from your work that shows you are an effective communicator.<br>給我一個例子，顯示出你的一個擅於溝通的人。<br>Give an example from your work that shows you are a responsible team member.<br>給我一個例子，顯示出你是一個負責任的小組成員。 |
| 假使你必須趕及一個你沒有把握的限期，你會如何做？ | What will you do if you have to meet a deadline that you don't have control over? |
| 如果小組成員待到接近限期才工作，你會怎樣做？ | If a team member doesn't work until the deadline is approaching, what will you do? |
| 如果有同僚總是落後於項目的進度，你會怎樣跟他説？ | How will you talk to a co-worker who is always behind the schedule of a project? |

effective communicator 擅於溝通的人　multitasks 多項任務
responsible team member 負責任的小組成員

# 一般對答（對上）

021.mp3

| | |
|---|---|
| 我的名字是佐治。過去五年，我在資訊技術公司，帶領三組項目。 | My name is George. In the last 5 years, I headed 3 project teams for an IT company. |
| 我當了很多年的程式員。 | I have spent many years as a programmer. |
| 我在顧客服務行業已有好些年。 | I have been in the customer service industry for several years. |
| 在這之前，我是在同一家公司當項目經理。 | Prior to that, I was a project manager in the same firm. |

謹記當對方問你擔當過的工作職位，必須以過去式表達；如果問及你的現職而你沒有辭掉的話，可考慮採用現在完成進行式（Present perfect continuous tense）。例如：

I've been working as an office assistant for 2 years. 我一直做了兩年的辦公室助理。

如果你覺得這樣說很複雜，或可以用現在完成式（Present perfect tense）而用 since 配合入職的年份：

I've been an office assistant since 2008.

從 2008 年開始我一直是辦公室助理。

| | |
|---|---|
| 我的前僱主又好又樂於助人。 | My previous employer was nice and helpful. |
| 我從前主管身上學習了很多。 | I learned a lot from my previous supervisor. |
| 他是我工作上的良師益友。 | He was my work mentor. |
| 他也鼓勵我找更好的機會。 | He also encouraged me to look for a better opportunity. |
| 我為以前的公司設計了新的會計程式。 | I've designed a new accounting programme for the previous company. |

022.mp3

| | |
|---|---|
| 三個月前，我準時完成一項項目。 | I completed a project on time 3 months ago. |
| 我在一季內增加10%營業額。 | I increased 10% sales revenue for a season. |
| 我大部分的經驗是處理顧客打進來的電話。 | Most of my experience was dealing with inbound customers' calls. |
| 我寧願到外面去找顧客，而不呆在桌上電腦後。 | I'd rather be visiting customers than stuck behind a desktop. |
| 現在我在 The Glam 集團任職。 | Right now I work at The Glam Corporate. |
| 我是市務部營業代表。 | I am a marketing sales representative. |
| 我的前職是在彩虹百貨公司工作。 | My previous job was at The Rainbow Department Store. |
| 我肯定能夠處理難以應付的顧客。 | I definitely can handle difficult customers. |
| 在我現時職位，我每天處理投訴的顧客。 | In my current position, I deal with complaining customers every day. |
| 我先讓他們發洩。 | I'd let them vent out first. |
| 我讓他們看到，公司關心他們的需要。 | I'd show them that the company cares their needs. |

# 離職原因（對上）

023.mp3

| | |
|---|---|
| 我享受前職。 | I enjoyed the previous job. |
| 工作環境不錯。 | The work environment was nice. |
| 同事們令辦公氣氛很愉快。 | People made the workplace approachable. |
| 我真的享受跟那裏的人一起工作。 | I truly enjoyed working with the people there. |
| 那裏的工作文化是開放而不拘禮節。 | The work culture there was open and casual.<br>在提出離職理由前，稱讚前公司的好處。 |
| 我的現職甚少晉升機會。 | Advancement opportunities are scarce at my current job. |
| 未來的晉升機會有限。 | Future advancement opportunities are limited. |
| 我覺得是時候到新公司迎接新挑戰。 | It is time for me to move to a firm with new challenges. |
| 公司重整了架構。 | The company reconstructed its organization system. |
| 它跟我的事業目標不一致。 | It wasn't consistent with my career goals. |
| 我喜歡得到一份有更多晉升機會的工作。 | I want a job with more opportunities for advancement.<br>同 I want a job with more opportunities for promotion. |
| 我從 2006 年開始從事現職。 | I've worked at my present job since 2006. |

024.mp3

| | |
|---|---|
| 我趁沒有工作的一年去旅遊，多認識這個世界。 | I took a break from my career for a year to travel to learn more about the world. |
| 這是由於部門改制。 | It was due to departmental changes. |
| 我決定先集中照顧孩子幾年。 | I decided to focus on my children for a few years. |
| 我覺得，舊職位再沒有晉升的空間。 | I feel that I have advanced as far as I can in my previous position. |
| 我在之前的公司看不到自己的未來。 | I didn't see a future for myself with the previous company. |
| 公司縮減規模。 | The company was downsized. |
| 我現在的職位被取消，因為公司縮減規模。 | My current position is being eliminated as a result of corporate downsizing. |
| 之前的公司在財政年度大幅減省開支。 | The previous company cut spending drastically for the fiscal year. |
| 我是年資最短的其中一個，所以我離職了。 | I was the one with the least amount of seniority. So I left. |
| 因為合併，我變成冗員。 | There was a merger and my position became redundant. |

# 應徵反問（對上）

025.mp3

| | |
|---|---|
| 你為這職位面試了多少人？ | How many people are you interviewing for this position? |
| 你會怎樣形容這機構的文化？ | How would you describe the culture of this organization? |
| 貴公司的長遠目標是甚麼？ | What are this company's long-term goals? |
| 你希望這職位多久之後就要開始工作？ | How soon do you see someone actually starting in this job? |
| 如果我做好這份工作的話，在公司裏我有甚麼發展機會？ | If I do a good job in this position, where can I go in this company? |
| 公司裏面有晉升機會嗎？ | Are there opportunities for advancement within the company? |
| 這職位的前任職員為甚麼離職？他做了多久？ | What happened to the last person who held this job? How long did he stay? |
| 目前市場有甚麼趨勢會影響此公司？ | What market trends are affecting the company at this time?<br>What economic factors are affecting the company at this time?<br>目前有甚麼經濟因素會影響公司？ |
| 擔任此職位的人會面對甚麼個別挑戰？ | What are the particular challenges the person hired for this position will face?<br>What are the specific difficulties the person hired for this position will face?<br>擔任此職位的人會面對甚麼具體的困難？ |
| 工作上我需要對誰匯報？ | To whom would I be reporting?<br>同 Who would I report to? |

026.mp3

| | |
|---|---|
| 我的工作日程是怎樣？ | What would my schedule be? |
| 可否告訴我有關工作日程？ | Can you tell me about the work schedule? |
| 我甚麼時候會聽到消息？ | When may I expect to hear from you? |
| 甚麼時候你會下決定？ | When will you be making your decision? |
| 我將會獨自工作，或是跟一組人一起合作？ | Would I be working alone or in a group?<br>類 Would I be working alone or as a member of a team?<br>我將會獨自工作，或是成為一組人的成員？ |
| 要求公幹的時間有多少？ | How much travel would be required?<br>How much travel would you expect?<br>你預期這工作會有多少公幹機會？ |
| 你們會提供在職訓練給員工嗎？ | Would you provide on-the-job training for staff?<br>類 Is there on-the-job training?<br>有在職訓練嗎？<br>Is on-the-job training provided?<br>提供在職訓練嗎？ |
| 我想知道多一點關於貴公司在中國市場中的發展。 | I'd like to know more about your company's development in the China market. |
| 這職位主要負責甚麼？ | What are the main duties of this position? |
| 我的主要責任是甚麼？ | What would my key responsibilities be? |
| 平日我將會做甚麼？ | What would I do in a typical day? |

# 個人強項（對上）

027.mp3

| | |
|---|---|
| 我希望多學市務運作，將來我可以開自己擁有的公司。 | I'm hoping to learn more about the marketing so that I may open my own company. |
| 我又勤奮又有效率。 | I'm hardworking and efficient. |
| 我有正面的願景，就是帶領一個研究小組。 | I have a positive vision that I'll lead a research team. |
| 我喜歡專注在一項任務，直至完成為止。 | I like to focus on a task until it's done.<br>I like to focus on......<br>我喜歡專注在……<br>I like to focus on details.<br>我喜歡專注在細節上。<br>I like to focus on efficiency.<br>我喜歡專注在效率。<br>I like to focus on getting a job done in a timely manner.<br>我喜歡專注在適當的時間內完成工作。 |
| 我有操作這軟件的實際經驗。 | I got hands-on experience in handling this software.<br>同 I got practical experience in handling this software. |
| 我擅於學習新事物。 | I'm good at learning new things. |
| 我有你們要的資歷。 | I have the qualifications you are looking for. |
| 我做事周密仔細。 | I'm thorough and detail-oriented. |
| 這些優點對市場研究是必須的。 | These qualities are essential for marketing research.<br>當我們說了一些個人強項和優點後，不妨再針對該行業強調這些優點的重要性。 |

028.mp3

| | |
|---|---|
| 我與其他人合作愉快。我可以推動別人更勤奮工作。 | I work well with people. I can motivate others to work harder.<br>有關人際溝通技巧，可採用以下動詞來做具體的例子：<br>Listen 聆聽<br>I can listen to customers patiently.<br>我有耐性聆聽顧客的説話。<br>Persuade 説服<br>I can persuade customers to buy products.<br>我能夠説服顧客購買產品。<br>Arrange 安排<br>I arranged social gatherings for co-workers.<br>我為同事安排社交聚會。 |
| 當我工作的時候，我總是做到該做的事情。 | When I have a job, I always do what I'm supposed to do. |
| 我的工作通常質素很高，很少出錯。 | I always do quality work with very few errors. |
| 我答應了的事就做得到。 | I delivered what I promised. |
| 顧客總是很滿意我解決問題的方法。 | Customers were always pleased with how I solved their problems. |
| 我在營業部中保持最高留客率。 | I held the highest customer retention rate in sales department. |
| 我能好好掌握英語，在日常情況中溝通流利。 | I have a good working knowledge of English and communicate fluently in everyday situations. |
| 客戶欣賞我對他們的盡心服務。 | Clients appreciate my dedication towards them. |
| 我相信我有一些技能可以轉移運用到這份工作上。 | I believe all the transferable skills I have can apply to the job. |

# 坦承不足（對上）

029.mp3

| | |
|---|---|
| 我處理資料庫往往緩慢，因為我希望確定那些資料是正確的。 | I tend to be slow at dealing with database because I'd like to make sure the data is accurate.<br>I tend to try to accomplish too much in a day.<br>我往往嘗試在一天之內完成太多工作。 |
| 與一些無法在限期內完成工作的人一起做事時，我會覺得煩惱。 | It's annoying when I work with someone who doesn't meet deadlines. |
| 如果有小組成員不如其他人那麼努力工作，我會感到困惱。 | I'd be frustrated if a team member doesn't work hard as others. |
| 如果我發現部門裏面有溝通問題，這會煩擾我。 | It bothers me if I find there's a communication problem in the department. |
| 我不是十分有彈性，因為我喜歡完全跟隨一個方向。 | I'm not very flexible because I like to follow a direction thoroughly. |
| 我偶爾頗固執。 | I'm quite stubborn at times.<br>I'm quite...... at times.<br>......critical 吹毛求疵<br>......nervous 緊張 |
| 我注意到自己經常墨守個人原則。 | I'm aware of the problem that I often stick to my principles. |
| 有時候，我發覺很難令工作符合自己的期望——工作上的完美主義是我的問題。 | Sometimes I find it hard to get a job done as my expectation of perfection is my problem. |

030.mp3

| | |
|---|---|
| 如果時間緊迫，我會忽略細節。 | If the schedule is tight, I'd overlook details.<br>同 If the schedule is tight, I'd pass over details. |
| 有時候，我太注重細節。 | Sometimes I pay too much attention to detail.<br>通常提及個人的弱點，提供發生的情況和細節，可避免對方斷章取義。例如，當你提到自己太注重細節的情況是：<br>......when I calculate costs.<br>當我計算成本。<br>......when I collect clients' data.<br>當我收集客戶的資料時。<br>......when I file documents.<br>當我為文件存檔時。<br>......when I order office supplies.<br>當訂購辦公室文具時。 |
| 我不懂拒絕。 | I don't know when to say no. |
| 如果有些事情聽起來我有興趣或需要去做的話，我會接受。 | I'd agree to take on anything that sounds interesting or needs to be done. |
| 然後，我察覺到自己不能扛起所有工作。 | Then, I find I can't afford everything. |
| 我只在不被侮辱時才接受批評。 | I can accept criticism only when I'm not offended. |

stubborn 固執
principles 個人原則
perfectionism 完美主義

# 期望待遇（對上）

031.mp3

| | |
|---|---|
| 如果你不介意的話，現階段我不想談及金錢。 | I'd rather not talk about money at this stage if you don't mind. |
| 我對薪酬範圍可以商量。 | My expectation for salary range is open to discussion. |
| 我的焦點是我可以為你做甚麼。 | My focus is on what I can do for you.<br>My focus is on what I can accomplish in your company.<br>我的焦點是我可以在貴公司完成甚麼。<br>My focus is on what I can establish in my career.<br>我的焦點是我可以在事業上成就甚麼。 |
| 我對得到經驗比獲得多少薪金更感興趣。 | I'm more interested in gaining more experience than the amount I'd get paid.<br>I'm more interested in working in an innovative environment than the amount I'd get paid.<br>我對在創新的環境工作比獲得多少薪金更感興趣。 |
| 在我成為你們團隊一員後，我相信我的薪酬會反映我的表現。 | I believe my salary will reflect my performance when I become a member of your team. |
| 金錢不是我唯一優先的考慮。 | Money is not my only priority.<br>Salary is not my only priority.<br>薪酬不是我唯一優先的考慮。 |
| 如果你能夠提供薪酬範圍，我便能夠告訴你那是否適合。 | If you can suggest your salary range, I may tell you where I think I fit. |

# 人脈連絡（一般）

032.mp3

| | |
|---|---|
| 我是雲妮的朋友。 | I'm Winnie's friend. |
| 她推介我來聯絡你。 | She referred me to contact you.<br>類 I was referred to contact you.<br>我被推介來聯絡你。 |
| 他告訴我，你會給我有用的指引。 | He told me that you may give my some useful guidance. |
| 我知道你在這行業浸淫了超過 20 年。 | I know you've been in this industry for more than 20 years. |
| 若你知道哪間公司在聘人，可否讓我知道？ | Could you let me know if you hear any job offers? |
| 你公司有職位空缺嗎？ | Are there any openings in your company? |
| 你是否介意替我告訴別人我在找工作？ | Would you mind telling people that I'm looking for a job?<br>類 Would you mind telling people that I'm a job seeker?<br>你是否介意告訴別人我是求職者？ |
| 我可以聯絡你介紹的那個人嗎？ | Can I contact the person you suggested? |
| 我可以告訴他你是推薦人嗎？ | May I use your name to contact him? |
| 我們可以見面喝杯咖啡嗎？ | Can we meet for a coffee? |
| 我想跟你約見。 | I'd like to set up an appointment with you. |
| 我想尋求你的專業意見。 | I want to seek your professional advice. |

# 回答求職者的要求（對外）

033.mp3

| | |
|---|---|
| 我與她相交多年。 | I've known her for years. |
| 她曾是我的下屬。 | She was my subordinate in the company. |
| 對，她跟我說了關於你的事。 | Yes, she's told me about you. |
| 我們的公司將會進行招聘。 | Our company is going to recruit. |
| 但我不肯定將有多少空缺。 | But I'm not sure how many vacancies there'll be. |
| 在不同的部門有5個職位空缺。 | There'll be 5 openings in various departments. |
| 現在內部正在招聘職位。 | Internal postings are available now. |
| 暫時他們只准許內部調職申請。 | They only allow internal transfer applications for now. |
| 當然，如果有職位空缺，我會告訴你的。 | Certainly, I'll tell you if there's an opening. |
| 不，我不介意跟別人說你在找工作。 | No, I don't mind telling people that you're looking for work. |
| 若你有更多問題請傳電郵給我。 | Email me if you have further questions.<br>為了防止對方來電太頻密而令自己不勝其煩，直接說出你寧願用其他方式來保持聯絡。 |
| 請隨意提及我的名字。 | Please feel free to mention my name. |

## 相關生字

求職面試中可提及不同的特殊技巧和強項：

| | |
|---|---|
| I am...... | 我是…… |
| ...... responsible | 負責任 |
| ...... ambitious | 有雄心 |
| ...... creative | 有創意 |
| ...... energetic | 充滿活力 |
| ...... patient | 有耐性 |
| ...... reliable | 可靠 |
| ...... willing to learn | 願意學習 |
| ...... organized | 有組織 |
| I have...... | 我有…… |
| ...... leadership | 有領導力 |
| ...... negotiating skills | 談判技巧 |
| ...... the ability to motivate | 推動別人的能力 |
| ...... interpersonal skills | 有人際關係的技巧 |
| ...... a positive attitude | 有積極的態度 |
| ...... work ethic | 職業道德 |
| ...... management experience | 管理經驗 |
| ...... customer service skills | 顧客服務技能 |

也可以直接用動詞，具體顯示自己的工作經驗，例如：

### 顧客服務

| | |
|---|---|
| I assisted clients. | 我協助客戶。 |
| I escorted visitors to the conference room. | 我帶訪客到會議室。 |
| I informed customers. | 我通知顧客。 |
| I serve the disabled. | 我服務殘疾人士。 |

### 行政文職

| | |
|---|---|
| I photocopied documents. | 我影印文件。 |
| I sorted files. | 我整理檔案。 |
| I prepared reports. | 我預備報告。 |
| I printed handouts. | 我打印講義。 |

## 面試貼士

面試模式大致有：結構式面試（Structured interview）、行為／情景方面的面試（Behavioural／Situational interview）、多人面試（Panel interview）、小組面試（Group interview）等不同形式。事先問清楚，讓自己做好心理準備。其實面試的問題大同小異，只要你做足準備，有助減少無可避免的緊張感。首先，深入研究（research into）該公司，嘗試設想他們招聘的目標（goal），衡量個人技能（skills）、經驗（experience）和學歷（qualification），參看刊登的職務說明（job description）。面試前多練習，最後是效果自然，給人感覺你熱切（enthusiastic about）得到這份工作。

# Chapter 2

# 日常事務

# 接聽電話（對外）

036.mp3

| | |
|---|---|
| 你好，E-Connect 公司。 | Hello, E-Connect Company. |
| 你早，這是珍妮花。 | Good morning. Jenny's speaking. |
| 我可以怎樣幫到你？ | How can I help you? |
| 我可以為你做甚麼？ | What can I do for you? |
| 可以把你的名字告訴我嗎？ | May I know your name please?<br>同 May I have your name please? |
| 請問是誰來電？ | Who's calling please? |
| 對不起，你説你的名字是甚麼？ | Sorry, what did you say your name was? |
| 請再説你的名字一遍？ | And your name again, please? |
| 你想找約翰。 | You want to talk to John.<br>如果不肯定對方想找誰可以重複一遍。如果真的聽錯了，對方自然會告訴你。 |
| 對不起，我沒有聽過這個名字。 | Sorry, I don't know anyone of that name. |
| 這裏沒有這個名字的人。 | There's no one of that name here. |
| 恐怕我們沒有這個部門。 | I'm afraid we don't have a research department. |
| 誰是你的聯絡人？ | Who was your contact person?<br>如果對方詢問一些事情，而你無法解答，最好是問清楚對方，哪一位同事曾經跟他聯絡。 |

# 無法接聽（對外）

037.mp3

| | |
|---|---|
| 她剛出去吃午飯。 | She just stepped out for lunch. |
| 她出去開會。 | She's out for a meeting.<br>同 She's gone for a meeting.<br>She's headed to a meeting. |
| 我們的經理出去了。 | Our manager is out. |
| 他還未到。 | He's not in yet. |
| 他大概 10 點鐘到。 | He'll be around 10 o'clock. |
| 我們預期他會隨時回來 | We're expecting him any minute. |
| 他今天不上班。 | He's out for the day.<br>如果同事請病假，可以婉轉告訴對方，他今天不在公司。如果同事遲遲還沒有到，又沒有打電話回來告假，跟對方說，他隨時回來。 |
| 我可以嘗試找某位同事幫你嗎？ | May I try someone else for you?<br>May I try...... for you?<br>我可以嘗試找……幫你嗎？<br>May I try a sales rep for you?<br>我可以嘗試找一位營業代表幫你嗎？<br>May I try a consultant for you?<br>我可以嘗試找一位顧問幫你嗎？ |
| 有其他人可以幫到你嗎？ | Can someone else help you? |
| 你想嘗試跟瑪莉談嗎？ | Do you want to try Mary instead? |
| 安娜可以幫你嗎？ | Can Anna help you? |
| 最能協助你的人是安娜。 | The best person who can help you is Anna.<br>當某位同事未能接聽，你可以提議另一位同事的名字，盡量滿足對方的需求。 |

# 電話轉線（對外）

038.mp3

| | |
|---|---|
| 他現在可以接聽你的電話。 | He can take your call now. |
| 你被接通了。 | You're through now. |
| （嘗試轉撥給其他同事後）恐怕接不上。 | I'm afraid there's no answer. |
| 他在講電話。 | He's on the line. |
| 他正在通話。 | His line is busy at the moment.<br>同 His line is engaged right now. |
| 你想稍候片刻嗎？ | Would you like to hold? |
| 你想留電話錄音的口訊嗎？ | Would you like to leave a voice mail message? |
| 請稍等一會。 | Please hold.<br>類 Could you please hold?<br>請問你可否稍候片刻嗎？ |
| 謝謝你的等候。 | Thank you for holding. |
| 你好，你在等保羅接聽嗎？ | Hello, are you holding for Paul?<br>有時候突然有很多來電，你不清楚誰在線上等候，你必須先問清楚，然後再轉撥到其他內線。 |
| 你介意再稍等嗎？ | Would you mind holding again? |
| 他現在沒能接聽。 | He's not available now. |
| 他在聽另一通電話。 | He's on the other line. |

Take a call 接聽電話
Pick up the phone 接電話
Hold a call 待接電話

# 溝通困難（對外）

039.mp3

| | |
|---|---|
| 請你說大聲一點？ | Could you speak up please? |
| 我聽不到。 | I didn't catch that. |
| 我不能正常地聽到你。 | I can't hear you properly.<br>類 I can't hear you clearly.<br>我不能清楚聽到你。 |
| 對不起，你說得太快了。 | I'm sorry. That's too fast for me. |
| 我不明白你在說甚麼。 | I can't understand what you're saying. |
| 請問你介意重複一遍嗎？ | Would you mind repeating that please?<br>類 Would you mind saying that again please?<br>請問你介意再說一遍嗎？ |
| 我仍然不懂你的意思。 | I still don't know what you mean. |
| 恐怕電話訊號很弱。 | I'm afraid the signal is weak. |
| 剛剛幾秒我聽不到你。 | I just lost you for a few seconds. |
| 可否把你的電話號碼給我？我立即會回撥給你。 | Could you give me your number? I'll call you back right away. |
| 你可否再打電話來，看看我們的通話訊號會否好一點？ | Could you ring again and see if we can get a better line? |
| 請慢慢把它拼出來。 | Please spell it out slowly. |

# 記下口訊（對外）

040.mp3

| | |
|---|---|
| 我可以記下你的口訊嗎？ | May I take a message? |
| 如果你喜歡的話，我可以記下口訊。 | I'll take a message if you like. |
| 你想我為你記下口訊？ | Would you like me to take a message? |
| 你想留下口訊嗎？ | Would you like to leave a message? |
| 等一下，待我拿一支筆。 | Just a moment while I get a pen. |
| 請別掛電話，待我找一張紙來？ | Could you please hold on while I find a piece of paper? |
| 你可否等一會兒？ | Could you wait a second? |
| 我可以記下你的口訊了。 | I'm ready to take your message. |
| 是 cat 的 C 嗎？ | Was that C for cat?<br>取得正確的名字是必須的，你最好習慣用一些簡單文字的首個字母來確定。例如：Mary 的 M、Nancy 的 N。 |
| 請你再慢慢說一遍好嗎？ | Could you say that again more slowly please? |
| 請你重複一遍？ | Would you repeat that please? |
| 你想早上10:00來，而不是9:00，對嗎？ | You'd like to come at 10 o'clock instead of 9 o'clock in the morning, right? |

| | |
|---|---|
| 你想他在會議後打電話給你。 | You'd like him to give you a call after the meeting. |
| 我可以檢查一下我是否聽對了？ | May I check I've got that right? |
| 讓我重述你講過的。 | Let me reword what you've said.<br>類 Let me confirmed what you've said.<br>讓我確定你説過的。 |
| 我説對嗎？ | Am I right? |
| 還有其他事情嗎？ | Anything else? |
| 謝謝你的來電。 | Thank you for your call.<br>Thank you for......<br>謝謝你……<br>Thank you for calling us.<br>謝謝你打電話給我們。<br>Thank you for calling E-Connect Company.<br>謝謝你打電話來 E-Connect 公司。 |
| 祝你有愉快的一天。再見。 | Have a good day. Good-bye.<br>同 Have a nice day. Good-bye.<br>Have a good one. Bye then.<br>（此句更不拘小節，適合跟熟絡的人説） |

Hold on 不掛斷電話
Just a moment. 等一下
Wait for a second 等一會兒

# 撥出電話（對外）

042.mp3

| | |
|---|---|
| 我可以跟瓊安講電話嗎？ | May I speak to Joanne?<br>同 May I talk to Joanne?<br>Could I speak to Joanne? |
| 請問羅倫斯在嗎？ | Is Lawrence here please?<br>同 Is Lawrence there please? |
| 勞駕，我想跟約翰通電話。 | I'd like to speak to John please. |
| 請轉到內線 123。 | Extension 123, please. |
| 約翰在嗎？ | Is John in? |
| 請問你可否把我轉接到尼爾遜？ | Could you put me through to Nelson please? |
| 這是 Tech 公司的雪莉。 | This is Shirley from Tech Company.<br>This is [name] from......<br>這是……的……（名字）。<br>This is Sam from Chicago.<br>這是芝加哥的森姆。<br>This is Thomas from the head office.<br>這是總公司的湯姆斯。 |
| 上個星期我們在會議中碰過面。 | We met at a conference last week. |
| 請告訴他我們昨天在巡迴展覽見過面。 | Please tell him that we met at a road show yesterday. |
| 今早他才打電話給我，現在我回覆他。 | He just rang me this morning and now I am getting back to him. |

| | |
|---|---|
| 我是她的客戶。 | I'm her client.<br>類 I'm her customer.<br>我是她的顧客。<br>I'm her buyer.<br>我是她的買家。 |
| 我打電話來是商討那個計劃。 | I'm calling to ask about the plan. |
| 我打電話來的原因是我需要一份報價單。 | The reason I'm calling is that I need a quotation. |
| 我不介意在線上等。 | I don't mind holding. |
| 好的，我想留給她電話錄音的口訊。 | Sure, I'd like to leave her a voice mail message. |
| 請問你可否把我轉到他的留言信箱。 | Could you please transfer me to his voice mail?<br>類 Could you please put me through to his voice mail?<br>請問你可否把我轉撥到他的留言信箱？ |
| 她不在。嗯，午飯後我再來電吧。 | She's not in. Well, I'll call again after lunch. |
| 請問你可否告訴他開會後致電給我？ | Can you please tell him to call me after the meeting?<br>Can you please tell him to call me after......?<br>請問你可否告訴他……後致電給我？<br>Can you please tell him to call me after the conference?<br>請問你可否告訴他會議後致電給我？<br>Can you please tell him to call me after the presentation?<br>請問你可否告訴他在工作匯報後致電給我？ |
| 你可否記下我的口訊？ | Could you take my message? |

044.mp3

| | |
|---|---|
| 他甚麼時候回來？ | When will he be back?<br>同 When will he be in?<br>When will he return? |
| 你知道她甚麼時候有空？ | Do you know when she'll be back? |
| 這個早上我致電給他幾次了。 | I called him a few times this morning. |
| 他沒有回覆。 | He didn't return a call. |
| 我一直在等他的電話。 | I was expecting his call. |
| 我需要在這個下午解決它。 | I need to fix it this afternoon. |
| 其實這是蠻急的。 | It's quite urgent actually. |
| 如果他三點前回覆我便好了。 | It'd be great if he gets back to me before 3pm.<br>對方一直沒有回覆電話，可向接線生表示事情迫切，嘗試要求對方甚麼時間要回覆。 |
| 有誰能夠幫我看一看那張發票？ | Can anyone help me check out the invoice?<br>Can anyone help me......?<br>有誰能夠幫我……？<br>Can anyone help me follow up the purchase order?<br>有誰能夠幫我跟進那購貨訂單？<br>Can anyone help me issue the receipt?<br>有誰能夠幫我發收據？ |
| 不如我跟米克講吧？ | Can I talk to Mick instead? |
| 我可以跟負責處理批發商的人嗎？ | Could I speak to someone who deals with wholesalers? |
| 我可以晚一點再打電話來。 | I may call back later. |

# 電話商談（對外）

045.mp3

| | |
|---|---|
| 你好嗎？ | How are you doing? |
| 生意如何？ | How's business? |
| 有新消息嗎？ | Any updates? |
| 上月我們開了新店鋪。 | We opened a new store last month.<br>類 We opened a new branch last month.<br>上月我們開了新分店。<br>We opened a new shop last month.<br>上月我們開了新店。 |
| 我們推出了新產品系列。 | We've launched a new product line. |
| 很高興聽到這好消息。 | Glad to hear the good news. |
| 讓我們談生意吧。 | Let's talk about business. |
| 我有一個關於上次交易的問題。 | I have a question about the last transaction. |
| 我來電是關於我的訂單。 | I'm calling you regarding my order. |
| 你收到我的傳真嗎？ | Did you receive my fax? |
| 我打電話來是跟進我的電郵。 | I'm calling to follow up my email.<br>I'm calling to......<br>我打電話來是……<br>I'm calling to change my purchase order.<br>我打電話來是查一查我的訂購單。<br>I'm calling to change our quotation.<br>我打電話來是改一改我的報價單。 |
| 我想訂購更多。 | I wanted to order more. |

046.mp3

| | |
|---|---|
| 你可以改到星期三送貨？ | Can you change the delivery to Wednesday?<br>類 Can you move the delivery to Wednesday?<br>你可以移到星期三送貨？<br>Can you arrange the delivery to be Wednesday?<br>你可以安排在星期三送貨嗎？ |
| 價錢看來太高了。 | The price seems too high. |
| 這個價錢沒有競爭力。 | The price isn't competitive. |
| 這個設計不合我們的顧客。 | The design isn't good for our consumers. |
| 對，早上收到傳真了。 | Yes, I received the fax in the morning. |
| 我對你在電郵中提及的產品感到興趣。 | I'm interested in the product you mentioned in the email.<br>同 I'm interested in the product you talked about in the email. |
| 我相信這產品在市場是可賣的。 | I believe the product is marketable. |
| 市場會接受這新產品。 | The market will accept the new product. |
| 大部分顧客喜歡那個樣本。 | Most of the customers like the sample. |
| 你明白我的意思嗎？ | Did you get my points? |
| 清楚嗎？ | Is that clear? |
| 請你重複說那個數量？ | Would you repeat the quantity please? |
| 你會提供大量訂購的折扣嗎？ | Can you offer bulk discount? |

# 預備掛線（對外）

047.mp3

| | |
|---|---|
| 那麼我會把細節電郵給你。 | So I'll send you the details by email. |
| 我會把報價單傳真給你。 | I'll fax you the quotation. |
| 收到送遞的貨物後，今午答覆你可以嗎？ | Can I answer you this afternoon after we've received the delivery? |
| 我明天回覆你。 | I'll get back to you tomorrow. |
| 遲些再聊。 | Talk to you soon. |
| 聽見這些真好。 | It's great to hear about that. |
| 跟你聊天真好。 | Nice talking to you. |
| 打電話給我喔。 | Give me a ring.<br>意思是保持聯絡。 |
| 代我問候他。 | Give my regards to him.<br>同 Give him my regards. |
| 謝謝你打電話給我。 | Thank you for calling me. |
| 謝謝你回覆我。 | Thank you for getting back to me. |
| 好的，我現在要掛線了。 | OK, I got to hang up now. |
| 對不起，我現在得繼續工作。 | Sorry, I got to get on now.<br>暗示將要掛線。 |
| 下個星期一你可以打電話給我嗎？ | Could you call me next Monday? |

# 提出約見（對外）

048.mp3

| | |
|---|---|
| 我可以約個時間跟你見面嗎？ | May I make an appointment to see you? |
| 我們可以約定見面嗎？ | Can we set up an appointment? |
| 嗨，你好嗎？很久不見。 | Hey, how are you? It's been a while.<br>若跟對方熟絡，語氣親切些，説句很久不見，大家相約見面就再自然不過了。 |
| 我們需要會面。 | We need a meeting. |
| 我想，我們應該見見面來討論。 | I think we should meet for discussion. |
| 讓我們約定一個會議吧。 | Let's set up a meeting. |
| 我想告訴你多些關於那個新產品。 | I'd like to tell you more about the new product. |
| 我對你的產品有興趣。 | I'm interested in your products. |
| 你的計劃聽起來是可行的。 | Your plan sounds workable. |
| 我們也許需要你的服務。 | We may need your service.<br>如果你對對方的建議、企劃、產品或服務感到興趣，在表達你的個人看法後，可約定會面時間。 |
| 面談會省時間。 | It'd save time to meet in person. |
| 我想讓你看看目錄。 | I'd like to show you the catalogue. |

| | |
|---|---|
| 我想看樣本。 | I want to see the samples.<br>當電話中沒法解決的時候，提議一些實質的提議。 |
| 如果你來我們的辦公室就更好了。 | It'd be better if you come to our office. |
| 哪一天你方便？ | Which day is good for you? |
| 明天你可以嗎？ | Would tomorrow suit you? |
| 不如二十五號？ | How about the 25th? |
| 明天如何？ | What about tomorrow? |
| 我在星期五有空。 | I'm available on Friday.<br>同 I'm free on Friday. |
| 下星期三我們能夠進一步討論嗎？ | Can we further discuss next Wednesday? |
| 你下星期四行嗎？ | Can you make it next Thursday? |
| 明天我可以來你的辦公室嗎？ | Can I come to your office tomorrow? |
| 我打算下個星期三來香港。我們可以見面嗎？ | I'm planning to be in Hong Kong next Wednesday. Can we meet? |

# 接受約見（對外）

050.mp3

| | |
|---|---|
| 請問你可否告訴我那是關於甚麼的呢？ | Would you tell me what's that about please? |
| 我可以問這是關於甚麼的嗎？ | May I ask what it's about? |
| 讓我看看自己的日程安排。 | Let me check out my schedule.<br>類 Let me check out my agenda.<br>讓我看看自己的工作日程。<br>Let me check out my organizer.<br>讓我看看自己的記事本。<br>Let me check out my calendar.<br>讓我看看自己的行事曆。 |
| 讓我看看是否能夠見你。 | Let's me just see if I can meet you. |
| 你會否介意來我們的辦公室嗎？ | Would you mind coming over to our office?<br>Would you mind......?<br>你會否介意……？<br>Would you mind meeting in a local restaurant?<br>你會否介意在本地餐廳會面？<br>Would you mind giving us a presentation?<br>你會否介意給我們一個口頭匯報嗎？ |
| 我們可以來一個午餐會議嗎？ | Can we go for a lunch meeting? |
| 那一天我的行程緊湊。 | I'll have a tight schedule that day. |
| 哪是星期幾？ | What day of the week is that? |
| 早上還是下午？ | Morning or afternoon? |
| 整天我都有空。 | I'm free all day. |

# 取消會面（對外）

051.mp3

| | |
|---|---|
| 我改了日程安排。 | I've changed my schedule. |
| 我重新安排了工作日程。 | I've rescheduled my agenda. |
| 那一天我必須留在辦公室。 | I'll have to stay in the office that day. |
| 我將會和經理有一個緊急會議。 | I'll have an urgent meeting with my manager. |
| 我不能按照原定安排來。 | I can't make it as we scheduled. |
| 我不能去這個會議。 | I won't be able to go to the meeting. |
| 我要取消約見。 | I've to cancel the appointment. |
| 我們可以重新編排會議嗎？ | Can we reschedule the meeting?<br>類 Can we rearrange the meeting?<br>我們可以重新安排會議嗎？<br>Can we postpone the meeting?<br>我們可以推遲會議嗎？<br>Can we delay the meeting?<br>我們可以延遲會議嗎？ |
| 你可以改另一天嗎？ | Would you make it another day?<br>同 Would you make it a different day? |
| 下星期怎麼樣？ | What about next week instead? |
| 我可以提議下星期五嗎？ | Can I suggest next Friday? |
| 下星期三下午你行嗎？ | Is Wednesday afternoon good for you? |
| 對此我很抱歉。 | I'm sorry about it. |

# 尋求協助（一般）

052.mp3

| | |
|---|---|
| 我想知道，你是否可以給我一分鐘。 | I was wondering if you can spare me a minute. |
| 你是否可以給我一分鐘？ | Could you spare me a minute? |
| 我知道你很忙，但是我需要你的意見。 | I know you are busy, but I need your advice.<br>I know you are busy, but......<br>我知道你很忙，但是……<br>I know you are busy, but it's urgent.<br>我知道你很忙，但是這是很急的。<br>I know you are busy, but you are the best person who can help me.<br>我知道你很忙，但是你是最能夠幫到我的人。 |
| 你會否介意告訴我那份報告放在哪裏？ | Would you mind telling me where the report is? |
| 你認為你可以幫我整理檔案嗎？ | Do you think you can help me sort out the files?<br>Do you think you can help me......?<br>你認為你可以幫我……？<br>Do you think you can help me save the file?<br>你認為你可以幫我存檔嗎？<br>Do you think you can help me answer the call?<br>你認為你可以幫我接聽這個電話嗎？ |
| 我找不到它。你看見嗎？ | I couldn't find it. Did you see it?<br>類 I lost it. Did you see it?<br>我不見它。你看見嗎？ |
| 我可以問你一條問題嗎？ | May I ask you a question? |
| 我有一條問題。 | I have a question. |

| | |
|---|---|
| 我有困難。 | I got a problem. |
| 我應該通知上司嗎？ | Should I inform the supervisor? |
| | 類 Should I report to the supervisor?<br>我應該向上司報告嗎？<br>Should I let the supervisor know?<br>我應該讓上司知道嗎？ |
| 我覺得不大清楚。 | I'm rather confused. |
| 我不肯定這個計算。 | I'm not sure about the calculation. |
| 我完全沒有頭緒。 | I have no clue at all. |
| | 同 I have no idea at all. |
| 請你可否再解釋一次嗎？ | Can you explain again please? |
| 你知道怎樣改報表嗎？ | Do you know how to correct the spreadsheet? |
| | Do you know how to......?<br>你知道怎樣……？<br>Do you know how to log on the system?<br>你知道怎樣登入系統嗎？<br>Do you know how to number the invoice?<br>你知道怎樣給發票編號嗎？ |
| 我需要幫手。 | I need a helping hand. |
| 嗨，我忘記了怎樣找數據…… | Hey, I forget how to find the data...... |
| 你可以示範給我看如何把它印出來嗎？ | Can you show me how to print it out? |
| 我在哪裏做錯了呢？ | Where did I go wrong? |
| 請問你可否指出錯處？ | Could you point out the mistake please? |

054.mp3

| | |
|---|---|
| 這裏有錯。我怎樣可以改正它呢？ | There's a mistake. How can I fix it? |
| 你找到這份報告的任何錯誤之處嗎？ | Did you find something wrong in the report? |
| 你可以解決它嗎？ | Can you solve it? |
| 你碰巧有那個數據嗎？ | Do you have the figure by chance? |
| 請問有解決方法嗎？ | Any solution please? |
| 我想不出解決方法。 | I can't come up with a solution. |
| 我不知道怎樣處理像他那樣難應付的顧客。 | I don't know how to deal with a difficult customer like him. |
| 在我們的網站，哪裏可以找到哪個圖表？ | Where can I find the chart on our website? |
| 你可以幫我一把嗎？ | Can you do me a favour? |
| 你想到甚麼方法嗎？ | Do you have any ideas? |
| 我真的感謝你的幫忙。 | I really appreciate your help. |
| 我很多謝你的協助。 | I'm grateful for your help. |
| 沒有你的幫忙，我做不成。 | I can't make it without your help. |

# 接受查詢（一般）

055.mp3

| | |
|---|---|
| 我可以怎樣幫到你？ | How can I help you? |
| 你有任何問題嗎？ | Do you have any questions? |
| 我們在同一組工作的嘛。 | We work in the same team. |
| 別覺得問我會不好意思。 | Please don't feel embarrassed to ask. |
| 我們應該守望相助。 | We should help each other.<br>若看見同事好像有疑問又難與啟齒，可主動詢問，看看他們有甚麼需要幫助，甚至說一些鼓勵話語，鼓勵對方說出來。 |
| 有甚麼地方你是不肯定的？ | Is there anything that you're not sure about?<br>Is there anything that......?<br>有甚麼地方……？<br>Is there anything that I can help?<br>有甚麼地方我可以幫忙？<br>Is there anything that you doubt?<br>有甚麼地方你覺得疑惑的？ |
| 有甚麼詢問？ | Any inquiries? |
| （解釋疑問後）清楚嗎？ | Is that clear? |
| 你需要澄清嗎？ | Do you need clarification?<br>類 Do you need me to clarify?<br>你需要我澄清嗎？ |
| 你想我再解釋嗎？ | Do you want me to explain again? |
| 你有甚麼要問的？ | Do you have anything to ask? |
| 我幫到你嗎？ | Can I do you a favour? |

056.mp3

| | |
|---|---|
| 你想聽我的看法嗎？ | Do you want to hear my views?<br>Do you want to hear my......?<br>你想聽我的⋯⋯？<br>Do you want to hear my advice?<br>你想聽我的意見嗎？<br>Do you want to hear my suggestions?<br>你想聽我的建議嗎？ |
| 我很高興你來問我。 | I'm glad to be asked.<br>類 I'm glad to hear your questions.<br>我樂意聽你的問題。 |
| 我樂意幫助你。 | It's my pleasure to help you. |
| 我準備好聽聽你的問題。 | I'm ready to listen to your question. |
| 你可否多說一次你的問題？ | Can you repeat your question? |
| 讓我總結我的見解。 | Let me summarize the points. |
| 你一直懂我的意思嗎？ | Can you follow what I'm saying? |
| 這聽起來並不簡單，不過我可以重複一次。 | It doesn't sound simple, but I may repeat it again. |
| 如果有疑問，請隨便問。 | Please feel free to ask if there is any doubt. |
| 你可以讓我知道你的困擾嗎？ | Can you let me know your trouble?<br>Can you let me know......?<br>你可以讓我知道⋯⋯？<br>Can you let me know what's bothering you?<br>你可以讓我知道甚麼正煩着你嗎？<br>Can you let me know what got you in trouble?<br>你可以讓我知道是甚麼使你陷入困難中嗎？ |

057.mp3

| | |
|---|---|
| 我解答到你的問題嗎？ | Can I answer your question? |
| 看，我在忙着一些事情。 | Look, I'm in the middle of something. |
| 其實我現在是挺忙的。 | I'm quite busy right now actually. |
| 我要去開會。 | I'm going to a meeting. |
| 我現在不能回答你，因為我先要看一遍這份報告。 | I'm not able to answer you right now because I need to go through the report first.<br>不能即時解答問題的時候，清楚說明理由，避免產生不必要的誤會。 |
| 我可以晚一點回答你嗎？ | Can I answer you later? |
| 我可以在打一個緊急電話後，再回答你嗎？ | May I answer you after I've made an urgent call? |
| 希望這能夠幫上忙。 | I hope it can help. |
| 如果你又遇到同樣問題，請來問我。 | Please come to ask me if you get the same problem again. |

View 看法
Suggestion 建議
Clarification 澄清（名詞）
Explanation 解釋（名詞）
Point 見解
Clarify 澄清（動詞）
Explain 解釋（動詞）

## 辦公室文具及儀器

| | | | |
|---|---|---|---|
| Bookend | 書夾／書擋 | Portfolio | 文件夾 |
| Desk tray | 書桌文件盤 | Clip board | 寫字夾板 |
| Filing box | 檔案盒 | Folder | 文件夾 |
| Stamp rack | 印章架 | Spiral binding | 膠線圈裝訂 |
| Stamp pad | 印台 | Fastener binder | 彈簧扣夾套 |
| Rubber stamp | 橡皮印章 | Clamp binder | 壓夾式活頁夾套 |
| Dater | 日期印章 | Ring binder | 鐵環夾套 |
| Numbering stamp | 數字印章 | Tab | 檔案分類索引 |
| Self-adhesive label | 自黏標貼 | Divider | 檔案分類卡 |
| Pencil sharpener | 鉛筆刨 | Glue | 膠水 |
| Paper punch | 打孔機 | Scissors | 剪刀 |
| Tape dispenser | 膠紙座 | | |
| Scotch tape | 膠紙 | | |

## 初到貴境

所謂「初到貴境」，當新人進入新的工作環境，必須言行謹慎，以免得罪任何人。所以，無論事情大小，遇到不清楚的地方，便要問個明白，而且，一定要保持禮貌，以免破壞別人對你的初步印象。“Please”這個字一定不可小看，少了這一個字，語氣聽起來會生硬而不夠客氣，禮多人不怪，如果同事跟你説不用客氣，你可以回答説：“I just wanted to show courtesy.”只要有人解答了你的疑問或幫你甚麼忙，務必要説“Thank you”，不要以為同事幫忙你是天經地義的事情，處處顯出友善有禮，有助你在新環境建立良好的人際網絡。有些人會出於好奇心而問及私人問題，例如你的婚姻狀況，這要視乎你自己願意透露多少才覺得舒服。畢竟，這是工作場合不宜花太多時間閒聊，你可以輕描淡寫説一兩句來回應，然後反問對方：“What about you? Are you married?”如果對方樂意長篇大論的話，待他説完後，你乘機轉換話題，或者問他一些公事上的事情。如果對方還是沒有知難而退，你可以説：“Can we talk about it later please?”或“I'm sorry. I really need to make a call now. Let's talk about it later.”來終止對話。至於，有些人不避嫌的問你薪金、福利或如何入職等敏感事情，最好是不要透露，直接説：“I think it's not appropriate to disclose the details. I'm afraid my supervisor won't be happy.”

# Chapter 3

# 內部會議

# 開始會議（對下）

060.mp3

| | |
|---|---|
| 我是約翰，我現在主持這個會議。 | I'm John and I'm chairing this meeting.<br>同 I'm John and I'm leading this meeting. |
| 我安排了這個會議來討論。 | I've organized this meeting to discuss. |
| 今天我是主席。 | I'm the chair today. |
| 我是主席，今天來主持這個會議。 | I'm the chair to lead this meeting today. |
| 謝謝出席這個會議。 | Thank you for attending this meeting. |
| 歡迎出席會議。 | Welcome to the meeting. |
| 我召開這個會議，為了討論各項選擇。 | I've called this meeting to discuss the options. |
| 在本週例會中，我希望大家能夠想出辦法。 | In this weekly meeting, I hope we could figure out a solution.<br>In this......meeting, ......<br>在這……會議，……<br>In this monthly meeting, we'll vote for some major projects.<br>在本月例會中，我們將會投票決議幾個重大項目。<br>In this ad hoc meeting, we've got to investigate into the issue.<br>在這個特別會議中，我們要深入研究那個問題。 |
| 期望大家能透過今天的討論制訂支出數目。 | We're expected to determine the expense after today's discussion. |

061.mp3

| | |
|---|---|
| 今天我們希望找出最好的選擇。 | Today we'd like to find out the best option. |
| 我們會檢討去年的特許經營生意。 | We'll review last year's franchising business.<br>會議主席在正式討論前，簡略説明會議的目的或重要議題。 |
| 既然大家都在，我們開始吧。 | As we're all here, let's get started. |
| 積克還沒到？我們等一等他吧。 | Jack isn't here yet? Let's wait for him then. |
| 有誰會知道他是否來？ | Does anyone know if he'll be coming? |
| 蘇珊今天不能與我們在一起，因為她正在國外公幹。 | Susan can't be with us today because she's working abroad at the moment. |
| 你們全都有上次會議的記錄？ | Do you all have the minutes of the last meeting?<br>類 Did you receive the minutes of the last meeting?<br>你們都收到了上次會議的記錄嗎？ |
| 你們全都有議程了。 | You've all had the agenda. |
| 請看看議程。 | Please have a look at the agenda. |
| 有任何人動議通過它嗎？ | Would anyone make a motion to adopt it?<br>同 Who would make a motion to adopt it? |
| 有誰附議？ | Would anyone second the motion? |
| 誰附議？ | Who will second the motion? |

062.mp3

| | |
|---|---|
| （珍舉手附議）謝謝你，珍。 | Thank you, Jane. |
| 我要說，動議全體一致通過。 | I'd say that the motion was carried unanimously.<br>類 I'd say that the motion was adopted without amendment.<br>我宣佈，動議不用修改地通過。 |
| 這個會議，珍妮會負責會議記錄。謝謝你，珍妮。 | For this meeting, Jenny will take the minutes. Thank you, Jenny. |
| 有任何人自願負責會議記錄嗎？ | Will anyone volunteer to take the minutes today? |
| 保羅，今天輪到你寫會議記錄。 | Paul, it's your turn to take the minutes today. |

Chair 會議主席
Discussion 討論（名詞）
Second 附議（動詞）
Agenda 議程
Discuss 討論（動詞）
Motion 動議（名詞）
Minutes 會議記錄

# 帶領討論（對下）

063.mp3

| | |
|---|---|
| 我們可以從新的事項開始討論嗎？ | Can we start with the new business? |
| 嗯，我們先來討論第一項吧。 | Well, let's start the first item. |
| 我們現在討論增加我們在中國的銷售量。 | We're here to discuss of increasing our sales in China. |
| 本會議的第一部分，我們會看看大衛的報告。 | For the first part of the meeting, we'd go over to David's report. |
| 大衛會匯報他的調查。 | David will present his survey. |
| 大衛樂於同意向我們報告有關在上海設立分行的事宜。 | David kindly agreed to give us a report on setting up a branch in Shanghai. |
| 大衛，請開始。 | David, please go ahead.<br>類 David, over to you.<br>大衛，以下交給你。<br>David, would you like to get the ball rolling?<br>大衛，你想開始嗎？<br>"get the ball rolling" 是俗語，意思是「開始進行」；也可以說："set the ball rolling" 或 "start the ball rolling"。另有相似的俗語 "keep the ball rolling"，意思是「繼續幹下去」。 |
| 讓我們略看一下森姆整理的背景報告。 | Let's get a quick look at the background from Sam. |
| 他將會談及推出新品牌的可能性。 | He'll talk about the possibility of launching a new brand. |

064.mp3

| | |
|---|---|
| 議程的下一項是籌備年度晚餐。 | The next item on the agenda is organizing the annual dinner. |
| 我們上週收到一些顧客的投訴。我們可以找到原因嗎？ | We've received some complaints from customers last week. Can we look for the reasons? |
| 我想聽聽你們的意見。 | I'd like to hear your opinions. |
| 請隨便發表意見。 | Please feel free to express your opinions. |
| 阿健，你那一組已經在比較各種產品。 | Ken, your team has worked on comparing products. |
| 你可以把結果告訴大家嗎？ | Would you tell us the result? |
| 你可以現在開始匯報那些比較嗎？ | Can you start to present the comparison now? |
| 關於這一部分，有問題嗎？ | Is there any question for this part?<br>類 Is there anything unclear in this part?<br>在這部分，有不清楚的地方嗎？ |
| 有誰想問彼得關於那些表現？ | Anyone wants to ask Peter about that performance? |
| 如果沒有其他問題，輪到下一項。 | If there's no more questions, let's move on to the next item. |
| 如果你們不介意，我想跳過下一項。 | If you don't mind, I'd like to skip the next item. |

# 工作報告（一般）

065.mp3

| | |
|---|---|
| 午安，今天我想報告上一季的銷售營業額。 | Good afternoon, today I'd like to report our sales turnover of last season. |
| 今天我會解釋那個新設計。 | Today I'm going to explain the new design.：<br>類 Today I'm going to discuss the new design in detail.<br>今天我會詳細討論那個新設計。<br>Today I'm going to show you the details of the new design.<br>今天我會給你們看那個新設計的細節。 |
| 我會講及中國市場的趨勢。 | I'll cover the trend in the China market. |
| 正如主席説，我今天在這裏匯報最近的調查結果。 | As the chair said, I'm here today to present the result of a recent survey. |
| 先讓我準備好手提電腦。 | Let me set up the laptop first.<br>Let me set up......<br>先讓我準備好……<br>Let me set up the screen.<br>先讓我準備好屏幕。<br>Let me set up the microphone.<br>先讓我準備好麥克風。 |
| 這是講義。 | This is the handout. |
| 請傳下去。 | Please pass around. |
| 在我開始前，僅代表總公司，感謝大家的參與。 | Before I begin, on behalf of the head office, I'd like to thank you for your participation. |
| 在我開始前，我想問你們一個問題。 | Before I start, I'd like to ask you a question. |

066.mp3

| | |
|---|---|
| 你們覺得我們的顧客服務如何？ | How do you feel about our customer service?<br>How do you feel about......?<br>你們覺得……如何？<br>How do you feel about our skin products?<br>你們覺得我們的護膚產品如何呢？<br>How do you feel about our corporate image?<br>你們覺得我們的企業形象如何呢？ |
| 首先，我想把顧客調查的結果告訴你們。 | First of all, let me tell you the result of the customers' survey. |
| 我們先從 XYZ 產品系列開始。 | Let's start from the XYZ product line. |
| 我將會先從統計開始。 | I'm going to begin by the statistics.<br>I'm going to begin by......<br>我將會先……開始。<br>I'm going to begin by showing a chart.<br>我將會先給你們看圖表來開始。<br>I'm going to begin by logistic issues.<br>我將會先從物流的問題開始。 |
| 營業額在上個月增加了百分之二。 | The sales turnover increased by 2% last month. |
| 這些數字根據一項研究而來。 | The figures are based on a study. |
| 我想引起你的注意。 | I'd like to draw your attention. |
| 請看一看屏幕。 | Please look at the screen. |
| 那麼我們可以怎樣改善質素呢？ | So how can we improve the quality? |

# 鼓勵建議（對下）

067.mp3

| | |
|---|---|
| 這是開放討論的。 | It's open to discussion. |
| 我的選擇是未定的。 | I keep my options open. |
| 我們的決定仍是懸而未決的。 | Our decision is still open. |
| 我們還在草擬這計劃。 | We're still drafting the plan.<br>類 We're still outlining the plan.<br>我們還在寫這計劃。 |
| 我們還未達成最後決定。 | We haven't reached the final decision. |
| 歡迎任何建議。 | Any suggestions are welcome. |
| 我們現在集思廣益。請發言。 | We're brainstorming. Go ahead please. |
| 你會給予甚麼意見？ | What advice would you give? |
| 瑪莉，你有任何見解嗎？ | Mary, do you have any ideas?<br>同 Mary, do you have any opinions?<br>瑪莉，你有任何意見嗎？ |
| 祖，你好像要說甚麼似的。 | Joe, you seem to have something to say. |
| 請表達你的看法。 | Please express your view. |
| 請問你可以給我們你更多深刻的理解嗎？ | Could you please give us more of your insights? |

068.mp3

| | |
|---|---|
| 你可否告訴我們，哪裏需要改進？ | Can you tell us where it needs to improve?<br>Can you tell us......?<br>你可否告訴我們……？<br>Can you tell us if it needs improvement?<br>你可否告訴我們這是否需要改善？<br>Can you tell us how we can do better?<br>你可否告訴我們怎樣可以做得更好？<br>Can you tell us the solution?<br>你可否告訴我們解決方法嗎？ |
| 我想知道，我們可以怎樣改善這份報告。 | I'd like to know how we can improve the report. |
| 我們該怎麼做，才能令這份建議書看來更好呢？ | How should we make the proposal look better? |
| 關於這一點，你可否給我們意見？ | Regarding the point, can you give us comments? |
| 上幾個月，我們流失了一些顧客。 | We've lost some customers in the last few months. |
| 我們需要儘快解決。 | We need a quick fix.<br>強調必須尋求最佳方案的迫切性。 |
| 我們的服務質素過去幾個月好像有點走下坡。 | The quality of our services seemed to go slightly downhill over the last few months. |
| 這使董事經理十分頭痛。 | It gave the directing manager a headache. |
| 總公司要求我們分行下個禮拜作出解釋。 | The head office requested our branch to explain next week. |

# 分配工作（對下）

069.mp3

| | |
|---|---|
| 我們的進度不錯，現在是時候實行了。 | Since we're making good progress, it's time to implement it.<br>同 Since we're making good progress, it's time to put it into practice.<br>Since we're making good progress, it's time to carry it out. |
| 現在是分配工作的時候。 | Now it's time to allocate tasks. |
| 看來我們擬定好計劃了。 | It seems that we've set the plan. |
| 既然我們已經定好了國際會議的日期，讓我來委派工作吧。 | Since we've set a date for the international conference, let me assign the jobs. |
| 接着，我想請你們挑選任務。 | Next, I'd like to ask you to pick a task. |
| 湯姆斯，你有很多實際的程式經驗。 | Thomas, you've got a lot of hands-on experience in programming. |
| 阿健，你是這方面領域的專家。 | Ken, you're an expert in this field. |
| 阿凱，你在他們當中資歷最高。 | Kat, you're the senior among them. |
| 你跟公關公司有聯繫。 | You have connections with PR companies. |
| 我需要一個有耐性的人……保羅，你可以處理那些投訴嗎？ | I need someone patient...... Paul, can you deal with the complaints?<br>分配工作前，先點出那位同事的優點和長處，讓人容易信服。 |

070.mp3

| | |
|---|---|
| 我想不出任何人能勝任，就只有你。 | I can't come up with anyone but you. |
| 我想你接受這項任務。 | I'd like to ask you to take this task. |
| 你是負責它的最佳人選。 | You're the best one to take care of it.<br>同 You're the best one to be responsible for it.<br>You're the best person to take care of it. |
| 你可以接受這項任務嗎？ | Can you take this task? |
| 你可以籌備會議的茶點嗎？ | Can you organize refreshments for the conference? |
| 你介意打電話各給賓客提醒他們嗎？ | Would you mind calling all the guests to remind them? |
| 請起碼預先在一星期前印出綱要。 | Please print out the rundown at least a week in advance. |
| 請問你可以去找最便宜的印務公司嗎？ | Could you look for the cheapest printing company please?<br>Could you look for...... please?<br>請問你可以去找……嗎？<br>Could you look for a reliable fabric supplier please?<br>請問你可以去找可靠的布料供應商嗎？<br>Could you look for a sponsorship please?<br>請問你可以去找贊助商嗎？ |

Allocate 分配
Implement 實行
Assign 委派
Task 任務／工作
Conference（大型）會議

# 財務預算（一般）

071.mp3

| | |
|---|---|
| 現在我們開始談談關於金錢的事情。 | Now we start to talk about the money matter. |
| 接下來讓我們討論部門預算案。 | Let's move on to the budget for the department. |
| 因為撥款即將到期，大家來討論一下吧。 | As the funding is going to expire, let's discuss it. |
| 總公司要求我們平衡預算。 | The head office asked us to balance the budget. |
| 我們可以怎樣從總公司得到更多錢呢？ | How can we get more money from the head office?<br>同 How can we get more funds from the head office? |
| 你們有誰可以建議一個數字？ | Can any of you suggest a figure? |
| 請給我們看看你的計算。 | Please show us your calculation. |
| 成本被高估了。 | Cost is overestimated.<br>反 Cost is underestimated.<br>成本被低估了。 |
| 我們估計明年成本會漲。 | We estimated that the cost will arise next year. |
| 東西可能比預期貴。 | Things may be more expensive than expected. |
| 物料價格會上升。 | Price of materials may go up. |
| 這是我們的初步估計。 | It's our initial estimate. |

072.mp3

| | |
|---|---|
| 成本上漲導致利潤下降。 | The rise in cost may lead profit to drop.<br>類 The rise in cost may cause profit to drop.<br>成本上漲引起利潤下降。 |
| 讓我們找出減少支出的方法吧。 | Let's look for methods to reduce expenses.<br>類 Let's figure out how to reduce expenses.<br>讓大家來想出如何減少支出吧。<br>Let's work out a way to decrease expenses.<br>讓我們想出減低支出的方法吧。 |
| 哪一項支出我們應該減省？ | Which expense item should we cut? |
| 運輸支出看來太高。 | Transportation expenses look too high. |
| 恐怕我們要買三台手提電腦，而不是五台。 | I'm afraid that we'll buy 3 laptops instead of 5. |
| 辦公室裝修應該要考慮。 | Office renovation should be considered. |
| 不可能取消旅遊一項。 | It's impossible to delete travel.<br>同 It's impossible to remove travel. |
| 我的意見是，我們不該訂商務客位。 | In my opinion, we should not book any business class. |
| 這可能幫助我們減少支出。 | It may help us minimize the expenses. |
| 我們應該預算更多宣傳費。 | We should budget more for promotion expense. |
| 也許，我們要縮減年夜飯的規模。 | Perhaps we shrink the scale of the annual dinner. |
| 這個項目可能會超出預算。 | The project may go over budget. |

# 決議（對下）

073.mp3

| | |
|---|---|
| 由於這件事情我們已停止討論，我要求投票。 | As there's no more discussion on this matter, I'm asking for a vote. |
| 我們無法在辯論中達成同意。 | We can't conclude an agreement in debate. |
| 我建議投票動議。 | I'd propose a motion for a vote. |
| 約翰動議。 | John moved a motion. |
| 現在我們來作決定。 | Now we've come to make a decision.<br>類 Now we've come to determine it.<br>現在我們來決定它。<br>Now we've come to resolve.<br>現在我們來議決。 |
| 我們需要一個人來動議通過。 | We need someone to make a motion for approval. |
| 我現在要求會議中的每一個人投票。 | I'm asking everyone in the meeting to vote. |
| 我們需要立即投票。 | We need a vote right away. |
| 你們有誰提議投票動議呢？ | Any of you may propose a motion for a vote? |
| 有人提出投票動議嗎？ | Will someone bring a motion to vote? |
| 瑪莉附和動議。 | Mary seconds the motion. |
| 那麼大家投票吧！ | Let's vote then! |

074.mp3

| | |
|---|---|
| 約翰是附議者。 | John is the seconder. |
| 讓我們投票修改動議。 | Let's vote on an amendment to the motion. |
| 我們將投票要求審議該報告的動議。 | We'll vote for a motion calling a review of the report. |
| 投票可以進行了。 | A go-ahead was given for voting.<br>以上一句較適合內部會議。 |
| 我想請各位為這項動議投票。 | I'd like to invite all of you to vote for the motion. |
| 請不要在票上寫上你的名字。 | Please don't write your name on the ballot. |
| 這是不記名的。 | It's anonymous. |
| 大多數人贊成這項動議。 | The majority voted for the motion. |
| 我們大部分人反對法蘭提出的動議。 | Most of us voted against the motion moved by Frank. |
| 動議被否決。 | The motion was turned down.<br>同 The motion was voted down. |
| 我宣佈動議通過。 | I declare that the motion passed. |
| 動議獲通過。 | The motion was adopted. |
| 一致通過它。 | The motion passed by unanimous vote. |
| 它以五票大多數通過。 | It was carried by a majority of five. |

# 爭辯（一般）

075.mp3

| | |
|---|---|
| 我不能接受你的論據。 | I can't accept your argument. |
| 我想馬上處理它。 | I'd like to deal with it straightaway. |
| 我要現在表達個人見解。 | I have to express my point now.<br>對某議題持不同觀點，最好是立即提出辯論或解釋。 |
| 這正是我的意思。 | That's exactly what I'm saying. |
| 我的意思是，這是不成的。 | What I mean is it doesn't work. |
| 我的看法是，這是不可能。 | In my view, it's impossible.<br>In my view, ......<br>我的看法是，……<br>In my view, it costs too much.<br>我的看法是，這帶來太高成本。<br>In my view, it can't increase the profit.<br>我的看法是，這不能增加利潤。 |
| 我看不到有足夠的證據。 | I didn't see that there is enough proof. |
| 為甚麼只有另一個選擇？ | How come there's one alternative only? |
| 我不明白為甚麼你會說它不受市場歡迎？ | I don't understand why you said it's not marketable. |
| 你肯定這個數字是準確嗎？ | Are you sure the figure is accurate? |
| 如果我們不進行市場調查，將會帶來風險。 | It's risky if we don't undergo a marketing survey. |

076.mp3

| | |
|---|---|
| 你怎知道我們的顧客不喜歡它呢？ | How can you tell our customers won't like it? |
| 讓我說白一點。這不是我的工作。 | Let me get it straight. It's not my job. |
| 請不要把所有事情扛在我的肩頭上。 | Please don't put everything on my shoulders. |
| 我沒有時間負責另一個項目。 | I can't afford time for another project. |
| 我沒有足夠的知識來處理這軟件。你可否提議其他人呢？ | I don't have fair knowledge in handling this software. Can you suggest anyone else? |
| 很抱歉，我必須拒絕。我已經負責三項計劃了。 | Sorry, I have to say no. I'm working on 3 projects already. |
| 暫時我有太多工作。我不能承擔這份工作了。 | I've had too much work for now. I can't take up the job. |
| 如果我被委派的話，我覺得自己不能在限期前完成。 | I don't think I can finish it by the deadline if I'm assigned. |

開會分配工作的時候，有些人總喜歡偷懶，拒絕承擔本身的工作，甚至會藉故推到你的身上。如果你已經有很重的工作負擔，明明知道自己沒有時間或能力完成老闆委派的任務，你要言詞堅定，說明正當有力的理由，當場婉拒。

| | |
|---|---|
| 相反，這研究顯示將會有需求。 | On the contrary, the study shows that there will be a demand. |

077.mp3

| | |
|---|---|
| 但是，另一個供應商如何呢？ | But, what about another supplier? |
| 那麼，對你來說，在十二月開會議沒有不妥的地方。 | So for you holding the conference in December can do no wrong.<br>暗示可能有對方未察覺的問題。 |
| 你講的那一點是對的，不過，這只是假設。 | You're right there, but it's just an assumption. |
| 為甚麼這不是一個錯誤？ | How is it that there is not a mistake? |
| 很多時候，你忽略了污染的代價。 | Most of the time, you neglect the cost of pollution. |
| 你可否告訴我為甚麼將會有短缺？ | Can you tell me why there'll be a shortage? |
| 你可否解釋為甚麼你寧願挑這個顏色？ | Can you explain why you prefer to pick this colour? |
| 「不利的結果」到底是甚麼意思？ | What does "an unfavourable result" mean exactly?<br>What does "......" mean exactly?<br>「……」到底是甚麼意思？<br>What does "an unexpected factor" mean exactly?<br>「沒有預期的因素」到底是甚麼意思？<br>What does "an irreversible effect" mean exactly?<br>「不可逆轉的影響」到底是甚麼意思？ |
| 你說的「進取的方法」到底是甚麼意思？ | What exactly did you mean by "an aggressive approach"? |
| 「經濟因素」指的是甚麼？ | What does "the economic factor" refer to? |

# 溫和反對（一般）

078.mp3

| | |
|---|---|
| 事實上，我會說相反的意見。 | In fact, I'd say the opposite.<br>In fact, I......<br>事實上，我……<br>In fact, I have a different opinion.<br>事實上，我有不同的意見。<br>In fact, I'd have another idea.<br>事實上，我有另一種見解。 |
| 大體而言，你的看法與事實相反。 | Generally speaking, the fact is contrary to your view. |
| 恐怕我不能同意你。 | I'm afraid that I can't agree with you. |
| 我有點不同意。 | I somewhat disagree. |
| 我有點不同意這一點。 | I kind of disagree on this point. |
| 看來我們的看法有衝突。 | There seems to be a conflict between our views. |
| 這是錯的，原因是缺乏證據。 | This is wrong for the reason of lack of evidence. |
| 我明白你的重點，不過很難認同。 | I understand your point, but I hardly agree.<br>類 I understand what you've expressed, but I hardly agree.<br>我明白你表達了的意見，不過很難認同。 |
| 很抱歉，但我得要說跟你不同的見解。 | Sorry, but I've got to say a different point from yours. |
| 你說的這一點很好，不過如果我們不減省成本的話會如何呢？ | You were making a good point, but what if we don't cut the cost? |

# 強烈反對（一般）

079 .mp3

| | |
|---|---|
| 我完全不同意你。 | I completely disagree with you. |
| 我強烈持有不同的看法。 | I strongly hold a different view. |
| 我完全不能接受你的觀點。 | I can't accept your viewpoint completely.<br>類 I can't accept your argument as a whole.<br>我不能接受你的整體辯論。 |
| 你根本無法説服我。 | You can't persuade me at all. |
| 我絕對反對你剛剛説的話。 | I absolutely object to what you said just now.<br>同 I totally object to what you said just now.<br>I entirely object to what you said just now. |
| 不會有我同意你的機會。 | There's not a chance that I'd agree with you. |
| 我不覺得你的建議合理。 | Your suggestion doesn't make sense to me.<br>雖然沒有明言反對，這句話的攻擊力是很強的，如非必要，不要如此決絕。 |

Opposite 相反　　Conflict 衝突／矛盾

# 強烈同意（一般）

080.mp3

| | |
|---|---|
| 我深信你是對的。 | I strongly believe that you're right.<br>I strongly believe that......<br>我深信……<br>I strongly believe that it can work.<br>我深信這是可行的。<br>I strongly believe that your prediction will come true.<br>我深信你的預測成真。 |
| 跟隨你的建議肯定是唯一的方法。 | This is surely the only way to follow your suggestion. |
| 我完全支持你。 | I fully support you. |
| 我毫無保留同意你的重點。 | I agree to your point without reservation. |
| 我一直完全認同你。 | I'm with you all the way. |
| 我絕對站在你那邊。 | I'm absolutely on your side. |
| 你可以相信我對你的支持。 | You can count on me for supporting you. |
| 我們對這一點的意見相符。 | Our views coincide at this point.<br>同 Our views match at this point.<br>Our views agree at this point. |
| 我們都同意。 | We're singing from the same hymn sheet.<br>"sing from the same hymn" 是俗語，意思是一群人公開表示同意某一事項或原則。<br>或可以説："We're singing the same tune." |
| 我們異口同聲，對於這一點看法一致。 | We speak with one voice on this point. |
| 我們看事情的方向完全相同。 | We have exactly the same way of viewing things.<br>同 We share exactly the same way of viewing things. |

# 溫和同意（一般）

081.mp3

| | |
|---|---|
| 我傾向同意。 | I tend to agree. |
| 我的看法幾乎跟你一樣。 | I see it almost the same way as you do. |
| 我也有相同的意見。 | I also have the same idea. |
| 很高興，我們也同意某一點。 | I'm glad that we agree to a certain point. |
| 我會這樣說，我部分同意你的見解。 | I'd say that I partly agree to your points. |
| 我同意你的一些要點。 | I'd agree on some of your points. |
| 我同意第一項，但我想更多討論其餘的。 | I agree to item 1, but I'd like to discuss more about the rest. |
| 似乎我們有相同的意見，但是你可以澄清那個理由嗎？ | It's likely that we share the same opinion, but can you clarify the reason? |
| 基本上我同意你的關注。你可否闡述更多？ | Basically I agree to your concern. Can you elaborate more?<br>縱使有些地方同意，但是對於不肯定的地方，還是提議對方清楚說明，讓自己能下更明智的決定。 |
| 我們快要意見一致。 | We're getting closer to consent. |
| 你大部分的要點說服了我。 | Most of your points persuaded me.<br>類 Most of your points were convincing.<br>你大部分的要點具說服力。 |
| 某程度而言，我同意那投資部分。 | To a certain extent, I agree to the investment section. |

# 表示保留（一般）

082.mp3

| | |
|---|---|
| 我要說，這並不符合我的期望。 | I'd say it's not up to my expectation. |
| 我沒有預期這樣的。 | I didn't expect that. |
| 這沒有我想過的那麼好。 | It's not as good as expected. |
| 我預期它應該是更好的。 | I expected that it should have been better.<br>不要直接說「糟糕」或「差勁」（bad, worse），說它不夠好已經讓人明白你的立場。 |
| 我對這個計劃有保留。 | I have reservations about the plan.<br>I have reservations about......<br>我對……有保留。<br>I have reservations about the research.<br>我對這項研究有保留。<br>I have reservations about your assumptions.<br>我對你的假設有保留。 |
| 我認為你的計劃不能帶給我們有利的結果。 | I don't think your plan got us anywhere near a favourable result. |
| 我不認為這會如你所說的，帶來有利的結果。 | I don't think it'll bring us a favourable result as you said. |
| 我沒有你那麼樂觀。 | I'm not as optimistic as you.<br>同 I'm not as positive as you.<br>I'm not as hopeful as you. |

083.mp3

| | |
|---|---|
| 我質疑它能否改善生產。 | I doubt that it can improve the production.<br>I doubt that it can......<br>我質疑它能否……<br>I doubt that it can upgrade our image.<br>我質疑它能否提高我們的形象。<br>I doubt that it can build up our reputation.<br>我質疑它能否它能否建立我們名聲。 |
| 對我來説，它看來不是完全合理的。 | It seems not completely sensible to me. |
| 當然這是我們的目標，但是看來不大有希望。 | Surely it's our goal, but it seems less hopeful. |
| 我鼓勵你細看那些隱藏的風險。 | I'd encourage you to look into the hidden risks. |
| 也許，你漏看了政治不穩引起的風險。 | Perhaps you overlook the risks due to political instability. |
| 聽我的意見——考慮他們的背景吧。 | Please take my advice-consider their background. |
| 我發現回顧部分有不妥的地方。 | I've found something wrong in the review section.<br>立場有所保留的時候，最好也説明哪裏你覺得有問題，讓對方有機會解釋或改善。 |
| 你可能忽略了一些重要因素。 | You may have ignored some of the essential factors.<br>You may have ignored......<br>你可能忽略了……<br>You may have ignored some determining causes.<br>你可能忽略了一些具決定性的原因。<br>You may have ignored some unexpected effects.<br>你可能忽略了一些沒有預期的影響。 |

# 延長會議（對下）

084.mp3

| | |
|---|---|
| 你也知道，我們已經討論很久了。 | As you can see, we had a long discussion. |
| 我們的會議比預期更長。 | Our meeting was longer than expected. |
| 我們無法在預定的時間前完成。 | We're not able to finish before the time we set. |
| 我們在會議中不大有進展。 | We were not making progress in the meeting. |
| 我們有很多不同的意見。 | We had so many different opinions there.<br>提出延長會議的原因時，盡量別提任何人的名字，以免任何人被其他同事責怪他拖延會議。 |
| 我們應該討論更多。 | We should discuss more. |
| 我們離開前，還是想一想解決方案。 | We'd better come up with a solution before we go. |
| 我不認為我們可以就此打住。 | I don't think we can stop here.<br>I don't think we......<br>我不認為我們……<br>I don't think we'll just leave it like that.<br>我不認為我們就這樣算了。<br>I don't think we want the meeting to come to an end.<br>我不認為我們我們想會議結束。 |
| 好可能我們需要多一個小時。 | It's very likely that we need one more hour. |
| 我們只餘下十五分鐘。 | We only have 15 minutes left. |

085.mp3

| | |
|---|---|
| 我們都熱烈參與討論。 | We've actively participated in discussion. |
| 看來我們想繼續下去。 | It seems that we want to go on. |
| 我們還沒有決定解決方法。 | We haven't determined the solution yet.<br>類 We haven't solved it yet.<br>我們還沒有解決它。 |
| 我幾乎忘掉了時間。 | I've almost forgotten the time. |
| 噢，我們花了整個早上了！ | Oh, we've spent the whole morning! |
| 已經是午飯時間，但是我們還沒完成。 | It's lunch time already, but we didn't get it done. |
| 現在已經是三點鐘！ | Now it's 3 already! |
| 你們有誰下午有約？ | Does anyone of you have an appointment this afternoon?<br>Does anyone of you......?<br>你們有誰……？<br>Does anyone of you have to leave for work?<br>你們有誰要回去工作？<br>Does anyone of you have to go?<br>你們有誰要走？ |
| 你們想多留一會兒嗎？ | Would you like to stay a little bit longer? |
| 你們可以留下來嗎？ | Can you all stay? |
| 有誰現在想走？ | Anyone has to go now?<br>同 Who has to go now?<br>Any person has to leave right away? |
| 你們可以多留三十分鐘嗎？ | Would you stay here for another 30 minutes? |

# 終止會議（對下）

086.mp3

| | |
|---|---|
| 時間不多了。 | Time is running out. |
| 我知道你們有些人不能留下來。 | I know some of you can't stay any longer.<br>類 I know some of you have to go now.<br>我知道你們有些人現在要走了。 |
| 我要說，我們只有很少時間。 | I'd like to say we have very little time. |
| 可惜，我認為討論無法繼續。 | Unfortunately, I don't think the discussion can go on.<br>同 Unfortunately, I don't think the discussion can continue. |
| 我建議在下次會議討論其他的。 | I'd suggest discussing the rest in the next meeting. |
| 我們要把這些留到下次會議。 | We have to leave that to the next meeting. |
| 如果沒有反對，我把討論推延到下次會議。 | If there's no opposition, I'd put off the discussion until the next meeting. |
| 我們可以跳過這一項，下次再討論嗎？ | Could we skip it and discuss next time? |
| 我們今天還是暫停討論。 | We'd better suspend the discussion for today. |
| 看來我們已經論及大部分議題。 | It seems that we've covered most of the items. |
| 看來主要的議題已經討論過了。 | It looks as if main items have been discussed. |

| | |
|---|---|
| 我們得要去會見客戶。 | We are due to meet the clients.<br>We are due to......<br>我們得要（離開的理由）。<br>We are due to head to another meeting.<br>我們得要動身往另一會議。<br>We are due to go to the exhibition.<br>我們得要去那個展覽。 |
| 有誰提出其他事項？ | Will anyone raise any other business? |
| 有其他事項嗎？ | Is there any other business?<br>在會議記錄中，"any other business" 多寫成 "AOB"。 |
| 如果沒有其他事項，就此打住吧。 | If there's no more other business, let's stop here. |
| 我相信我們已經討論了所有議題。 | I believe that we've discussed all the items. |
| 我們可以定下次會議的日期嗎？ | Can we fix a date for the next meeting? |
| 下個星期五你們都行嗎？ | Is next Friday good for all of you? |
| 大家如常九點開會吧。 | Let's meet at 9 as usual. |
| 每個人都行嗎？ | Is that ok for everyone? |
| 那麼下次會議在星期一九點舉行。 | So the next meeting will take place at 9 on Monday. |
| 結束前，我想謝謝你們的貢獻。 | I'll finish by thanking you for your contributions. |

## 相關生字

| | |
|---|---|
| Deficit | 赤字 |
| Surplus | 盈餘 |
| Meeting | （一般、內部）會議 |
| Conference | （大型）會議 |
| Convention | （大型）會議 |
| Exhibition | 展覽 |
| Unanimous | 全票一致 |
| Anonymous | 不記名 |
| Approval | 批准 |
| Consent | 意見一致 |
| Assumption | 假設 |
| Clarification | 澄清 |
| Conclusion | 結論 |
| Consequence | 結果 |
| Discussion | 討論 |
| Persuasion | 說服 |
| Elaboration | 闡述 |
| Explanation | 解釋 |
| Result | 結果 |
| Suggestion | 提議 |

## 表達技巧

促使工作環境和諧是維持良好人際關係的重要一環。不過，當我們開會的時候，往往是唇槍舌劍的戰場。我們會有不同的意見和看法，這時候必須保持尊重別人的態度；否則，很容易讓人覺得你跋扈囂張，日後給其他同事孤立而不自知。本章中表達反對意見的部分，讀者務必小心使用。雖然我們一般認為，西方人崇尚個人主義，認為必須表達自己的想法，但是這不代表你「想到甚麼，便説甚麼」。他們反而在表達異議的時候，十分客氣，儘可能保存同事的顏面，冷靜分析彼此之間不同的地方。首先，鋪陳大脈絡，提出自己的看法，然後才指正不同意的地方。而主持會議的時候，盡量邀請所有與會同事發言，公平地讓每個人也有發表意見的機會；如果有人離題的話，藉故問他一些相關問題，或直接提醒他，別把會議拖延太長——誰想開一個無休止的會議？這樣做令人更信服你的領導和管理能力。

# Chapter 4

# 工作權益

# 面對壓力（一般）

090.mp3

| | |
|---|---|
| 我無法處理那麼多任務。 | I was unable to handle so many tasks. |
| 我失去控制是因為要接聽那麼多電話。 | I just lost control in picking up so many phone calls. |
| 想到那個被縮短的限期，我就覺得壓力重重。 | I'm stressed out when thinking of the shorter deadline. |
| 找解決方法令我很有壓力。 | It's stressful to find a solution. |
| 我有時對處理投訴沒有信心。 | I sometimes don't feel confident about handling the complaints. |
| 我在工作中發揮有困難。 | I had trouble functioning in my job. |
| 我想心中更平靜。 | I want more peace of mind. |
| 我感到更大壓力。 | I feel more stressed. |
| 我正在受很大的壓力。 | I'm under a lot of stress. |
| 一切事情真的使我感到壓力重重。 | All the things really stress me out. |
| 我恐怕我趕不上限期。 | I'm afraid that I can't meet the deadline. |
| 顧客聲稱要投訴。 | The customer claimed to complain. |
| 我曉得怎樣向主管解釋。 | I don't know how to explain to the supervisor. |
| 我如何用英文解釋得更好？ | How can I explain better in English? |

091.mp3

| | |
|---|---|
| 我要說服那位顧客有困難。 | I have trouble persuading the customer. |
| 使人壓得透不過氣來。 | It was overwhelming. |
| 快到的限期使我感到壓力沉重。 | I feel overwhelmed by the upcoming deadline.<br>I feel overwhelmed by......<br>使我感到壓力沉重。<br>I feel overwhelmed by the huge task I have on hand.<br>手上的一大件工作使我趕到壓力沉重。<br>I feel overwhelmed by the big task ahead of me.<br>面前的一大件工作使我趕到壓力沉重。 |
| 很有挑戰性。 | It's challenging. |
| 我正處於困難的時刻。 | I'm having a hard time. |
| 他們刁難我。 | They just gave me a hard time. |
| 項目到期了。 | The project is due. |
| 我預料我要處理很多工作量。 | I can foresee that I'll manage a huge workload. |
| 我不斷覺得緊張。 | I constantly feel tense. |
| 我無法控制情況。 | I can't take control of the circumstances. |
| 我可以怎樣使這個問題沒有那麼困難？ | How can I make the issues less problematic? |
| 這個問題認真大。 | The problem is really big. |
| 我本該拒絕他。 | I should've said no to him.<br>同 I should've refused him.<br>I should've turned him down. |

# 鼓勵同事（一般）

092.mp3

| | |
|---|---|
| 正面些吧。 | Be positive. |
| 誰可以分擔你的工作？ | Can anyone share your work? |
| 別太勉強自己。 | Don't push yourself to the limit. |
| 別把所有事情塞在太少時間裏完成。 | Don't cram everything into too little time. |
| 現在休息一下吧。 | Take a break now. |
| 你一直工作勤奮，別埋怨自己了。 | You've been working hard and don't blame yourself. |
| 我們都知道這是很棘手的個案。 | We all knew that it's a difficult case. |
| 我明白你的感受。 | I understand your feelings. |
| 我也經歷過。 | I've experienced it. |
| 放鬆，讓我弄一杯茶給你吧。 | Relax, let me make you a cup of tea. |
| 暫且把它擱在一旁。 | Put it aside for now. |
| 你快要耗盡自己的精力。 | You'll risk burning out. |
| 看來這太困擾你了 | It seems to bother you too much. |
| 別想負面的那一面。 | Stop thinking about the negative side. |

093.mp3

| | |
|---|---|
| 或者你能夠準時完成。 | Maybe you can finish on time. |
| 別去想那個重擔吧。 | Put the burden out of your mind. |
| 這是真正的挑戰。 | It's a real challenge. |
| 你想要額外幫助嗎？ | Do you want additional help? |
| 你會讓別人幫忙嗎？ | Would you allow someone to help? |
| 這是時候你要學習把自己的一些工作分配給別人。 | It's time you learn to assign people to take on some of your tasks. |
| 有人能夠幫到你嗎？ | Is there anyone who can help you? |
| 敢言些，讓別人不會蹂躪你。 | Be assertive and people won't walk all over you. |
| 直接表達你的感受。 | Be direct about your feelings. |
| 你本該告訴他們，你已經有太多工作。 | You should've told people that you had too much work already. |
| 別擔心。你那一組很有效率的。 | Don't worry. Your team is efficient. |
| 說「不」不表示你壓制了別人。 | Saying no doesn't mean that you steamroll over others. |
| 當你滿手工作的時候，拒絕接手任何事情。 | Refuse to take over anything when your plate is full. |
| 你太投入了。 | You're overcommitted. |

# 要求加薪（對上）

094.mp3

| | |
|---|---|
| 我可以跟你預約會面，討論我的報酬？ | Can I set up a meeting with you to discuss my compensation? |
| 我可以和你討論加薪事宜嗎？ | May I discuss a pay raise with you? |
| 我們可以安排一次關於加薪的會議嗎？ | Can we schedule a meeting for a pay raise? |
| 我們可以在星期五見面嗎？ | Can we meet up on Friday?<br>跟上司相約商談加薪的事情，要給對方好些時間準備，他也要看看市場的薪酬趨勢或垂詢人事部有關政策。 |
| 我知道，要談這些事情很難找時間。 | I know, it's hard to find time to talk about these things. |
| 我真的需要這方面的答案。 | I really need an answer on this. |
| 甚麼時候方便你談論它？ | When is it a good time for you to talk about it? |
| 謝謝你今天跟我會面。 | Thank you for meeting me today. |
| 今天，我想要求加薪。 | Today, I'd like to ask you for a pay raise.<br>同 Today, I'd like to request for a pay raise. |
| 我希望我們有坦誠的討論。 | I hope that we'll have an open discussion. |
| 我們也看得見，市場現在愈來愈好。 | As we can see, the market is getting better now. |
| 我們的生意改善了。 | Our business has improved. |

095.mp3

| | |
|---|---|
| 我應該獲得加薪的。 | I deserve a raise. |
| 公司似乎更能夠加薪給我。 | The company is more likely to afford a pay raise for me. |
| 我理解公司的薪酬措施。 | I understand the company's pay practices. |
| 我明白，我們通常每年檢討薪酬一次。 | I know we usually review the pay rate annually. |
| 你們每年年底給我們加薪。 | You offer a salary increase by the end of each year. |
| 在你公佈全公司加薪前，我想向你商討爭取更多薪金。 | I want to negotiate more money before you announced the pay raises for everyone. |
| 由於去年公司減了我們的薪金，這是時候商討加薪了。 | As the company froze our salary last year, it's time to discuss a raise. |
| 這就是我預備的一份清單，關於我在公司的建樹。 | Here you go. I've prepared a list of my accomplishments in the company. |
| 這是支持我要求加薪的文件。 | It's a supporting document. |
| 我蒐集了一些資料來支持我的要求。 | I've collected some data to support my request. |

096.mp3

| | |
|---|---|
| 我已經達成符合公司要求的目標。 | I've achieved goals that matched the company's requests. |

要求加薪前，想一想自己對公司貢獻過甚麼，然後列出一份清單來跟上司討價還價，例如：

Set-up of cost – saving system 設立節省成本的系統

Major projects completed successfully 成功完成重大項目

A rise in sale turnover 營業額上升

Productive team under my supervision 本人管理具生產力的小組

An increase in bills handled 處理的帳單增加

More responsibility: takeover of a team from another supervisor 更多責任：從另一主管接受一組人

如果有實際數字支持的話，則更理想。

| | |
|---|---|
| 我已經研究市場薪酬。 | I've researched the market pay rates. |
| 我的薪金市低過市場薪酬。 | My salary is under the market rate. |
| 我是按員工手冊印刊的程序。 | I've followed the process printed in the employee handbook. |
| 我建議加 2%。 | I'd suggest a 2% increase. |
| 它可以反映我對公司的貢獻。 | It may reflect my contributions to the company. |
| 這是合理的數字。 | It's a reasonable figure. |
| 這是接近市場的薪酬。 | It's close to the market-based pay rate. |
| 我對如何獲取補償這一點很有彈性。 | I'm flexible on how I'm compensated. |

097.mp3

| | |
|---|---|
| 我知道銀根緊缺。 | I know that money is tight. |
| 不如大家別只關注人工。 | Let's not focus on salary only. |
| 如果我有額外假期，我會考慮 6%。 | I'd consider 6% if I have extra vacation days. |
| 你會考慮它嗎？ | Are you open to that? |
| 這是根據市場薪酬的估計。 | It's an estimate based on market rate. |
| 我從 2009 年開始擔任很多工作。 | I've taken on more jobs since 2009. |
| 我被分配很多責任。 | I was assigned more responsibilities. |
| 這是我工作的紀錄。 | That's the review of my work. |
| 它顯示我過去五年的表現。 | It shows last five years of my performance. |
| 請看一下。 | Please take a look. |
| 我相信我是有價值的員工。 | I believe I'm a valuable employee. |
| 我把自己的工作表現分析在這份數據表上。 | I've analyzed my job performance on this spreadsheet. |
| 你看到我在過去六個月找到的客戶有增加。 | You can tell the increase in clients I found in the last six months. |

# D 應加薪（對下）

098.mp3

| | |
|---|---|
| 好的，找一天來見面談談。 | Sure, let's meet up some day. |
| 我明白，星期四談談它吧。 | I see, let' talk about it on Thursday. |
| 我知道你很關注這一點，但是我們可否在隔一週後會面？ | I know it's a major concern, but can we meet the week after next? |
| 如果你不介意的話，我想請人事部主任參與我們的會面。 | If you don't mind, I'd ask a Human Resources officer to join the meeting.<br>一些公司對於加薪實施既定的程序，或許必須通知人事部。 |
| 我知道，這會涉及你的私隱，不過另外有人在場更是明智。 | I know it may involve your privacy but it's wiser to have someone else there. |
| 我也想邀請一位人事部同事。 | I prefer to invite a colleague from Human Resources as well. |
| 根據員工手冊，人事部參與這過程是必須的。 | According to the employee handbook, it's necessary to get Human Resources involved. |
| 雖然仍是初步階段，我應該通知人事部。 | Although it's a preliminary phase, I ought to inform Human Resources. |
| 他們應該知道你的要求。 | They should know about your request. |
| 我需要聯絡人事部。 | I'll need to contact Human Resources. |

099.mp3

| | |
|---|---|
| 如果有第三者在場會更好。 | It'd be better if there's a third party.<br>類 It'd be better if a third party attends the meeting.<br>如果有第三者參與會面的話會更好。 |
| 我們開始來商討吧。 | Let's start to discuss it. |
| 你可以把你的要求告訴我嗎？ | Can you tell me your request?<br>類 Can you tell me your suggestion?<br>你可以把你的提議告訴我嗎？<br>Can you tell me your proposal?<br>你可以把你的建議告訴我嗎？ |
| 你準備了支持你要求加薪的文件嗎？ | Did you prepare any documents which support your request? |
| 你有任何數字證明你所說的嗎？ | Do you have any figures to prove what you said? |
| 有你的工作總結嗎？ | Is there any summary of your work? |
| 我們重視你的貢獻。 | We value your contribution. |
| 我們需要考慮更多因素。 | We need to take a lot of factors into consideration. |
| 我會考慮你的建議。 | I'll take your proposal into consideration. |
| 我想補償你的勤奮表現。 | I'd like to compensate your hard work.<br>類 I'd like to compensate your effort.<br>我想補償你的努力。 |
| 聽起來它比現在的市場薪金更高。 | It sounds higher than the current market rate. |
| 你知道，我現在不能提出任何薪酬數字。 | You know, I'm not able to offer you any rate for now. |

# 請假（一般）

100.mp3

| | |
|---|---|
| 你今年有甚麼計劃？ | What is your plan for this year? |
| 這個夏季有任何重大項目嗎？ | Will there be any major project during the summer? |
| | 在請假前，先諮詢上司公司未來的計劃，避免撞期。 |
| 我想向你請假。 | I'd like to ask you for time off. |
| 我想今年放假一次。 | I want to take a vacation this year. |
| 我可以下個月放假嗎？ | Can I get time off next month? |
| 請批准我要求的時間。 | Please approve my requested time. |
| 去年我無法放假。 | I wasn't able to have a vacation last year. |
| 我想請兩個星期的假期，五月一日至十四日。 | I'd like to request a 2-week vacation between May 1st and 14th. |
| 請批准我更多無薪假期。 | Please grant me more time off, which is unpaid. |
| 你可否告訴我，在我計劃假期的時候怎樣安排一切？ | Would you tell me how to arrange things when I'm planning a vacation? |
| 我可以把一些有薪病假轉為假期？ | May I convert some paid sick days to vacation days? |
| 我可以預留五月第二個星期嗎？ | Can I reserve the second week of May? |

101.mp3

| | |
|---|---|
| 我想到外面走走休息一下。 | I want to get away for a break. |
| 我可以怎樣做，在我放假時才不會影響到其他人？ | What can I do to make my time away disruptive to others? |
| 我想請八天假期。 | I'd like to take 8 vacation days. |
| 放假前，我會打點好一切。 | I'll take care of everything before the holiday. |
| 我沒有打算完全跟你們斷絕聯絡。 | I'm not ready to disconnect completely. |
| 我會跟客戶保持聯絡。 | I'll keep in contact with the clients.<br>盡量跟同事交代清楚及進行協調，並表示歡迎同事隨時聯絡你，請假的機會自然大增。 |
| 大衛會代理我的職務。 | David will cover me. |
| 我放假期間，森姆會取代我。 | Sam will fill in when I'm on vacation. |
| 我會跟瑪莉查查看，我們不會同時放假。 | I've checked with Mary that our vacation time won't overlap. |
| 我度假期間，她不會放假。 | She won't take time off during my vacation. |
| 我放假的時候，她不會缺席。 | My time off won't overlap with her absence. |
| 我們不在同一個星期放假。 | We don't take the same week off. |

# 向同事交代（一般）

102.mp3

| | |
|---|---|
| 我正在計劃旅行。 | I'm planning a trip. |
| 我不在的時候，會每星期電郵聯絡一次。 | I'll check in once a week by email while I'm away. |
| 我走了以後，也可以找到我的。 | I can be reached while I'm gone. |
| 我會在六月二十四日離開。 | I'll be gone on June 24th. |
| 我想回到辦公室也知道發生了甚麼事情。 | I'd like to stay on top of events back at the office. |
| 我會在星期一去度假。 | I'll leave on vacation on Monday. |
| 下星期三我會走了。 | I'll be going away next Wednesday. |
| 我會放假。 | I'll take time off. |
| 我會放假一個星期。 | I'll take a week off for holiday. |
| 別擔心。我不會最後一分鐘才通知你們放假。 | Don't worry. It won't be a last-minute absence. |
| 那個旅遊套餐很划算。 | The package is affordable. |
| 我買機票，得了很多優惠。 | I got a great deal on airfare. |
| 度假期間我會看電郵。 | I'll catch up on the emails on vacation. |

# 辭職通知（對上）

103.mp3

| | |
|---|---|
| 你可以坐下來跟我對談嗎？ | Can I have a sit-down conversation with you? |
| 我可以進來，跟你談三十分鐘？ | May I come in and talk to you for 30 minutes? |
| 我可以在今天完結前跟你面談？ | Can I meet you before the end of the day?<br>下班前跟上司作口頭辭職通知，會面後立即發辭職信。第二天才告訴其他同事。 |
| 我明白公司需要控制成本。 | I understand the need to control costs. |
| 找人替代一個好職員總是成本不少。 | Replacing a good worker is always costly. |
| 雖然經濟不景，我值得更高的薪金。 | I'm worth a higher pay in spite of the bad economy. |
| 我肯定你也同意我是勝任這個職位。 | I'm sure you agree that I'm a good fit for the position. |
| 如果我離開，找一個新人來做我的工作會很昂貴。 | If I leave, it'd be more expensive to hire someone new to do my job.<br>若在加薪談不攏的情況下，先鋪陳理據，然後才冷靜地提出辭職。 |
| 我考慮了這裏的各樣選擇。 | I was considering my options here. |
| 我不會接受低於我應得的條件。 | I won't settle for anything less than I deserve. |
| 人工不是唯一的理由。 | Salary isn't the entire reason. |
| 我想告訴你，我要離職。 | I'd like to tell you I'll quit the job. |

104.mp3

| | |
|---|---|
| 我在找新工作。 | I'm looking for a new job.<br>I'm looking for......<br>我在找……<br>I'm looking for a new career path.<br>我在找新的職業路向。<br>I'm looking for a better prospect.<br>我在找更好的前景。 |
| 我真的喜歡這裏，但我想找更多升職機會。 | I really like it here, but I look for more chances in advancement. |
| 我喜歡這裏，也認為自己稱職。 | I like it here and think I am good at my job. |
| 這是我改變的時候。 | It's time for me to make change. |
| 我決定這是我前進的時候。 | I've decided it is time for me to move on. |
| 我想追尋更多機會。 | I'd like to pursue more opportunities. |
| 我明白，你會覺得驚訝。 | I know it may shock you. |
| 請明白，我想了一些時間。 | Please understand that I was thinking about it for some time. |
| 我要給一個月通知。 | I must give my one month's notice. |
| 我今天要給你一個月通知。 | I need to give you my one month's notice as of today. |
| 如果我上班最後一天是八月十五日，你認為行嗎？ | Does it work for you if my last day is August 15th? |
| 我不知道你有沒有聽過關於這件事。 | I don't know if you've heard about it. |

105.mp3

| | |
|---|---|
| 但已經有另一家公司接觸我。 | But I've been contacted by another company. |
| 我要離職，接受另一家公司的新職位。 | I'll be leaving to accept a new position with another company. |
| 我頗想留下來，但他們的邀約讓我想接受它。 | I'd rather stay, but their offer made me think to accept it. |
| 我手頭上有更高薪的職位邀約。 | I have an offer in hand for a better-paying position. |
| 我寧願想要多些訓練。 | I would have preferred more training. |
| 我很感謝在這裏的機會。 | I am grateful for the opportunities here. |
| 離開這麼愉快的工作環境很困難。 | It's hard to leave this pleasant work environment. |
| 我真的享受這裏的工作。 | I have really enjoyed working here. |
| 我要讓你知道，有公司聘請我擔任新職位。 | I need to let you know that I have been offered a new position at another company. |
| 我現在要辭職接受另一家公司的職位。 | I am resigning to take a position at another company. |
| 在這裏的整體經驗都是正面。 | The overall experience here has been positive. |
| 有新挑戰，我覺得興奮。 | I feel excited to have new challenges. |

106.mp3

| | |
|---|---|
| 我想讓你知道，我是多麼享受與你工作。 | I wanted to let you know how much I've enjoyed working with you. |
| 謝謝你幫助我發展我的事業。 | Thank you very much for helping me develop my career. |
| 我會掛念每一位。 | I'll miss everyone here. |
| 他們是好同事，我懷念他們。 | They're a good team and I'll miss them. |
| 我從你身上獲益良多。 | I've learned a lot from you. |
| 或者我可以幫你找人代替我。 | Maybe I can help you find my replacement. |
| 我會留下進度報告給你和同事。 | I'll leave progress reports for you and colleagues. |
| 謝謝你的反建議。 | Thank you for your counteroffer. |
| 我想告訴你，我拒絕你的建議。 | I want to tell you that I'd decline the offer. |
| 你可以為我寫一封推薦信嗎？ | Can you write a letter of recommendation for me? |
| 你可以做我的推薦人嗎？ | Would you be my reference? |
| 今天我將會預備辭職信。 | I'll prepare a letter of resignation today. |
| 我會在明天遞交辭職信。 | I'll submit a letter of resignation tomorrow. |

# 廣傳消息（一般）

107.mp3

| | |
|---|---|
| 你認識市務部的保羅嗎？ | Do you know Paul from marketing? |
| 他會被調到生產部？ | He'll be transferred to the production department. |
| 他們説丹尼會領導小組。 | They said Danny will be the team leader. |
| 他們會在下次會議宣佈。 | They'll announce it in the next meeting. |
| 他的秘書告訴我。 | His secretary told me. |
| 我相信這是真的。 | I believe it's true. |
| 我是從某人打聽來的。 | I heard it from someone else. |
| 消息來源很可靠呢。 | The source of information is reliable. |
| 為甚麼你不信？ | Why don't you believe that? |
| 他們剛否決全體加薪。 | They just denied a pay raise across the board. |
| 明年我們會被凍薪。 | We'll have our pay frozen next year. |
| 信不信由你，他們會給我們加薪10%！ | Believe it or not, they'll raise our pay 10%! |
| 他們會減我們的人工嗎？ | Will they cut our salaries? |
| 他們會引入按表現發放的花紅制度！ | They'll introduce performance-linked bonus! |

108.mp3

| | |
|---|---|
| 我們很可能又被凍薪一年。 | We'll most probably experience another year of pay freezes. |
| 快到十二月。為甚麼他們還不宣佈加薪？ | It's almost December. Why don't they announce a pay raise? |
| 他今天看來不開心。他可能被要求退出那個項目。 | He looks unhappy today. He was possibly asked to quit the project. |
| 在會議裏，她被要求退出小組。 | She was asked to leave the team in the meeting. |
| 她真的好尷尬。 | She was really embarrassed. |
| 他們說，當時很尷尬。 | They said it was so embarrassing. |
| 他們說每個人在會議裏噤若寒蟬。 | They said everyone is silent as the dead in the meeting.<br>俗語"silent as the dead"的意思是像個死人一樣，完全沉默，也暗示不願意多談一些不愉快的事情。 |
| 經理很生他的氣。 | The manger was so angry with him. |
| 嗨，主管看上去很生氣。發生了甚麼事？ | Hey, supervisor looks mad. What's happened? |
| 她又不能趕及限期了。 | She can't meet the deadlines again. |
| 噢，他又搞錯訂單了！ | Oh, he made a wrong order again! |
| 你是說雪莉，我們的新經理嗎？ | Did you mean Shirley, our new manager? |

# D 應流言（一般）

109.mp3

| | |
|---|---|
| 你怎麼知道？ | How can you tell? |
| 你肯定？ | Are you sure? |
| 你肯定這是他的錯？ | Are you sure it's his fault? |
| 當中有誤會吧？ | Is there a misunderstanding? |
| 你從哪裏打聽來的？ | Where did you hear about that? |
| 個人來説我不大認識他，但我曾跟他通電話。 | I don't know him personally, but we've talked over the phone. |
| 為甚麼他們調走他？ | Why did they transfer him? |
| 你説真的？ | Do you mean it? |
| 你是認真的嗎？ | Are you serious? |
| 不是開玩笑。 | No kidding. |
| 我不認為他們會加薪給我們。 | I don't think that they'll award a pay raise. |
| 我們在過去三年只加薪一次。 | We've just received one pay rise in the last three years. |
| 很抱歉聽見這個消息。 | I'm sorry to hear that. |
| 我為這個誤會而感到遺憾。 | I'm sorry for the misunderstanding. |

110.mp3

| | |
|---|---|
| 或者，他不曉得按上層的意思做人吧。 | Maybe he doesn't know how to play the game. |
| 噢，你不該這樣說。 | Oh, you shouldn't have said that. |
| 這不該發生。 | It shouldn't have happened. |
| 嗯，這些是總會發生。 | Well, these things happen. |
| 這不會叫人驚訝。 | That's not shocking. |
| 太陽底下無新事。 | There's nothing new under the sun. |
| 這很難判斷。 | It's hard to judge. |
| 他們會很快公佈。 | They'll announce it very soon. |
| 噢，真的嗎？ | Oh really? |
| 我不認為是這樣。 | I don't think so. |
| 我未曾聽過。 | I haven't heard about that. |
| 她是一個好領導人。 | She was a good leader. |
| 我會懷念她。 | I'll miss her. |
| 我們也無能為力。 | There's nothing we can do. |

source of information 資料來源
embarrassed 尷尬
misunderstanding 誤會

# 抱怨（一般）

111.mp3

| | |
|---|---|
| 今天工作很長。我已經努力工作得快些，但…… | It's been a long day. I've tried to work fast, but...... |
| 他們去年沒有加薪給我。 | They didn't give me a raise last year. |
| 項目還沒完成，我覺得很沮喪。 | I'm frustrated that the project isn't completed yet. |
| 我擔心不能準時完成工作。 | I'm worried about getting the job done on time. |
| 為甚麼你不告訴我你不明白程序呢？ | Why didn't you tell me that you didn't understand the procedures? |
| 影印機壞了……誰決定訂購它的？ | The photocopier is down again...... who decided to order it? |
| 誰拿了我的原子筆？ | Who took my pens? |
| 為甚麼最後用的人不補充紙張？ | Why didn't the last user refill the paper? |
| 我們的辦公室一片混亂。 | Our office is a mess. |
| 桌子很混亂。 | The desk is messy. |
| 到底這個世界上有誰來幫我解決這個問題？ | Isn't there anyone under the sun who can help me with this problem? |
| 我還可以撐多久？ | How far can I go? |

112.mp3

| | |
|---|---|
| 我可以怎樣撐到極限嗎？ | How can I go to the limit? |
| 事情不如人意。 | Things didn't go my way. |
| 檔案愈疊愈高…… | Files are piling up...... |
| 我的桌面有一大堆工作。 | There's a pile of work on my desk. |
| 顧客要求很多。 | The customers are demanding. |
| 為甚麼我總是遇到難搞的顧客？ | How come I always get difficult customers? |
| 他們真的令我筋疲力盡。 | They really caused my burnout. |
| 他們從不聽我的。 | They never listen to me. |
| 他們從來沒有滿意過。 | They're never satisfied. |
| 他忘記處理我的訂單，這不是第一次了。 | He forgot to process my order and it wasn't the first time. |
| 我無法忍受他更多的錯誤。 | I can't tolerate any more of his mistakes. |
| 為甚麼印出來之前，他不仔細看一遍？ | Why does he never go through it before printing it out? |
| 我不知道我可以忍耐這些大意的錯誤多久。 | I don't know how long I can stand these careless mistakes. |

# 訓斥（對下）

113.mp3

| | |
|---|---|
| 我不在乎你怎樣做。在星期三完成它。 | I don't care how you'll do it. Just get it done by Wednesday. |
| 我要今天看到這份文件完成。 | I want to see the document get done today. |
| 如果你下星期沒有完成它，我會找另一個人接手。 | If you don't get it done next week, I'll ask someone else to take it over. |
| 你進行的進度太慢。 | The progress you made was too slow. |
| 我不會延長限期。 | I won't extend the deadline. |
| 我已經延長這個項目三次了。 | I've already extended the project for three times. |
| 請問你可否加快速度？ | Can you speed it up please? |
| 你已經有一位助理。 | You had an assistant already. |
| 我們不滿意你最近的業績。 | We're not satisfied with your recent performance. |
| 你只有令我失望。 | You just let me down. |
| 你的表現沒有達到我們的期望。 | Your performance isn't up to our expectation. |
| 你的營業額數字令人失望。 | Your sale figures are disappointing. |

114.mp3

| | |
|---|---|
| 你應該再開始打電話找新客人。 | You should start to make cold calls again. |
| 多些聯絡你的客戶。 | Make more contact with your clients. |
| 我希望你更努力工作。 | I hope you can work harder. |
| 你不明白的時候，別只管猜。過來問我。 | When you don't understand, don't guess. Come to ask me. |
| 你不清楚這項目的時候，別假設甚麼。 | Don't assume when you're not sure about the project. |
| 你應該多認識我們的產品。 | You should get to know more about our products. |
| 你從不做你工作的份兒。 | You never do your share of your work. |
| 你把一切扛到拍檔的肩頭上。 | You've put everything on your partner shoulders. |
| 記住，跟進帳單是你的工作。 | Remember, following up the bills is your job. |
| 公平些，做你自己的工作。 | Be fair, do your job. |
| 你請病假很多次，卻沒有醫生信。 | You've asked for sick leaves many times but didn't show any doctors' notes. |
| 你是必須呈交醫生信。 | You're required to submit a doctor's note. |

115.mp3

| | |
|---|---|
| 那樣跟顧客説謊是不道德的。 | It's not ethical to lie to a customer like that.<br>同 It's unethical to lie to a customer like that. |
| 那位顧客不滿意你的態度。 | The customer isn't satisfied with your attitude. |
| 那位顧客投訴你的服務。 | The customer complained about your service. |
| 瑪莉投訴你，因為你不做自己的工作。 | Mary complained about you because you don't do you job. |
| 他們向我投訴，你沒有按時回覆電話給他們。 | They complained to me that you don't call them back in a timely manner.<br>They complained to me that you......<br>他們向我投訴，你……。<br>They complained to me that you don't follow up their orders.<br>他們向我投訴，你沒有跟進訂單。<br>They complained to me that you ignore their requests.<br>他們向我投訴，你沒有理會他們的要求。 |
| 他來向我投訴。 | He has come to complain to me. |
| 這是無法忍受。 | It's intolerable. |
| 這在我們的辦公室是不能接納的。 | It's not acceptable in our office.<br>同 It's unacceptable in our office. |
| 如果你沒有經驗處理它，別聲稱你有這方面的經驗。 | If you didn't have experience in handling this, please don't claim that you had. |
| 很明顯，你不知道怎樣去做。 | It's obvious that you didn't know how to do it. |

# 警告（對下）

116.mp3

| | |
|---|---|
| 所有職員不允許上班時間使用手提電話。 | All the staff are not permitted to use their cell phones on the job.<br>同 All the staff are not permitted to use their mobile phones on the job. |
| 請不要再這樣做。 | Please don't do it again. |
| 別重複同樣錯誤。 | Don't repeat the same mistake. |
| 你看到問題所在嗎？ | Do you see your problem? |
| 我們已經談及它幾次。 | We've talked about it for a few times. |
| 你持續重複犯錯。 | You kept repeating the mistakes. |
| 明顯地，你沒有接納我之前的意見。 | Apparently, you didn't take my previous advice. |
| 有甚麼你想解釋的？ | Is there anything that you want to explain?<br>發出警告前，給機會對方解釋，也關心對方有甚麼難處，不要使人覺得你不近人情。 |
| 但是我仍想聽聽你的解釋。 | But I'd still like to listen to your explanation. |
| 改正你的工作習慣有困難嗎？ | Do you have difficulty correcting your work habits?<br>Do you have difficulty correcting your work habits?<br>……你有困難嗎？<br>Do you have difficulty being punctual?<br>準時上班對你來説困難嗎？<br>Do you have difficulty meeting the deadlines?<br>按期完成對你來説有困難嗎？ |

117.mp3

| | |
|---|---|
| 別影印你的私人文件。 | Don't make any photocopies of your personal documents. |
| 我們不准在上班時間在網上跟朋友聊天。 | We're not allowed to chat with friends online during work hours.<br>We're not allowed to......<br>我們不准⋯⋯<br>We're not allowed to copy personal documents.<br>我們不准影印私人文件。<br>We're not allowed to share our own login password to anyone else.<br>我們不准跟任何人分享自己的登入密碼。 |
| 我會考慮把你降低職位。 | I'll consider moving you to a lower grade of job. |
| 下一步會削減你的佣金。 | Next step would be to cut your commission. |
| 這不是我第一次的警告。 | This is not my first warning. |
| 當我們發第三封信，你被建議辭職。 | When we issue a third warning letter, you're advised to resign. |
| 這發出口頭警告的會議。 | This is a verbal warning meeting. |
| 我希望你會計劃改善這個問題。 | I hope you'll plan to correct the issue. |
| 我已經在上個月發出口頭警告。 | I've issued a verbal warning last month already. |
| 根據我的月曆，第一封警告信是在十一月二十五日。 | According to my calendar, the first warning letter was issued on Nov 25th. |
| 情況完全沒有改善。 | The situation didn't improve at all. |

### 相關生字

| | |
|---|---|
| Backpay | 欠薪 |
| End-of-contract gratuities | 約滿酬金 |
| Job placement | 實習 |
| Medical allowance | 醫療津貼 |
| Paid annual leave | 有薪年假 |
| Pay cuts | 減薪 |
| Pay trend | 薪金趨勢 |
| Pay level | 薪金水平 |
| Frozen pay | 凍薪 |
| No pay leave | 無薪假期 |
| Minimum wage | 最低工資 |
| Starting salaries | 起薪點 |
| Suspension from duty without pay | 停薪留職 |
| Performance-linked bonus | 按表現發放的花紅（制度） |
| Unpaid overtime | 無薪加班 |
| Well-paid | 薪酬不錯的 |
| Year-end bonus | 年終雙糧 |

有同事在你身邊明查暗訪的時候，你要考慮自己跟同事的關係如何，因為你每說一句話，別人可以拿來當情報，然後跟別人交換消息。如果你凡事置身事外，你會是永遠最後的一個人知道公司的小道消息；但這也是無法避免的，畢竟這也是公司裏非正式溝通管道（informal channels of communication）。有些公司會利用這種消息流傳的遊戲，來試探非正式的回應（informal feedback）。

不論是要求加薪或提出辭職，必須先要做好預備工夫。把要說的話寫下來，多唸幾遍直到自然順暢；跟家人或朋友綵排更是最好不過。提出辭職的時候，老闆一定會問你為甚麼要辭職。記住，這不是你的申訴聚會（a venting session）。別以為要趁這個機會，肆意批評其他同事或老闆本人，山水有相逢，說不定明天又有合作的機會。我們要保持優雅離場（graceful departure）的姿態，不應該截斷自己的後路（you should never burn any bridges）。

# Chapter 5

# 聊天與流言

# 下午茶（一般）

120.mp3

| | |
|---|---|
| 大家來喝杯咖啡休息吧。 | Let's go for a coffee break. |
| 你想喝咖啡嗎？ | Do you want a coffee? |
| 一起到樓下喝咖啡吧。 | Let's go downstairs for a coffee. |
| 你想我叫外賣嗎？ | Do you want me to order take-out? |
| 他們會送到我們的辦公室的。 | They deliver to our office. |
| 我們應該休息一下。 | We should take a break. |
| 你想點甚麼？ | What do you want to order? |
| 我要拿鐵。 | I'd go with latte. |
| 請替我點冰牛奶咖啡。 | Please order me iced coffee with milk. |
| 那一家是你喜歡的茶室？ | Which is your favourite café? |
| 我喜歡的飲品是摩卡。 | My favourite beverage is mocha. |
| 這杯咖啡有點烤焙過度。 | This coffee tastes a bit too roasted. |
| 他們沖製新鮮的咖啡。 | They brew fresh coffee. |
| 他們知道如何好好混合咖啡豆。 | They know how to blend coffee beans well. |

121.mp3

| | |
|---|---|
| 你放牛奶進咖啡嗎？ | Would you put milk in your coffee? |
| | Would you put ...... in your coffee?<br>你放……進咖啡嗎？<br>Would you put sugar in your coffee?<br>你放糖進咖啡嗎？<br>Would you put cream in your coffee?<br>你放奶油（忌廉）進咖啡嗎？ |
| 我不喝濃咖啡。 | I can't drink strong coffee. |
| 他們有味道淡的咖啡嗎？ | Do they have weak coffee? |
| 我喝黑咖啡。 | I drink my coffee black. |
| 這杯咖啡喝起來，跟嗅到的味道一樣香。 | This coffee tastes as good as it smells. |
| 我可以要一杯小的卡布其諾，不甜的，勞駕？ | Can I have a small cappuccino, unsweetened please? |
| 我渴望吃一些甜的東西。 | I'm craving for something sweet. |
| 我推介他們的下午茶餐。 | I'd recommend their afternoon tea set. |
| 套餐包括咖啡嗎？ | Is coffee included in the set? |
| 我不能喝含咖啡因的飲品。 | I can't take caffeine beverages. |
| 我想要不含咖啡因的。 | I want a decaf one. |
| 他們有栗子蛋糕嗎？ | Do they have chestnut cakes? |
| 我想吃糖霜巧克力杯蛋糕。 | I want a frosted chocolate cupcake. |

# 測試反應（一般）

122.mp3

| | |
|---|---|
| 你對瑪莉的建議有甚麼感想？ | How do you feel about Mary's suggestion? |
| 你有聽到關於約翰的評估？ | Did you hear about John's appraisal? |
| 嗨，我有一些壞消息…… | Hey, I've got some bad news...... |
| 我不肯定這是否真實。 | I'm not sure if it was true. |
| 我收到來自非常可靠來源的消息。 | I received the information from a very reliable source. |
| 有人找到加利輸入錯誤的資料……你認為他會怎樣？ | Someone just spotted that the wrong data Gary entered...... What do you think will happen to him? |
| 她看來不喜歡他。 | She seems not to like him. |
| 她看來很不情願跟他說話。 | She looks compelled to talk to him. |
| 她跟他說話的時候都不看他的。 | She doesn't look at him when talking to him. |
| 你知道他為甚麼獲升職？ | Do you know why she was promoted? |
| 她跟高層管理有關係。 | She has connections with the top management. |
| 你覺得她丟臉嗎？ | Isn't it a shame about her? |
| 我收到有趣的消息。 | I caught a juicy piece of news. |

| | |
|---|---|
| 我知道你不會告訴其他人，而我知道你想知道的…… | I know you won't tell anyone but I know you'll want to know...... |
| 你想聽有趣的消息嗎？ | Do you want to hear a juicy piece of news? |
| 它幫你了解辦公室的人事互動。 | It helps you understand office dynamics. |
| 你有聽過西門會在下週離開？ | Have you ever heard that Simon will be away next week? |
| 你知道他去哪裏？ | Do you know where he's going? |
| 你知道一些關於他的事情嗎？ | Do you want to know something about him? |
| 我剛收到這消息。 | I just got that. |
| 一些人告訴我為甚麼她上星期沒有上班。 | Someone has told me why she was away last week. |
| 她是財務總監的女兒。 | She's the Financial Controller's daughter. |
| 我一定要跟你分享…… | I'll have to share this with you...... |
| 我聽到關於她的傳聞。 | I've heard a rumour about her. |
| 我現在告訴你的是真的。 | What I'm going to tell you is true. |
| 這怎會是錯的呢？ | How could it be wrong? |

# 桃色八卦（一般）

124.mp3

| | |
|---|---|
| 你猜誰偷偷跟瑪莉約會？ | Guess who's dating Mary on the sly? |
| 他們常常暗地裏離開辦公室。 | They always leave the office furtively. |
| 你知道他們去哪裏嗎？ | Do you know where they go? |
| 你能想像她的約會對象是約翰嗎？ | Can you imagine John is her date? |
| 他們可能只是約會。 | They're just probably dating. |
| 我知道他們每個禮拜下班後去戲院。 | I know they go to cinema after work every week. |
| 你見到他們幾乎每天去吃午飯嗎？ | Did you see that they go out for lunch almost every day? |
| 但是，經理已婚的了。 | But, the manager is married. |
| 他們私下有戀情。 | They have an affair. |
| 你認為有人看到她的訂婚指環？ | Do you think anyone has noticed her engagement ring? |
| 你認識他的太太嗎？ | Don't you know about his wife? |
| 嘉倫懷孕了。你説是嗎？ | Karen's pregnant. Don't you think so? |
| 她發胖了。她懷孕了嗎？ | She's put on weight. Is she pregnant? |

125.mp3

| | |
|---|---|
| 她的男朋友也是經理。 | Her boyfriend is one of the managers.<br>Her boyfriend is one of the......<br>她的男朋友也是……。<br>Her boyfriend is one of the directors.<br>她的男朋友也是董事。<br>Her boyfriend is one of the owners.<br>她的男朋友也是老闆。 |
| 這個月她經常請病假。 | She's on sick leave frequently this month. |
| 為甚麼她要那麼頻密看醫生？ | Why does she need to see a doctor so often? |
| 她最近看來面色蒼白。她病了嗎？ | She looks pale recently. Is she sick? |
| 你結婚了嗎？ | Are you married? |
| 你仍是單身？ | Why are you still single? |
| 告訴我多些關於你的未婚妻？ | Tell me more about your fiancée. |
| 請給我看看你未婚夫的照片。 | Please show me a picture of your fiancé. |
| 你在哪裏遇上你的另一半？ | Where did you meet your significant other? |
| 他是個好男人嗎？ | Is he a nice guy? |
| 你的太太在哪裏工作？ | Where is your wife working? |
| 他們告訴我，你的伴侶也在同一座大廈工作。 | They told me that your partner works in the same building. |

# 批評工作（一般）

126.mp3

| | |
|---|---|
| 他們常常很快溜走。 | They often slip out the door quickly. |
| 他又早走。 | He left early again. |
| 他知道老闆不在嘛。 | He knew that the boss isn't here.<br>同 He knew that the boss is away. |
| 這就是為甚麼今天完全不工作。 | That's why he doesn't work at all today. |
| 看，她多輕鬆。 | Look, she's laid-back. |
| 她整天跟他的私人助理聊天。 | She's chatted with his personal assistant for the day. |
| 她完全沒有經驗。 | She isn't experienced at all. |
| 她沒有技術上的知識。 | She doesn't have the technical knowledge. |
| 她常常過來問工程師。 | She always comes to ask the engineers. |
| 我們想知道她如何得到這份工作。 | We wondered how she can get the job. |
| 我們的項目被她的領導不濟所拖慢。 | Our project dragged just because of her poor leadership. |
| 他不給清晰指示。 | He didn't give clear instructions. |
| 我們如何跟隨他的方法？ | How can we follow his way? |

127.mp3

| | |
|---|---|
| 自從他負責之後，更多有經驗的職員已經離開。 | More experienced staff has left since he was in charge. |
| 他們埋怨領導層。 | They blame the leadership. |
| 他們經歷了低士氣。 | They experienced low morale. |
| 他們投訴辦公室裏的低士氣。 | They have complained about low morale in the office. |

They have complained about...... in the office.
他們投訴辦公室裏的……。
They have complained about unfairness in the office.
他們投訴辦公室裏的不公平。
They have complained about the new policy in the office.
他們投訴辦公室裏的新政策。

| | |
|---|---|
| 我們對獎賞不予寄望。 | We feel no hope for reward. |
| 他不知道怎樣去做。他是假裝的。 | He doesn't know how to do it. He just fakes it. |
| 他不感謝我們非常長時間努力工作。 | He didn't appreciate that we worked hard for a very long time. |
| 高層管理從不聽我們的聲音。 | The top management never listen to our voice. |
| 全是假的。 | It's all fake. |
| 他很少做重大工作，居然仍然獲加薪。 | He does less than major work and somehow still gets a raise. |

# 批評為人（一般）

128.mp3

| | |
|---|---|
| 避開她。 | Stay away from her. |
| 她表面看來友善。 | She seems to be friendly on the surface. |
| 別讓她友善的態度蒙騙你。 | Don't be cheated by her friendly manner. |
| 她在你面前裝友善。 | She's friendly to your face. |
| 他幫助你的時候，有隱情的。 | He has a hidden agenda when he helps you. |
| 他其實不是真的想幫你的。 | He doesn't mean to help you actually. |
| 他只想利用你。 | He just wants to take advantage of you. |
| 他惡待我們大部分人。 | He abused most of us. |
| 他只為了自己開心而批評我們。 | He criticises us for his pleasure only. |
| 他經常想我們發洩怒氣。 | He often spills his anger over us.<br>同 He often spills his wrath over us. |
| 他喜歡向我們大聲嚷。 | He likes to yell at us. |
| 他有壞脾氣。 | He has a bad temper. |
| 他很刻薄。 | He's mean. |
| 他不耐煩。 | He's impatient. |
| 他在辦公室裏不受歡迎。 | He's not popular in this office.<br>同 He's unpopular in this office. |
| 大家迴避他。 | People avoid him. |

129.mp3 

| | |
|---|---|
| 別在她面前開玩笑。她受不了的。 | Don't crack a joke in front of her. She can't take it.<br>同 Don't make a joke in front of her. She can't take it. |
| 她受不了別人對她開玩笑。 | She can't take a joke. |
| 他在別人背後說是非。 | He stabs people in the back. |
| 她喜歡在別人背後說他們的壞話。 | She likes to talk badly about people behind their backs. |
| 你跟她說話時，小心用詞。 | Watch your words when talking to her. |
| 別逗弄他。 | Don't tease him.<br>Don't...... him.<br>別……他。<br>Don't laugh at him.<br>別取笑他。<br>Don't make fun of him.<br>別戲弄他。 |
| 你永不知道她在其他人面前怎樣說你。 | You'll never know what she'll be talking about you in front of others. |
| 經理幾乎從來不會讚賞我們的工作。 | The manager almost never praises our work. |
| 別認為這是針對個人。 | Don't take it personally. |
| 別相信他。 | Don't trust him. |
| 別相信他說的。 | Don't believe what he said. |
| 他不可靠。 | He's not reliable. |

# 婉轉暗示（一般）

130.mp3

| | |
|---|---|
| 你想要喝一杯咖啡嗎？ | Do you want to get a coffee? |
| 噢，我剛遇到疑難。我可以尋求你的意見嗎？ | Oh, I just got a problem. Can I seek your advice? |
| 我現在要處理一些事情。 | I need to take care of something now. |
| 對不起，我在忙着一些事情。 | Sorry, I'm in the middle of something. |
| 對不起，我要工作。 | Sorry, I've got to work. |
| 噢，對不起，我現在要打電話。 | Oh sorry, I have to make a call now.<br>嘗試轉換話題，以避免捲入是非的圈子。 |
| 晚一點我再跟你聊。 | Let me catch up with you later. |
| 我沒有留意到。 | I didn't notice that. |
| 惟有你告訴我這件事。 | You are the only one telling me about this. |
| 我沒有聽過關於約翰的事情。 | I hadn't heard that about John. |
| 我們問他吧。 | Let's go ask him. |
| 你肯定？ | Are you sure? |
| 我沒有跟她合作過。 | I haven't work with her before. |

131.mp3

| | |
|---|---|
| 但她對我們所有人很好的呢。 | But she's very nice to all of us. |
| 其實她是頗友善的。 | She's quite friendly actually. |
| 我想知道，有甚麼事情煩着你呢。 | I want to know what is really bothering you. |
| 這件事使你煩惱嗎？ | Does it bother you? |
| 看來它有點煩着你，不是嗎？ | It seems to bother you a bit, doesn't it? |
| 為甚麼你告訴我這個消息？ | Why are you telling me this information? |
| 就算新經理來管理部門，我仍是照樣工作。 | I'll work the same way even if a new manager heads the department. |
| 所以我覺得沒關係。 | So it doesn't matter to me. |
| 老實説，我沒法做任何事阻止別人離開。 | To be honest, I can't do anything when someone's gone. |
| 我想你可以向他的主管報告。 | I think you may report to his supervisor. |
| 你很會觀察。 | You have a good observation. |
| 對，他有時候會大聲嚷嚷，但所有人都會有情緒高低的時候。 | Yes, he sometimes yells, but everyone has mood swings. |
| 她很嚴格，但不會針對人。 | She is strict but it's not personal. |

132.mp3 

| | |
|---|---|
| 我真的不知道他們的關係。 | I really don't know their relationship. |
| 我從來沒有問她的婚姻狀態。 | I've never asked about her marital status. |
| 但她從來沒有提及前夫。 | But she never mentioned about her ex-husband. |
| 她很專業，沒有談及離婚。 | She's professional and doesn't talk about the divorce. |
| 我不知道她是老闆的女兒。 | I didn't know she's my boss's daughter. |
| 她沒有利用到那些關係。 | She didn't make use of the connection. |
| 她很好人，從不表現態度惡劣。 | She's nice and never gives us an attitude. |
| 讓我們採取觀望態度吧。 | Let's take a wait-and-see approach. |
| 她跟我們一起工作時很合作。 | She was cooperative when we were working together. |
| 事實上，她對這個項目貢獻良多。 | In fact, she contributed a lot to the project. |
| 我們的小組真的很感謝她努力工作。 | Our group really appreciates her hard work. |
| 在我來看，她沒有利用關係爬上高位。 | It seems to me that she didn't use the connection to position herself for higher status. |
| 依我的意見，她不像他們說的那樣急進。 | In my opinion, she isn't as aggressive as they said. |

133.mp3

| | |
|---|---|
| 如果她知道我們這樣說她，我不肯定她會有甚麼感覺。 | I'm not sure how she'd feel if she knew we were talking about her. |
| 你在開玩笑！ | You're joking! |
| 你一定在開玩笑！ | You must be joking! |
| 請別說笑。 | No kidding please. |
| 在辦公室裏，沒有誰比誰更好。 | Nobody is better than anybody in this office. |
| 或者她被誤會。 | Maybe she is misunderstood. |
| 他們可能不太了解她。 | They may not understand her very well. |
| 這是由於缺乏互相了解。 | It's due to a lack of mutual understanding. |
| 這會毫無因由而產生衝突。 | It'll create conflict for no reason. |
| 如果有人告訴她你說的事情，你可能會後悔。 | You may feel sorry to say these things if someone tells her. |
| 這個流言可能會惹得你一身麻煩。 | The rumour will probably come back to haunt you. |
| 別浪費時間擔心這件事。 | Don't waste time worrying about it. |
| 這可能不會發生。 | It may not come to pass. |

# 表明抗拒（一般）

134.mp3

| | |
|---|---|
| 我想保持集中在我的工作上。 | I'd like to stay focus on my job. |
| 我想先處理重要事情。 | I want to deal with my main priority. |
| 對不起，我忙得很。 | Sorry, I'm tied up. |
| 坦白說，這是錯的。 | Frankly, it's wrong. |
| 這是傳聞。 | It's a rumour. |
| 要談及這件事我覺得不舒服。 | I'm not comfortable talking about it. |
| 我不大想談及這個題目。 | I'd rather not talk about that topic. |
| 我沒有時間繼續聽你的，對不起。 | I can't afford the time to keep listening to you, sorry. |
| 不如把我們的對話換個跟工作有關的主題。 | Let's move the conversation back to a work-related subject. |
| 流言必須停止。 | The gossip must stop. |
| 流言惹來麻煩。 | Gossiping causes trouble. |
| 流言為辦公室帶來破壞的影響。 | Gossip may bring damaging effects to our office. |
| 傳聞的漣漪效應會傷害人。 | The ripple effects of a rumour may harm people. |

135.mp3 

| | |
|---|---|
| 流言會為工作環境帶來負面影響。我不想這樣。 | Gossip creates a negative work environment. I don't want that. |
| 不如轉換話題。 | Let's change the subject. |
| 這聽起來是人身攻擊。 | It sounds like a personal attack. |
| 這對她不公平，因為缺乏證據。 | It isn't fair to her as there is no proof. |
| 我不想談及其他人，因為我不喜歡人家談及我。 | I don't like talking about other people because I don't like them talking about me. |
| 如果我們不能正面論及彼此，就讓我們完全不要談及其他同事。 | If we cannot speak positively about each other, let us not speak about other coworkers at all. |
| 應該當面把傳聞告訴給主角。 | The rumour should be delivered to the person being talked about in person.<br>類 The rumour should be delivered to the person being talked about directly.<br>應該直接把傳聞告訴給主角。 |
| 我寧願當事人在場才談論他。 | I'd prefer to talk about that person when they are present. |
| 讓我們等到他可以親身在這裏才討論吧。 | Let's wait to discuss that until he can be here in person. |
| 如果你繼續談及它，會即時引起辦公室的衝突。 | It may cause an instant office conflict if you keep talking about it. |

136.mp3

| | |
|---|---|
| 你想不想別人知道關於你的這類消息？ | Would you want other people to know that kind of information about you? |
| 如果你不想別人在你背後說同樣的事情，那麼你別說了。 | If you don't want anyone to say the same thing behind your back, then don't say anything. |
| 你也想有人背地裏這樣說你嗎？ | Would you like to have someone share that about you without you knowing? |
| 除非當事人參與討論，要不然我不想談及他們的負面事情。 | I don't want to talk about others negatively unless they are involved in the discussion. |
| 這會危害別人的聲譽。 | It can put someone's reputation in jeopardy. |
| 在她不在場的時候談及她，令我覺得不舒服。 | I feel uncomfortable talking about her while she is not here. |
| 等她可以跟我們在一起才討論。 | Let's wait until she can be with us to continue this discussion. |
| 我不認為這樣討論他很適當。 | I don't think it is appropriate to discuss him in this way. |
| 他不在場，無法把他的看法告訴我們。 | He isn't here to give us his side of the story. |
| 這不是我們恰當的位置來為他編作故事。 | It isn't our place to be making up a story for him. |

🎧 137.mp3 

| | |
|---|---|
| 我不喜歡這樣聽見別人的事情。 | I dislike hearing about another person in this way. |
| 這使我好奇，如果我不在你身邊，你會怎樣説我的事情。 | It makes me wonder if you'd talk about me like this when I'm not around. |
| 如果他在的話，你會這樣説嗎？ | Would you be talking like this if he is here? |
| 正如俗語説，來説是非者，便是是非人。 | As the Chinese saying goes, "Whoever gossips to you, he is the ringleader" |
| 你這樣説別人，別人也照樣説你。 | What goes around comes around. |
| 誰跟你説是非，也會説你的是非。 | Who gossips with you will gossip of you. |
| 若我們散播傳聞，害人會終害己。 | When we spread rumours, it will end up coming back to hurt us. |
| 我嘗試不在人家背後説是非。 | I'm trying not to talk about people behind their backs. |
| 除非這是真的，要不然我不會去想它。 | I don't want to think about that until I know it's true. |
| 無論發生甚麼事情，我也應付到。 | I can handle whatever happens. |

# 自我闢謠（一般）

138.mp3

| | |
|---|---|
| 你有一分鐘嗎？我們需要談談。 | Have you got a minute? We need to talk. |
| 我想跟你談。 | I wanted to talk to you. |
| 我聽聞你一直如以下般說我。 | I heard that you've been saying the following about me. |
| 你說我跟老闆有私情。 | You said I had an affair with my boss. |
| 你說我常常在6點前離開。 | You said I always left before 6. |
| 你告訴他們我被辭掉。 | You told them that I'd be fired. |
| 你可以拿出證據嗎？ | Can you show any proof? |
| 如果你不能證明你說過的，請停止繼續說。 | If you can't prove what you said, please stop saying that. |
| 你可以想像到那影響有多破壞力？ | Can you imagine how damaging the effect was? |
| 你告訴同事，我沒有好好領導小組。 | You told the coworkers that I didn't lead the group well. |
| 我可以聽聽你個人意見嗎？ | Can I have your own comments? |
| 你可以重複你跟每一個人說過的嗎？ | Can you repeat what you've told everyone? |
| 我樂於開放討論。 | I'm open to discussion. |

139.mp3

| | |
|---|---|
| 請告訴我哪裏可以做得更好。 | Please tell me where I can do better.<br>如果對方批評你的工作表現，盡量和氣地請對方提出哪裏不妥。態度認真要求他別再背後批評你，建議他日後直接跟自己說，好讓自己有改善的機會。 |
| 希望你明白我是認真的。 | I hope you understand that I'm serious. |
| 將來，請直接把我的錯誤告訴我。 | In the future, please tell me about my fault directly. |
| 我想直接聽取你的建設性意見。 | I'd like to have your constructive advice directly. |
| 我歡迎你善意的意見。 | Your kind comments are welcome. |
| 這是人身攻擊。 | It's a personal attack. |
| 這對我不公平。 | It's not fair to me. |
| 在我不在場的時候，你談及我。 | You talked about me when I wasn't present. |
| 我聽到一個關於我的流言。 | I've heard about a gossip about me. |
| 我沒有引誘任何人。 | I didn't seduce anyone. |
| 如果他的太太聽見，會破壞某人的婚姻。 | It will damage someone's marriage if his wife hears about it. |
| 我聽到你說我的是非。 | I've heard that you gossiped about me. |

140.mp3

| | |
|---|---|
| 我沒有親身聽見的時候，你直接把意見告訴我，我很感謝你。 | While I wasn't there to hear you, I would appreciate your coming to me directly with any comments. |
| 請停止在我背後說我的家人。 | Please don't talk with my family behind my back.<br>Please don't talk with my...... behind my back.<br>請停止在我背後說到我的……。<br>Please don't talk with my friends behind my back.<br>請停止在我背後說到我的朋友。<br>Please don't talk about my private life behind my back.<br>請停止在我背後說到我的私生活。 |
| 我不知道你是否聽過有關於我的傳聞流傳。 | I don't know if you've heard the rumours going around about me or not. |
| 這真是擾人。 | It's really disturbing. |
| 如果你聽見有任何人說我的壞話，你叫他們收口的話，我會很感激。 | If you hear of anyone talking about me, I would appreciate it if you would ask them to stop. |
| 我希望我的私隱權被尊重。 | I hope my right to privacy is respected. |
| 我已經成為負面流言的主角。 | I've have been the source of negative gossip. |
| 如果你繼續對我暗箭傷人，我會寫信給我的主管。 | If you continue back stabbing me, I'll write a letter to my supervisor. |
| 我將會採取行動，讓經理知道。 | I'll take action to let the manager know. |

141.mp3

| | |
|---|---|
| 我會尋求主管的意見。 | I'll seek my supervisor's advice. |
| 我會把發生了的細節告訴他。 | I'll tell him the details of what happened. |
| 我不欣賞你談及我。 | I don't appreciate your talking about me. |
| 這帶來傷害的感覺。 | It causes hurt feelings. |
| 無論這是否有意圖，它傷害了我的感受。 | No matter it's intentional or not, it hurts. |
| 我現在要求你注意日後的説話。 | I'm asking you to pay attention to what you'll say. |
| 它破壞了我的名譽。 | It'll ruin my good reputation. |
| 它是我成為同事之間的笑柄。 | It made me the butt of jokes among my co-workers. |
| 我的名譽因失實傳聞受損。 | My reputation was hurt by the false rumour. |

Constructive advice 建設性意見
Good reputation 名譽
Negative gossip 負面流言
Kind comment 善意的意見
False rumour 失實傳聞

# 公餘聯誼（一般）

142.mp3

| | |
|---|---|
| 會議完結了。輕鬆一下吧！ | The meeting is over finally. Let's relax! |
| 匯報前休息一下。 | Let's take a break before the presentation. |
| 你們想怎樣？ | What do you think? |
| 已經 8 點了。是時候收工了。 | It's 8 pm. It's time to knock off for the day. |
| 大家下班吧 | Let's stop working. |
| 我們收工了。別再談公事。 | We're off now. Please don't talk shop. |
| 我想喝些酒。 | I'd like to go have a drink. |
| 大家去街角的酒吧吧。 | Let's go to the bar around the corner. |

Let's go to the......
大家去……吧。
Let's go to the café across the street.
大家去街上咖啡室吧。
Let's go to the karaoke on the next block.
大家去鄰街的卡拉 OK 吧。

| | |
|---|---|
| 我們正要去酒吧。 | We're heading to the bar. |
| 我們去哪裏？ | Where are we going? |
| 今天工作了很久。 | It's been a long day. |
| 你挑你喜歡的地方。 | You pick a place you like. |
| 哪裏也好。 | Anywhere is fine. |
| ABC 酒吧好嗎？ | What about ABC Bar? |

143.mp3

| | |
|---|---|
| 這是一定要試的酒廊。 | It's a must try lounge. |
| 我們去卡拉OK吧。 | Let's go for karaoke. |
| 我非常餓。你們想一起吃晚飯嗎？ | I'm so hungry. Do you want to have dinner together? |
| 你想吃哪類食物？ | What kind of food do you want to eat? |
| 一人火鍋如何呢？ | How about one-man hot pot? |
| | How about......?<br>……如何呢？<br>How about a steakhouse?<br>扒房如何呢？<br>How about an Italian bistro?<br>意大利餐廳如何呢？ |
| 喂，大家去任點任食日本餐廳囉！ | Hey, let's go to an all-you-can-eat Japanese restaurant! |
| 街口咖啡室的咖啡沒有味道。 | The cafe down the street has no taste in coffee. |
| 你想到好去處嗎？ | Can you think of a good place? |
| 你知道另一個地方？ | Do you know another place? |
| 你想推介另一個地方嗎？ | Would you recommend another place? |
| 它接近地鐵嗎？ | Is it near the subway? |
| 這是個好去處。 | It's a nice place. |
| 好極，我喜歡唱歌。 | Great, I love singing. |

# 酒吧餐廳（一般）

144.mp3

| | |
|---|---|
| 我們沒有預約而來的。 | We just walked in. |
| 我們沒有預約。 | We didn't make a reservation. |
| 我們可以取一張桌子嗎？ | Can we get a table? |
| 有桌子嗎？ | Is there a table available? |

Is there a...... available?
有……嗎？
Is there a booth available?
有雅座嗎？
Is there a room available?
有房間嗎？

| | |
|---|---|
| 我們甚麼時候可以取房？ | What time can we get a room? |
| 我們要等很久嗎？ | Do we have to wait for a long time? |
| 我們要等多久？ | How long do we have to wait? |
| 等候多久？ | Will the wait be long? |
| 嗯，我們到酒吧等吧。 | Well, we'll wait in the bar. |
| 你們預備好的話，請叫我們。 | Please call us when you're ready. |
| 我們想坐在一起。 | We'd like to sit together. |
| 請問你可以把這兩張桌子放在一起？ | Can you please put these two tables together? |
| 我們有 10 個人。 | We are a party of 10. |

145.mp3

| | |
|---|---|
| 你想喝甚麼？ | What would you like to drink? |
| 你想要啤酒嗎？ | Do you want a beer? |
| 你想喝哪種啤酒？ | What kind of beer do you want to drink? |
| 淡啤酒，勞駕。 | Lager, please. |
| 你有哪個啤酒牌子？ | What brand of beer do you have? |
| 我們有青島、嘉士伯和喜力。 | We have Tsing Tao, Carlsberg and Heineken. |
| 請給我青島。 | Please give me a Tsing Tao. |
| 一品脱還是一杯？ | A pint or a glass? |
| 你預備好點菜了沒有？ | Are you ready to order? |
| 請給我們一點時間。 | Please give us a moment. |
| 給我們時間決定。 | Give us time to decide. |
| 好的，我們先來點些飲料吧。 | Ok, let's order some drinks first. |
| 有一個人會晚一點來。 | One person will come later. |
| 我們還有一個人。 | We have one more person. |
| 他可以有座位嗎？ | Can he get a seat? |

# 娛樂消遣（一般）

146.mp3

| | |
|---|---|
| 你閒時喜歡做甚麼？ | What do you like to do in your spare time? |
| 週末你做甚麼？ | What do you do on weekends? |
| 你喜歡哪部電影？ | What is your favourite movie? |
| 你喜歡剛才看的電影嗎？ | Do you like the movie you just saw? |
| 上個星期你看甚麼電影？ | What movie did you see last week? |
| 你有看蝙蝠俠最新的電影嗎？ | Have you seen the new Batman flick? |
| 你喜歡哪類型電影？ | What kind of movies do you like? |

What kind of...... do you like?
你喜歡哪類型……？
What kind of music do you like?
你喜歡哪類型音樂？
What kind of novels do you like?
你喜歡哪類型小說？

| | |
|---|---|
| 你下載了 Lady Gaga 新歌嗎？ | Did you download Lady Gaga's new song? |
| 你通常在哪裏下載歌曲？ | Where do you usually download songs? |
| 你看過她新的音樂 MV 嗎？ | Have you seen her new music video? |
| 我常去看浪漫喜劇。 | I often go to see romantic comedies. |
| 我喜歡動作片。 | I like action films. |

🎧 147.mp3

| | |
|---|---|
| 所有蝙蝠俠電影都是賣座片。 | All the Batman movies were blockbusters. |
| 有一部新電影是畢彼特主演的。 | There's a new movie with Brat Pitt in the lead role. |
| 這是必看的電影。 | It's a must see movie. |
| 哪位明星嘉賓你會更興奮想看的呢？ | Which guest stars are you more excited to see? |
| 你看了第一集沒有？ | Did you watch the first episode? |
| 你明天會看那場比賽嗎？ | Are you watching the game tomorrow? |
| 我期待看 24 新一季的第一集。 | I'm looking forward to the premiere of a new season of 24. |
| 我沒辦法耐着性子看完結局誰被殺了。 | I can't sit through the finale to see who was killed. |
| 結局裏最佳片段是哪一段？ | What are the best moments in the finale? |
| 明天是結局了。 | It wraps up tomorrow. |
| 誰在「奪寶奇 show」最後一集中贏了？ | Who won in the Amazing Race's finale? |
| 你打賭誰贏了？ | Who's your bet for the big win? |
| 誰會是勝利者？ | Who will be the winner? |

🎧 148.mp3

| | |
|---|---|
| 她從不落後到最後位置，我很驚訝。 | I was surprised that she never came to the last place. |
| 他們勝利是應得的。 | They deserve to win. |
| 我不在乎誰在結局中贏了。 | I don't care who won the finale. |
| 這是很不錯的結局。 | It was a great ending. |
| 這會是大團圓結局。 | It'll be a happy ending. |
| 這絕對是棒極了。 | This is absolutely awesome. |
| 我為這流行音樂着迷。 | I'm obsessed with the smash hit. |
| 這是很搞笑的節目。 | It was a hilarious show. |
| 故事情節很刺激。 | The storylines are exciting. |
| 我愛看真人秀（真人騷）。 | I love watching reality TV. |
| 這是最差的一集。 | It's the worst episode. |
| 這是最好的電視節目。 | It's the best show on TV.<br>同 It's the best program on TV. |
| 我從一開始便愛上它。 | I've loved it from the start. |
| 現在播放的節目中，沒有一個比得上它。 | There's nothing on the air that competes with it. |
| 有誰跟我看法一樣？ | Is anyone with me on this? |

149.mp3

| | |
|---|---|
| 打從第一日開始我便是影迷了。 | I've been a fan since day one. |
| 它將要播放完畢了。 | It's going to be taken off the air. |
| 新系列節目的第一集令我印象深刻。 | I'm impressed by the premiere of the new series. |
| 那些倒敘只是浪費時間。 | The flashbacks just wasted my time. |
| 我喜歡所有參賽者。 | I like all the contestants. |
| 今晚的淘汰賽會是令人震驚的一集。 | Tonight's elimination would be another shocker. |
| 他會在「全美一叮」被淘汰嗎？ | Will he be eliminated from American's Got Talent? |
| 你昨晚有看「星隨舞動」嗎？ | Did you see Dancing with the Stars last night? |
| 她被淘汰了。 | She was eliminated. |
| 她不應該走的。 | She shouldn't have left. |
| 她應該留下。 | She should have stayed. |
| 他表演得很好，滿有體面的離開。 | He did a great job and left with great dignity. |
| 我真享受觀賞她的舞蹈。 | I really enjoy watching her dancing. |
| 那對參賽者應該多留一個禮拜。 | The couple could have stayed one more week. |

150.mp3

| | |
|---|---|
| 看她落選很傷心咧。 | I was sad to see her go. |
| 他及不上其他參賽者。 | He wasn't as good as other contestants. |
| 但其他舞者更好。 | But the other dancers are much better. |
| 最後一隊到達的會被淘汰。 | The last team to check in will be eliminated. |
| 這一集蠻重要喔。 | This episode is pretty crucial. |
| 他不會贏的。 | He's never going to win it. |
| 這已經是第 10 季了。 | It's been season 10 already. |
| 急不及待等下一季呢。 | I can hardly wait for the next season to begin. |
| 播放新一季，我好開心， | I'm happy to see its return. |
| 這是結局前的第一集。 | It's the second to the last episode of the season. |
| 官方劇情預告不會道破結局的。 | The official synopsis won't tell the ending. |
| 我喜歡在劇院看話劇。 | I enjoy watching drama in theatre. |
| 你看了預演嗎？ | Did you see the preview? |
| 我在 Youtube 看了預告片。 | I watched the trailers on Youtube. |
| 它每逢星期四播放「迷」。 | It's airing with Lost on Tuesday nights. |

151.mp3

| | |
|---|---|
| 「歡樂合唱團」今晚播放新一季。 | Glee returns tonight. |
| 誰是你喜歡的歌手？ | Who is your favourite singer? |
| 你不聽流行歌。很少見呢。 | You don't listen to pop music. That's rare. |
| 我喜歡爵士音樂。 | I like jazz music. |
| 那麼你有彈奏甚麼樂器嗎？ | So do you play any instruments? |
| 我彈吉他。 | I play guitar. |
| 你在公司工作了多久？ | How long have you been in the company? |
| 你曾經做過最不尋常的工作是甚麼？ | What's the most unusual job you've had? |
| 如果你要在餘生看三本雜誌，那會是甚麼？ | If you had to choose three magazines to read for the rest of your life, what would they be? |
| 你第一次買的股票是甚麼？ | What was the first stock you invested in? |
| 你喜歡旅遊嗎？ | Do you like to travel? |
| 你去過哪些國家？ | Which countries have you travelled? |
| 你喜歡那個國家嗎？ | Do you like that country? |
| 為甚麼你喜歡那個城市？ | Why do you like the city? |

## 相關生字

| | |
|---|---|
| Still wine | 無氣泡酒 |
| Sparkling wine | 氣泡酒 |
| Bourbon | 波本威士忌 |
| Gin | 杜松子酒／氈酒 |
| Tequila | 龍舌蘭 |
| Vermouth | 苦艾酒 |
| Vodka | 伏特加酒 |
| Beef tenderloin | 牛柳 |
| Veal filet | 菲力／牛仔柳 |
| Lobster | 龍蝦 |
| Foie gras | 鵝肝 |
| Garlic bread | 蒜味麵包 |
| Caesar salad | 凱撒沙拉 |
| Escargo | 焗田螺 |
| Lamb chop | 羊排 |
| Pork loin | 豬柳 |
| Roast pork knuckle | 烤豬腳 |
| Salmon steak | 三文魚排 |
| Chocolate fondue | 巧克力火鍋 |
| Crème brulee | 法式燉蛋 |
| Lemon meringue pie | 檸檬蛋白批 |

## 講是講非

辦公室內有人搬弄是非或散播傳聞，是無可避免的。當有人跟你評論別人的個性、為人、外表等等針對個人評價時，最好還是避之則吉。因為這些評論往往是這個「是非者」（gossiper）用做打擊當事人的武器，趁別人沒有問你的看法前，藉故離開，總比留在現場支吾以對來得容易，否則你自己的信譽（credibility）也會受損。當你聽到這些流言主角（subject of gossip）是自己的時候，首先要找出搬弄是非的元凶（ringleader），然後找機會私下跟他對質（confront），表明自己不喜歡再聽到這些壞話（harmful words），如果是與工作有關（work-related），向他請教改善之道，保持態度冷靜而克制。這些造謠者（rumourmonger）通常是欺善怕惡，只要你暗示可能向老闆投訴的話，他們便不敢太過份。

# Chapter 6

# 商務招待

# 歡迎客人（對外）

154.mp3

| | |
|---|---|
| 你好嗎，高士比先生？ | How are you, Mr. Crosby? |
| 我很好，謝謝。你好嗎？ | Great, thank you. How are you?<br>同 Good, thank you. And you? |
| 請叫我傑夫。 | Please call me Jeff. |
| 好，傑夫，我是伊麗莎。 | OK, Jeff. And I'm Eliza. |
| 再見你真好。 | Great to see you again. |
| 嗨，你是阿健嗎？ | Hey, are you Ken? |
| 很久沒見了。 | Long time no see. |
| 好一段時間不見了。 | It's been awhile. |
| 我們很久沒見了。 | We haven't met for a long time. |
| 我們有一段長時間彼此不見了。 | We haven't seen each other for a long time. |
| 我們不見了多久？ | How long has it been since we met? |
| 哇，已經六個月了。 | Wow, it's been 6 months. |
| 不經不覺呢。 | I didn't realize it. |
| 旅途順利嗎？ | How was the trip? |
| 從機場出來的交通如何呢？ | How was the traffic from the airport? |

| | |
|---|---|
| 容易找到我們的辦公室嗎？ | Did you find our office easily?<br>如果客人遲到的話，問一問他的行程和交通情況，除了寒喧一番，也可以稍作安慰説："Better late than never."（遲到總比不到好。）或"Oh, it's pretty normal."（噢，這蠻正常，馬路總是塞滿車。） |
| 班機延誤了。 | The plane was delayed.<br>類 late 遲到。例子：The train was late. 火車遲來了。 |
| 交通很繁忙呢。 | The traffic was busy. |
| 歡迎來我們的辦公室。 | Welcome to our office.<br>Welcome to our......<br>歡迎到我們的……<br>Welcome to our gala.<br>歡迎到我們的慶典晚會。<br>Welcome to our exhibition show.<br>歡迎到我們的展覽會。 |
| 請坐。 | Please take a seat. |
| 請自便。 | Please help yourself. |
| 請看一看我們今年的年刊。 | Please take a look at our current yearbook. |
| 請等候，隨便看雜誌。 | Please feel free to flip through the magazines while waiting. |
| 掛牆衣帽架在門後面。 | A wall-mounted coat rack is behind the door. |
| 衣帽架在那個角落。 | A coat rack is at the corner. |
| 讓我替你掛起大衣。 | Let me hang your coat on it. |
| 我可以幫你掛起它嗎？ | May I help you hang it up? |

156.mp3

| | |
|---|---|
| 你可以把袋子放在我們的接待處。 | You may leave your bags at our reception. |
| 請記得離開前取回它。 | Please remember to collect it before you leave. |
| 衣帽間在大門口旁邊。 | The cloakroom is next to the main entrance. |
| 有人看管寄存的大衣。 | Coat checks are attended. |
| 但請勿留下貴重物品在那裏。 | But please don't leave any valuable belongings there. |
| 你的袋子會保管安全。 | Your bags are stored securely. |
| 請別拘束。 | Make yourself comfortable. |
| 我想我們不曾碰過面。 | I don't think we've met before. |
| 我見過你嗎？ | Did I meet you somewhere else? |
| 你想喝點甚麼？ | Do you want something to drink? |
| 你想在會議前喝一杯咖啡嗎？ | Do you want to drink a cup of coffee before the meeting? |
| 來一杯咖啡如何？ | What about a cup of coffee? |
| 我們準備了茶點。 | We've prepared some refreshments. |
| 請在開會前取些三文治。 | Please take sandwich before the meeting. |
| 今天是我們首次見面。 | This is the first time we meet today. |

# 介紹來賓（對外）

157.mp3

| | |
|---|---|
| 南茜，我想你向你介紹傑佛瑞・高士比。 | Nancy, I'd like to introduce you to Geoffrey Crosby.<br>同 Nancy, I'd like you to meet Geoffrey Crosby.<br>Jeff is our company consultant. He's taking care of the investment projects.<br>Take care of 除了解作照顧人，也可以是「處理、負責」事情，尤其是一些困難的情況。 |
| 聽説你來自美國。 | I hear you're from the States.<br>閒談中，多稱美國為 the States，而不是 the United States 或 USA。 |
| 到目前為止，你覺得這裏怎樣？ | How do you like it here so far? |
| 你來自哪裏？ | Where are you from? |
| 讓我來向你介紹積奇。 | Let me introduce Jack to you. |
| 他今早才剛到香港。 | He just arrived in Hong Kong this morning. |
| 今天他是我們的客人。 | He's our guest today. |
| 她是其中一位賓客。 | She's one of our guests. |
| 很榮幸有她來做主旨演講人。 | It's an honour to have her as the key note speaker. |
| 她是在職訓練的導師。 | She's an instructor of the on-the-job training session.<br>在職訓練也可簡稱為“OJT”。 |
| 主管替我們報名訓練課程。 | The supervisor enrolled us in his training class. |

158.mp3

| | |
|---|---|
| 他是上海分行主管。 | He's the head of Shanghai branch. |
| 她是一位專業訓練導師。 | She's a professional trainer.<br>She's a professional......<br>她是一位專業……。<br>She's a professional consultant.<br>她是一位專業顧問。<br>She's a professional IT specialist.<br>她是一位專業資訊科技專家。 |
| 別錯過這個尋求她意見的機會。 | Don't miss this chance to seek her advice. |
| 請隨便諮詢他。 | Please feel free to consult him. |
| 很高興邀請她為我們的訓練導師。 | We're glad to invite her to be our trainer. |
| 他會發表演講。 | He'll deliver a speech. |
| 他專程為特別會議而來。 | He came for the special meeting. |
| 他協助我們的項目。 | He'll help us with the project. |
| 他是總部的代表。 | He's a representative of our head office. |
| 獲得這些新資訊很不錯呢。 | That's great to know the new information. |
| 你是第一次來這裏的嗎？ | Is it your first time being here? |
| 你以前曾來香港旅遊嗎？ | Have you travel to Hong Kong before? |

# 介紹公司（對外）

159.mp3

| | |
|---|---|
| 敝公司在 1979 成立。 | Our company was founded in 1979. |
| 我們的首個辦事處設立在銅鑼灣。 | Our first office was set up in Causeway Bay. |
| 五年前我們搬到這個新地點。 | We moved to this new location five years ago.<br>當我們介紹公司的歷史時，記得用過去式（Past tense）來表示。 |
| 今年，我們慶祝公司成立 20 週年誌慶。 | This year, we celebrated the 20th anniversary of our company's foundation. |
| 我們是領導本行業的製造商。 | We are a leading manufacturer in the industry. |
| 我們是本國中最好的製造商之一。 | We are one of the best manufacturers in this country. |
| 我們是資訊科技產品的全球製造商。 | We are a global manufacturer of information technology products. |
| 本公司定位為領導市場的品牌。 | This company is positioned to be one of the leading brands. |
| 作為良心企業，我們對公平工資持堅定的信念。 | As an ethical company, we hold strong belief regarding fair wages. |
| 在 1985 年，我們更改了商標。 | The change in the logo took place in 1985. |

160.mp3

| | |
|---|---|
| 很高興為大家介紹，我們是高性能器具製造商。 | We're pleased to introduce ourselves as a manufacturer of high-performance appliances. |
| 我們設立網上商店有三年了。 | We've launched the online store three years ago.<br>同 We've set up the online store three years ago.<br>We've established the online store three years ago. |
| 我們在過去兩年擴充了業務。 | Our company expanded its business in the last two years. |
| 本公司跟日本供應商拍檔。 | The company partnered with a Japan-based supplier. |
| 我們是中型公司。 | Our company is a medium-sized business. |
| 董事會現由 12 名董事組成。 | Our Board of Directors is now made up of 12 members. |
| 董事們負責業務運作。 | The Directors are in charge of business operations. |
| 他們也監督商務活動以保持工作效率。 | They also monitor the activities for efficiency. |
| 他們也鼓勵員工坦誠溝通。 | They also encourage open and honest communication among the staff. |
| 我們關注企業社會責任。 | We're concerned about corporate social responsibility. |
| 他們致力確保有效率的運作。 | They work to ensure efficient operation. |
| 我們有三間集團屬下公司。 | We have 3 group companies.<br>類 We have 3 subsidiaries.<br>我們有三間子公司。 |

# 吩咐訂票（對下）

161.mp3

| | |
|---|---|
| 我將到澳洲公幹。 | I'm going on a business trip to Australia. |
| 下個星期我又到外地公幹。 | I'll travel again next week. |
| 這對生意很重要。 | It's very important for business. |
| 請替我訂一張往澳洲的來回機票。 | Please book me a round ticket to Australia. |
| 立即去做，趁早買到優惠機票。 | Do it now to take advantage of advance-booking fares. |
| 便宜的機票會先售罄。 | Cheap tickets sell out first. |
| 把它的價錢跟其他便宜機票網站比較。 | Compare its rate to those bargain sites. |
| 瀏覽航空公司網站，因為他們可能會提供網上購票優惠價。 | Browse airline websites because they may offer lower internet-only fares. |
| 請問你可以打電話給旅行社職員？ | Can you call the travel agent please? |
| 請嘗試網上訂票。 | Please try to book a ticket online. |

Please try to......
請嘗試……。
Please try to book a flight online.
請嘗試網上訂位。
Please try to look for a budget airline.
請嘗試找廉價航空公司。

| | |
|---|---|
| 這間航空公司安全可靠？ | Is this airline safe and reliable? |
| 我通常買最便宜的機票坐飛機。 | I usually fly on the cheapest ticket. |
| 我只想乘搭安全的航空公司。 | All I want is to fly with a safe airline. |
| 我會在倫敦坐火車到巴黎。 | I'll travel from London to Paris by train. |
| 我不介意有中途站。 | I don't mind a stopover. |
| 這航空公司在領行李區很快輸出我的行李。 | This airline delivers my bags fast at the baggage claim area. |
| 請查看手提行李的重量限制。 | Please check the weight limit of hand luggage.<br>同 Please check the weight limit of carry-on luggage. |
| 手提行李最大尺碼是多少？ | What's the maximum size of hand luggage? |
| 你推介那間酒店？ | Which hotel would you recommend? |
| 你會推介另一間酒店嗎？ | Would you recommend another hotel? |
| 我滿意上次去的那間酒店的服務。 | I would satisfied with the services of the hotel I stayed at last time. |
| 請找一間可靠的酒店。 | Please look for a reliable hotel. |
| 他們上次沒有處理我的預定。 | They didn't process my reservation last time. |

# 回答訂票（對外）

163.mp3

| | |
|---|---|
| 我負責公司的公幹事宜。 | I'm in charge of the company's business travel. |
| 你想我替你訂機票嗎？ | Would you like me to book a ticket for you? |
| 我們用廉價航空公司是新政策。 | There's a new policy that we use budget airlines. |
| 我們去年開始用廉價航空公司。 | We started to use budget airlines last year. |
| 公司改變亞洲內飛行的政策。 | The company has changed its policy on flights within Asia. |
| 所有員工不准乘坐商務客位。 | All staff are not allowed to fly business class. |
| 我聽説航空公司減價。 | I heard that an airline reduced their fares. |
| 你在哪裏逗留？ | Where will you stay? |
| 你會在哪裏逗留？ | Where will you be staying? |
| 你甚麼時候回來？ | When would you like to come back? |
| 旅程會是多久？ | How long will the trip be? |
| 你正打算留多久？ | How long are you planning to stay? |
| 你曾經去俄羅斯公幹嗎？ | Have you ever visited Russia on business? |

164.mp3

| | |
|---|---|
| 你曾到國外公幹嗎？ | Have you ever travelled abroad on business? |
| 你喜歡那間航空公司？ | Which airline do you prefer? |
| 哪間航空公司你經常乘搭？ | Which airline do you frequently fly with? |
| 因為你現在是副經理，你可以訂商務客位。 | Since you're deputy manager now, you may book the business class. |
| 你有座位偏好嗎？ | What's your seat preference? |
| 你有加入他們的飛行里數計劃嗎？ | Did you join their mileage club? |
| 你可以給我你的會籍號碼嗎？ | May I have your membership number? |
| 對不起。飛行里數會算進公司的帳號。 | I'm sorry. The mileage will put into the company account. |
| 你計劃好整個行程沒有？ | Have you planned the entire travel itinerary yet? |
| 你介意乘搭中途停站的航班嗎？ | Would you mind a flight with a stopover? |
| 我會跟 ABC 酒店預定一間單人房。 | I'll book a single room with ABC Hotel. |
| 他們的價錢不錯。 | Their price is good. |
| 酒店接近會議場地。 | It's close to the conference venue. |

# 入住酒店（對外）

165.mp3

| | |
|---|---|
| 我想登記入住。 | I'd like to check in please. |
| 我來登記入住。 | I'm checking in. |
| 我想要一間房間。 | I'd like a room please. |
| 我預訂了房間。 | I have a reservation. |
| 我想要一間套房。 | I'd like a suite. |
| 你們的房間價錢如何？ | How much are your rooms? |
| 單人房每晚價錢如何？ | How much is the single room per night? |
| 你説的價錢是多少？ | How much did you say it was? |
| 你們的房租多少？ | What are your rates? |
| 我要一間小的單人房。 | I'd go with a small single room. |
| 我事先付款了。 | I've paid in advance. |
| 我要預先付款嗎？ | Do I have to pay upfront?<br>同 Do I have to pay in advance? |
| 可以看看那房間嗎？ | Would it be possible to see the room? |
| 你有更明亮的房間嗎？ | Do you have a brighter room? |
| 你們有游泳池嗎？ | Do you have a pool? |

166.mp3

| | |
|---|---|
| 這裏有商業服務中心？ | Is there a business services centre? |
| 你們有禮賓部服務？ | Do you have concierge service here? |
| 今晚還有房間嗎？ | Are there any rooms available tonight? |
| 單人房的房租多少？ | What's the rate for a single room? |
| 噢，好極了。我要它。 | OK, that's perfect. I'll take it. |
| 冰箱裏的汽水價錢多少？ | How much is the soft drink in the mini bar? |
| 價格包括早餐嗎？ | Is breakfast included in the price? |
| 幾點鐘有早餐吃？ | What time can I have breakfast? |
| 我想要炒蛋。 | I'll have them scrambled. |
| 我想多留一個晚上。 | I'd like to stay one more night. |
| 我只逗留兩晚。 | I'm only here for 2 nights. |
| 我會逗留一個星期。 | I'm going to be staying for a week. |
| 甚麼時候要退房？ | What time is check out? |
| 你們有送餐服務嗎？ | Do you have room service? |
| 房間裏有保險箱嗎？ | Is there a safe in the room? |
| 保險箱的密碼組合是甚麼？ | What's the combination of the safe? |

# 接待櫃檯（對外）

167.mp3

| | |
|---|---|
| 你想要單人房還是雙人房？ | Would you like a single or a double? |
| 有海景的房間每晚 $1,200。 | The rooms with a harbour view are $1,200 per night. |
| 我們的房租由 $500 單人房起至套房 $1,500。 | Our rooms start at $500 for a standard single room and go up to $1,500 for a suite. |
| 你想要有街景或海景的房間？ | Would you like a room facing the street or the sea? |
| 請告訴我你的名字，可以嗎？ | May I have your name, please? |
| 請問你可以拼出來嗎？ | Could you spell that please? |
| 多少人入住？ | How many are in your party? |
| 你會住多少個晚上？ | How many nights would you like to stay? |
| 你會在我們這裏住多久？ | How long will you be staying with us? |
| 你何時退房呢？ | When will you check out? |
| 你想要這房間多少天？ | How many days would you like the room for? |
| 你會住 4 晚，對嗎？ | You'll be staying for 4 nights, right? |
| 我們為你預留 803 號房。 | We have you booked in room 803. |

168.mp3 

| | |
|---|---|
| 因為它正向街道，會有點吵。 | As it faces the street, it's a bit noisy. |
| 你會如何付款？ | How will you be paying? |
| 可以把你的信用卡號碼告訴我嗎？ | Can I have your credit card number? |
| 你的 visa 卡號碼是甚麼？ | What is your visa card number? |
| 那麼我可以知道你萬事達卡號碼嗎？ | May I get your master card number then? |
| 你需要電話喚醒服務？ | Would you like a wake-up call? |
| 我們供應自助式早餐。 | We serve breakfast buffet style. |
| 你想怎樣煮那些雞蛋？ | How would you like the eggs? |
| 這是餐券。 | This is the meal coupon. |
| 請填這份登記表格。 | Please fill out the registration form. |
| 含稅共 $1,850。 | The total comes to $1,850 after tax. |
| 先生，這是你房間的鑰匙。 | Here's your room key, sir. |
| 1206 號房在十二樓。 | This room 1206 is on the twelfth floor. |
| 我會叫服務員把你的行李拿上房間。 | I'll have the bellboy bring up your bags. |

# 商務聚餐（對外）

169.mp3

| | |
|---|---|
| 你喜歡甚麼（菜）？ | What would you like? |
| 你喜歡哪一類的食物？ | What kind of food do you like? |
| 想喝一杯飲料嗎？ | Would you like a drink of something? |
| 你有海鮮敏感嗎？ | Are you allergic to seafood? |
| 你對牛奶有不良反應嗎？ | Do you have a milk intolerance? |

國外很多人對不同的食物有敏感反應，為了安全起見，務必事先問清楚對方。例如：堅果類敏感（nut allergy）。

| | |
|---|---|
| 我跟從糖尿病飲食。 | I'm on a diabetic diet. |
| 我不吃糖。 | I avoid sugar. |
| 我傾向清淡的餐食。 | I prefer to take a light meal. |
| 我要戒吃高脂肪食物。 | I have to avoid high-fat food. |
| 我是素食者。 | I'm vegetarian. |
| 請煮得清淡些。 | Please make it mild. |
| 我不能吃蝦。 | I can't eat shrimps. |

I can't eat......
我不能吃……。
I can't eat raw food.
我不能吃生的食物。
I can't eat peanuts.
我不能吃花生。

| | |
|---|---|
| 我想嘗試本地的特色菜。 | I'd like to try a local specialty. |

170.mp3

| | |
|---|---|
| 菜牌上有些真正的本土菜。 | There's some real local on this menu. |
| 我可以看看餐牌嗎？ | May I see the menu? |
| 你有甚麼有好介紹？ | What would you recommend? |
| 這是哪類菜式？ | What kind of dish is this? |
| 這是用甚麼材料來做的？ | What comes with that? |
| 你愛香港嗎？ | Do you like Hong Kong? |
| 這是你第一次來香港嗎？ | Is this your first visit to Hong Kong?<br>第一次招待國外來賓，用餐的時候不一定立即談及業務，先聊一些軟性的話題，例如對本地的觀感。 |
| 你想要甚麼來作餐前酒？ | What would you like to have as an aperitif? |
| 你會推介甚麼來作餐前酒？ | What do you recommend for an aperitif? |
| 雞尾酒如何呢？ | What about a cocktail? |
| 讓我們來喝香檳作餐前酒。 | We'll have champagne for an aperitif. |
| 哪類飲品你喜歡？ | What kind of drinks do you like? |
| 你想喝一杯高級葡萄酒嗎？ | Do you want a glass of fine wine? |
| 他們有哪個啤酒牌子？ | What brand of beer do they have? |
| 讓我問他們有甚麼牌子。 | Let me ask them what brands they have. |

171.mp3

| | |
|---|---|
| 我會問他們來一份酒水單。 | I'll ask them for a wine list. |
| 我可以為你點一杯紅酒嗎？ | May I order a glass of red wine for you? |
| 我想嘗試本地酒。 | I'd like to try local wine. |
| 哪類食物配合這白酒？ | What kind of food does this white wine go well with? |
| 他們有哪類餐酒？ | What kind of house wines do they have? |
| 這梅鹿紅酒是從哪裏來？ | Where is this merlot from? |
| 我可以多點一杯布根地紅酒嗎？ | Can I have another glass of burgundy please? |
| 威士忌加冰，勞駕。 | Whiskey on the rocks, please. |
| 請為我的威士忌加冰。 | Please bring ice for my whiskey. |
| 我酒量很淺。 | I'm a poor drinker. |
| 我酒量一般。 | I'm a moderate drinker. |
| 我很會喝。 | I like to drink a lot. |
| 一點點酒也讓我臉紅。 | A little wine can make my face red. |
| 乾杯！ | Cheers! |
| 你今天晚上有什麼打算嗎？ | Do you have any plans tonight? |
| 我想邀請你出外吃飯。 | I'd like to invite you to dine out. |
| 餐廳在市中心裏。 | The restaurant is in downtown. |

172.mp3

| | |
|---|---|
| 我肯定你會喜歡那些食物。 | I'm sure you'll enjoy the food. |
| 先讓我們在會後稍作休息，然後去吃晚飯的地方。 | Let's take a rest after the meeting and then go to the dinner place. |
| 今晚會有歡迎晚宴。 | There'll be a welcoming dinner tonight. |
| 幾點鐘到酒店來接你方便呢？ | What time would be good to pick you up at the hotel? |
| 6 點來接你方便嗎？ | Is it good for you if I pick you up at 6? |
| 我在大堂見你。 | I'll meet you in the lobby. |
| 我會安排接送你。 | I'll arrange a ride for you. |
| 我的助理會接送你。 | My assistant will give you a ride. |
| 希望你今晚度過了一段好時光。 | I wish you had a good time tonight. |
| 各位來賓，請一起來向 E-Connect Corporate 的行政總裁祖・巴刻先生祝酒！ | Ladies and Gentlemen, please join me in the toast to Mr. Joe Parker, the CEO of E-Connect Corporate! |
| 為我們的成功和高興而乾杯！ | Please raise your glasses for a toast to success and happiness! |

# 租車行職員招呼客人（對外）

173.mp3

| | |
|---|---|
| 請問你有旅行社發出的收據嗎？ | Do you have the voucher form your travel agency? |
| 你要自動排檔的，還是手排檔的？ | Would you rather drive an automatic or a manual?<br>同 Would you rather drive an automatic or a stick-shift?<br>Would you rather drive an automatic or a standard? |
| 你最喜歡那種，手排檔或自動排檔車？ | Which do you like best, the standard or automatic shift car? |
| 大型、中型或小型？ | Full-size, mid-size or compact? |
| 你想要哪類車？ | What kind of car do you prefer? |
| 你可以駕駛手排檔的汽車嗎？ | Can you drive a manual shift car? |
| 每天 $90，不限里數。 | $90 a day with unlimited mileage. |
| 這是我們的目錄。 | Here's our catalogue. |
| 你可以在這一欄挑選小型款式。 | You may choose a compact model in this section. |
| 你是司機嗎？ | Are you the driver? |
| 還另有司機嗎？ | Is there an additional driver? |
| 你想用多少天？ | How many days would you like to use it? |

174.mp3

| | |
|---|---|
| 我可以看看你的駕駛執照嗎？ | May I see your driver's license? |
| 你想要全保的話，每天是 $6。 | If you want full insurance, it'll be $6 per day. |
| 你有購買 PLPD 嗎？ | Will you be taking PLPD? |
| 法律要求最起碼的個人責任和財物損害保險。 | Personal liability and property damage, the minimal insurance required by law. |
| 它包括碰撞損失免除保險和個人意外保險。 | It includes a collision damage waiver and personal accident insurance. |
| 在你的國家，交通流向是怎樣？ | On which side does traffic drive in your country? 是在哪一邊駕駛？ |
| 在你國家是哪邊駕駛？ | What side of the road do you drive in your country? |
| 請填這份表格。 | Please fill in this form. |
| 請你劃上這格欄？ | Can you check this box please? |

automatic 自動排檔的
driver' s license 駕駛執照
manual/standard 手排檔的
full insurance 全保

# 租車顧客垂詢職員（對外）

175.mp3

| | |
|---|---|
| 我四天前預先租了一輛車子。 | I have a car reserved for four days. |
| 這是預先付款的。 | It's pre-paid. |
| 我想租車。 | I'd like to rent a car. |
| 租金多少？ | What's the rate? |
| 我想買保險。 | I'd like to have insurance. |
| 我有國際駕駛執照。 | I have an international license. |
| 國際駕駛執照行嗎？ | Is the international driving licence fine? |
| 甚麼是 PLPD ？ | What does PLPD stand for? |
| 在香港，我們是左上右下。（註：駕駛盤在右方。） | In Hong Kong, we drive on the left.<br>在北美地區，交通流向是右上左下，駕駛盤在左方。 |
| 高速公路的時速限制是多少？ | What are the speed limits on the highway? |
| 我會用三天。 | I'll use it for 3 days. |

# 旅行社或航空公司職員接聽（對外）

176.mp3

| | |
|---|---|
| 這是來回機票還是單程？ | Would that be a round-trip or one-way ticket? |
| 來回還是單程？ | Will this be round-trip or one-way? |
| 你想要一張單程機票，而不是來回，對嗎？ | You wanted a one-way ticket, not round-trip, right? |
| 哪裏是你的目的地？ | Where's your destination? |
| 你一個人旅遊？ | Are you traveling alone? |
| 有其他人與你一起嗎？ | Will anyone travel with you? |
| 你想甚麼時候離開？ | When would you like to depart? |
| 你想哪一天回來？ | Which day would you like to return? |
| 一班航機在 8:30，另一班是 19:00。 | There's a flight at 8:30 and one at 19:00 hours. |
| 每週我們有七班往台北航機。 | We have seven flights to Taipei every week. |
| 星期一和星期三的航班是直航的。 | The flights on Monday and Wednesday are direct. |
| 你想乘搭哪一班航機？ | Which flight would you like? |
| 你想坐哪種客位？ | How would you like to fly? |

177.mp3

| | |
|---|---|
| 你要經濟、商務或頭等客位？ | Would you prefer economy, business class or first class? |
| 這是中途停站新加坡的航班。你介意嗎？ | This is a flight with a stopover in Singapore. Do you mind? |
| 你寧願要直航？ | Would you prefer direct? |
| 回程的日子是哪一天？ | What about the return date? |
| 你心中有固定日子嗎？ | Do you have a fixed date in mind? |
| 你想要不設回程日子的機票嗎？ | Do you want an open ticket? |
| 你想在那天幾點鐘啟程？ | What time of day do you want to depart? |
| 請給我幾分鐘看看有沒有座位。 | Please give me a few minutes while I check availability. |
| 你喜歡甚麼座位？ | Do you have a seating preference? |

Window seat 靠窗的座位
Aisle seat 靠過道的座位
除了座位偏好，膳食方面也可以事先預定，例如：
Diabetic meal 糖尿病飲食
Fruit platter meal 水果餐
Gluten intolerant meal 無麩質飲食
Low calorie meal 低卡路里飲食
Low cholesterol meal 低膽固醇飲食
Vegetarian oriental meal 東方素食

| | |
|---|---|
| 你可定特別膳食，而不用另付任何費用。 | You may place a special meal order at no extra charge. |

# 預訂機票（對外）

178.mp3

| | |
|---|---|
| 嗨，我想買一張來回柏林的機票。 | Hi, I'd like to have a round ticket to Berlin. |
| 下星期四你們有去挪威的航班嗎？ | Do you have any flights to Norway next Thursday? |
| 我一個人去。 | I'm traveling alone. |
| 我會逗留 5 天。 | I'll be staying 5 days. |
| 我想訂一個去上海的座位。 | I'd like to reserve seat  for a flight to Shanghai. |
| 請訂最便宜的機位。 | Please look for the cheapest one. |
| 你可以告訴來回機票賣多少元？ | Could you tell me how much a return flight costs? |
| 我不介意中途站。 | I don't mind stopovers. |
| 我想要不停站的商務客位。 | I want a business class ticket without any stopovers. |
| 我要經濟客位。 | I'd better go economy class. |
| 有多少中途站？ | How many stopovers would be there? |
| 不停站航班票價多少？ | What's the fare for a non-stop flight? |
| 這是去杜拜的直航班機嗎？ | Is it a direct flight to Dubai? |
| 我甚麼時候會收到電子機票？ | When will I receive the e-ticket? |

179.mp3

| | |
|---|---|
| 你不發傳統機票？ | You don't issue paper tickets? |
| 如果我要傳統機票，你另外收取費用嗎？ | So you'll charge me an extra fee if I want a paper ticket? |
| 在前排位置有靠近窗口的座位嗎？ | Do you have a window seat in one of the front rows? |
| 不，別為我訂位。我會去其他地方查詢。 | No, don't book for me. I have a few places to check. |
| 對，我有座位偏好。 | Yes, I have my seat preference. |
| 我想知道座位的靠背是否能調教高低？ | I wonder if the seats on this plane can recline. |
| 這個座位是否有更多空間舒展雙腳嗎？ | Is there a seat with more leg room? |
| 因為不肯定甚麼時候辦妥生意，回程的日期可以改嗎？ | Can I change the return date as I'm not sure when my business will be finished? |
| 我會在接着的星期二回程。 | I'd like to return the following Tuesday. |
| 我要在星期四離開，因為星期五有重要的商務會議。 | I have to leave by Thursday because there'll be an important business meeting on Friday. |
| 我用 visa 信用卡付款。 | I'd pay by visa. |
| 我可以用 visa 信用卡付款嗎？ | Can I pay by visa? |

# 道別（一般）

180.mp3

| | |
|---|---|
| 很高興與你一起工作。 | I've enjoyed working with you. |
| 我很享受這次的到訪。 | I've enjoyed my visit. |
| 我很高興認識你。 | I enjoyed getting to know you. |
| 你幫了我很多忙。 | You've been very helpful. |
| 真愉快。 | It was a pleasure. |
| 請替我問候萊恩。 | Give my regards to Ryan.<br>同 Give Ryan my best wishes. |
| 希望不久再見。 | I hope to see you again soon. |
| 期待我們再見。 | I'll look forward to it. |
| 保重，保持聯絡。 | Take care and keep in touch.<br>同 Take are and stay in touch. |
| 我好想繼續聊下去，但是…… | I'd love to continue this conversation, but...... |
| 跟你會面很高興。 | It was a pleasure meeting you.<br>It was a pleasure......you.<br>跟你……很高興。<br>It was a pleasure seeing you.<br>跟你見面很高興。<br>It was a pleasure talking to you.<br>跟你聊天很高興。 |
| 保重。 | Take care. |
| 日後見。 | See you later. |
| 再見。 | Good bye. |

181.mp3

| | |
|---|---|
| 拜 | Bye.<br>非常熟絡才這樣道別。 |
| 再見 | So long. |
| 遲些再聊。 | Talk to you later. |
| 那麼，再見。 | Goodbye then. |
| 下回再會。 | Until next time. |
| 嗯，我不想再佔用你的時間。 | Well, I don't want to take up any more of your time. |
| 是時候坐飛機了。 | It's time to catch the flight. |
| 我現在得走了。 | I've got to go now. |
| 對不起，但我現在該走了。 | Sorry, but I should be going now. |
| 我恐怕是時候我們要離開。 | I'm afraid it's time we got to leave. |
| 適當時候再見你。 | I'll see you in due course. |
| 如俗語所説，一切美好的事情總有終結。 | As the saying goes, all good things come to an end. |
| 你下次一定要再來。 | You must come to us next time. |
| 跟你聊天真不錯。 | I had a great time talking to you. |
| 今天的會面真好。 | It was great meeting up today. |
| 臨別贈言，祝你安好，再見。 | There's nothing for it but simply to wish you well and say goodbye. |

## 相關生字

| | |
|---|---|
| Double room | 雙人房（一張大床） |
| Twin | 雙人房（兩張單人床） |
| Suite | 套房 |
| Sunny-side up | 太陽蛋 |
| Over-easy | 兩面煎蛋（另一面嫩煎的） |
| Poached | 水煮雞蛋 |
| Scrambled | 炒蛋 |
| Omelet / omelette | 奄列、煎蛋餅 |
| Corporate social responsibility | 企業社會責任 |
| Decision-making process | 參與決策過程 |
| Ethical company | 良心企業 |
| Fair trade | 公平貿易 |
| Franchise chain | 特許聯營 |
| Management system | 管理制度 |
| Management philosophy | 管理理念 |
| Organizational culture | 機構文化 |
| Outsourcing | 外判 |
| Quality-control procedure | 品質管理程序 |
| Quality management | 質量管理 |
| Safety standard regularly | 安全標準 |

## 稱呼與飲食

有一些教科書採用“How do you do?”，語氣非常客套。不過，這反而容易長生隔閡感，所以辦公室裏面很少用這句話。一般而言，我們以“How are you?”來打招呼，聽起來可以令人覺得親切隨和。未得到對方同意，必須稱呼對方的姓氏（Last Name）與頭銜（Title），例如：Mr Hussain 或 Ms Andres。若對方明確表示你可以稱呼他們的名字（First name），你才直呼他們的名字。當你介紹自己的時候，簡單說“I'm...... ”，不用說“My name is...... ”。

一些國外酒店不一定供應自助式早餐。他們通常提供兩款早餐：英式早餐（English breakfast）或歐陸早餐（Continental breakfast）。英式早餐比歐陸式豐富，包括煎蛋和火腿（ham）或煙肉／醃肉（bacon），歐陸式早餐只有圓麵包（rolls）、吐司／多士（toasts）和咖啡（coffee）。當你點菜的時候，侍應生會問你要怎樣的煎蛋或水煮蛋，請參考相關生字。

# Chapter 7

# 商務往來

# 跟業務夥伴寒喧（對外）

184.mp3

| | |
|---|---|
| 嗨，我想跟營業人員談。 | Hi, I'd like to speak to someone in sales. |
| 請找一位營業代表來我的辦公室。 | Please ask a sales rep to visit me. |
| 如果現在我們能討論它，那就好極了。 | How great it would be if we can talk about it now. |
| 我來這裏是要會面一位營業主任。 | I'm here for meeting a sales officer. |
| 我約見了營業經理。 | I have an appointment with the sales manager. |
| 我在網上找到你的網站。 | We found your website online. |
| 我們對你們的服務感興趣。 | We're interested in your services. |
| 我想知道更多關於你們的業務。 | I'd like to find out more about your business.<br>I'd like to find out more about……<br>我想知道更多關於……。<br>I'd like to find out more about your event planning service.<br>我想知道更多關於你們籌劃活動的服務。<br>I'd like to find out more about the new technology you used.<br>我想知道更多關於你們用的新科技。 |
| 我們在昨天的展銷會見過面了。 | We met in a fair trade yesterday. |

185.mp3

| | |
|---|---|
| 你記得那次活動嗎？ | Do you remember the event?<br>Do you remember......?<br>你還記得我……嗎？<br>Do you remember our first deal?<br>你還記得我們的第一次交易嗎？<br>Do you remember where we met?<br>你還記得我們在哪裏第一次見面嗎？ |
| 我們在那裏首次碰面。 | We met there for the first time. |
| 自第一次交易後，已經有三年了。 | It's been three years since the first transaction. |
| 你幫了很大的忙才令交易成功。 | You helped a lot to make the deal. |
| 我們沒有碰面三個月了。 | We haven't met for three months. |
| 生意如何？ | How's business? |
| 我們合作了一段長時間了。 | We've cooperated for a long time.<br>同 We've worked together for a long time. |
| 時間過得真快。 | Time flies. |
| 你一向跟我們合得來。 | You're always on good terms with us. |
| 我們仍然維持合作愉快。 | We still maintain good terms. |
| 我們已經是長期的業務夥伴。 | We've been long-term business partners. |
| 我們建立了成功的合作關係。 | We've built up a successful partnership. |
| 你是可信賴的夥伴。 | You're a trustworthy partner. |

# 首次接觸（對外）

186.mp3

你們賣甚麼的？
What do you sell?

你們有哪類新服務？
What kind of new services do you have?

我從鍾斯先生那裏聽聞到你們的服務。
I heard about your service from Mr. Jones.

我聽説，你們是有名的分銷商。
I've heard that you are a well-known distributor.

I've heard that you are......
我聽説，你們是……。
I've heard that you are an experienced event organizer.
我聽説，你們是蠻有經驗的活動策劃人。
I've heard that you are an artistic florist.
我聽説，你們是具有藝術氣息的花店。

鍾斯先生大力推薦你們的服務。
Mr. Jones highly recommended your services.

莎拉告訴我，她多麼滿意你們的產品。
Sara told me that she was so satisfied with your products.

她説，你們的服務為滿足她的需要而適當調整。
She said that your service is tailored to her needs.

你們有甚麼特別的服務？
Any special services do you have?

你們跟其他供應商有甚麼不同？
How are you different from other suppliers?

它跟市場上其他產品比較，有何不同？
How does it compare with other products on the market?

187.mp3

| | |
|---|---|
| 我想知道當中的分別。 | I'd like to know the difference. |
| 已經有好些供應商了。你有甚麼地方有別於人呢？ | There are a number of suppliers already. What makes you different?<br>為了找到適當的業務夥伴，問對方有別於其他競爭者的地方，多了解他們的強項和市場定位，幫助自己決定雙方是否適合合作。 |
| 你們有適合我們的服務嗎？ | Do you have services suitable for us? |
| 你可以解釋你們的服務細節嗎？ | Can you explain the details of your service? |
| 你會為我們從頭寫一套程式嗎？ | You will write a program for us from scratch? |
| 有整套服務嗎？ | Is there a package available? |
| 它包括甚麼？ | What does it include? |
| 你認為我們可以在網上銷售嗎？ | Do you think we can sell online? |
| 你剛剛説在網上銷售較為容易？ | Did you say that it's easy to sell online? |
| 請告訴我更多關於你們提供的技術支援。 | Please tell more about technical support you provide. |
| 如果我們遇到問題，你們會多久才解決？ | If we get a problem, how long will it take for you to fix it? |
| 我們可以怎樣告訴顧客，網上付款是安全的？ | How can we tell the customers that it's safe to pay online?<br>同 How can we tell the customers that it's safe to make an online payment? |

# 進入正題（對外）

188.mp3

| | |
|---|---|
| 讓我們繼續討論有關大家合作的機會。 | Let's continue our discussion of our cooperation. |
| 讓我們探索合作生意的可能性。 | Let's explore the possibility of our business. |
| 是討論細節的時候了。 | It's time to go through the details. |
| 大家來談談生意吧。 | Let's talk about the business. |
| 上一次，我們在決定日期前結束了。 | Last time, we've stopped before we decided the date. |
| 我們已經討論了一些重點。 | We've discussed some of the points. |
| 在前一次會議中，你提及擴充你的市場佔有率的可能性。 | In the previous meeting, you mentioned the possibility of expanding your market share. |
| 我想，我們可以幹些甚麼來實現它。 | I think we can do something to make it possible. |
| 我樂意告訴你有關我們的新產品。 | I'm pleased to tell you about our new products. |
| 我們鎖定年輕夫婦來打進市場。 | Let's push our way into the market by targeting the young couples. |
| 他們願意買我們既安全又有教育功能的玩具給孩子。 | They are willing to buy our safe and educational toys to their children. |

189.mp3

| | |
|---|---|
| 信我吧，他們現在更關注安全。 | Trust me, they're more concerned about safety now. |
| 我們將會展開大型廣告活動。 | We'll launch a huge advertising campaign. |
| 大家會認識到我們的品牌，然後到你們的商店購買。 | People will know our brand and buy them at your stores. |
| 我們派一些有經驗的推廣員來回答他們的問題。 | I'll assign some of our experienced promoters to answer their questions. |
| 對我來講，任何事情都可以實現的，只要我們有共同的商務願景。 | To me, everything is possible as long as we share the same business vision. |
| 我已經準備了價目表。 | I've prepared the price list. |
| 這就是了。請留意價格的變動。 | Here you go. Please notice that there's a change in prices. |
| 你可以在這本目錄找到我們的產品。 | You may find our products from this catalogue. |
| 我們認為質量是最重要的。 | What we think of as most important is quality. |
| 我們每一件產品都是高品質的。 | Everything we produced is of high quality. |
| 我們決定給你八折優惠去訂購新產品系列。 | We've decided to offer you a 20% discount on the new product lines. |

190.mp3

| | |
|---|---|
| 你的顧客會因為我們的批發價獲折扣而受惠。 | Your customers will benefit from more discounts on our wholesale prices. |
| 有我們更低的批發價，你不用擔心其他對手。 | With our cheaper wholesale prices, you don't need to worry about other competitors. |
| 我保證，我們不會向同區零售商發售產品。 | I promise, we won't sell the products to other retailers in your area. |
| 你也知道，我們只向你供應那些貨品。 | As you know, we just supply these goods to you. |
| 你是我們授權的經銷商。 | You are our authorized dealer. |
| 作為授權經銷商，你必須每個月訂貨超過 $100,000 元。 | As an authorized dealer, you have to make orders of more than $100,000 every month. |
| 我想告訴你貨運時間必須的改變。 | I'd like to tell you some of the necessary changes in shipping time. |
| 我可以給你更多資料。 | I may give you more information. |
| 我們會每個星期下訂單。 | We'll make orders every week. |
| 我們最近的銷貨很快。 | Our turnover is quick recently. |
| 顧客現在需求更多你們的產品。 | Customers are now demanding more of your products. |

191.mp3

| | |
|---|---|
| 我恐怕，顧客無法明白怎樣使用你們的設備。 | I'm afraid that customers may not be able to know how to use your equipment. |
| 他們想儘快買到那些產品。 | They want to buy the products as soon as possible. |
| 一些熱門貨品，我們想以快遞送來。 | For some hot items, we'd like to have them sent by express delivery. |
| 日本的快遞服務成本是多少？ | How much is the cost of express delivery in Japan? |
| 我仍然擔心運費。 | I'm still concerned about the shipping cost. |
| 我想以電郵收到那本目錄。 | I'd like to receive the catalogue by email. |
| 你有把產品的照片放在網上嗎？ | Do you put the pictures of products online? |
| 請問你可否把最新的目錄寄給我？ | Can you send me the latest catalogue please? |
| 請把你們的小冊子寄給我。 | Please send me your brochure. |
| 你送貨需時多久？ | How long does it take you to send the goods? |
| 你可以為他們打折嗎？ | Can you offer a discount on them? |
| 我們會負責那些收費。 | We'll cover the charges. |
| 或者我們可以遲些研究吧。 | Maybe we can look at that later. |

# 商定議程（對外）

192.mp3

| | |
|---|---|
| 現在我們可以決定下次會議的議程嗎？ | Now can we decide on the agenda for the next meeting? |
| 我們沒有完成討論。 | We haven't finished the discussion. |
| 對，我們需要深入研究那些詳細內容。 | Yes, we need to look into the details. |
| 是的，我們沒有計算出確切的數字。 | Right, we didn't figure out an exact number. |
| 你認為我們應該加入新的商討項目嗎？ | Do you think that we should add some new items? |
| 讓我想一想……提升系統的可能性如何呢？ | Let me think...... what about the possibility of upgrading the system? |
| 零件的百分比……我們跳過了沒有討論。 | The percentage of parts...... we have skipped it. |
| 我們今天沒有討論所有事項。 | We didn't cover everything today. |
| 噢，我們忘記了第四項！ | Oh, we forgot item 4! |
| 哎呀，我們沒有注意到它。 | Oh my, we overlooked it. |
| 謝謝提醒我。 | Thanks for reminding me. |

193.mp3

| | |
|---|---|
| 我們可否在下次會議只是繼續討論而不加入新議題？ | Can we just try to continue instead of adding new items for the next meeting? |
| 在下次會議，我們會進一步討論貨運事宜。 | In the next meeting, we'll further discuss about the shipping matters. |
| 我想討論到原料的成本。 | I'd like to cover the cost of the raw material. |
| 我們下次是否應該談及新的廣告活動？ | Should we cover a new ad campaign next time? |
| 關於處理發票的程序，我不大清楚。 | I'm not sure about the procedures of handling the invoices. |
| 你下次可以解釋發票事宜嗎？ | Can you explain the invoicing next time? |
| 我們應該在下次見面時，再討論它。 | We should go through it again next time when we meet again. |

We should...... again next time when we meet again.
我們應該在下次見面時，再……。
We should investigate the possibility again next time when we meet again.
我們應該在下次見面時，再研究那可能性。
We should work at it again next time when we meet again.
我們應該在下次見面時，再努力成事吧。

| | |
|---|---|
| 有甚麼議題你想我們在下次會議重複一遍的？ | Is there any item that you want us to repeat in the ncxt meeting? |
| 下個星期我們可以給你那些細節。 | We may give you more details of it next week. |

# 磋商技巧（對外）

194.mp3

| | |
|---|---|
| 謝謝你們來這個協商會議。 | Thank you for coming to this negotiation meeting. |
| 今天，我們會面是要討論達成協議。 | Today, we're meeting to discuss reaching an agreement. |
| 現在我們來到談判桌。 | Now we've come to the table for negotiation. |
| 我們已經商討了多個月。 | We've discussed for months. |
| 很明顯，我們對那份建議書有很強烈的看法。 | Obviously, we have strong views about the proposal. |
| 我們自四月以來便一直討價還價。 | We've been bargaining since April. |
| 讓我們來達成協議吧。 | Let's hammer out an agreement.<br>同 Let's hammer an agreement out. |
| 進展不理想。 | It wasn't good progress. |
| 讓我們來消除談判障礙吧！ | Let's unblock the negotiations. |
| 如果我們能夠產生協議來便好了。 | I'd be great if we can create an agreement. |
| 我相信任何事情皆可磋商。 | I believe everything is negotiable.<br>開始談判前，說一些積極的說話來緩和緊張場面。 |
| 我們仍然期望雙贏局面。 | We're still looking forward to a win-win situation. |
| 這項計劃可以協商的。 | This project is negotiable. |

195.mp3

| | |
|---|---|
| 會有解決這個問題的方法。 | There'll be a solution to the problem. |
| 彼此互相遷就可以移除障礙。 | Mutual give and take may remove the hurdle. |
| 如果我們互相遷就，會達成協議的。 | We may reach an agreement if we give and take.<br>常用詞組 "give and take" 解作互讓互惠或公平交換。 |
| 彼此讓步可解決它。 | It may be settled by mutual concession. |
| 如果我們達成可接受的條件便令人滿意了。 | It's desirable if we can work out acceptable terms. |
| 我們會致力作出極優惠的條件。 | We'll work out highly favourable conditions. |
| 也許我們在今天結束前得到好結果。 | Perhaps we may get good result at the end of the day. |
| 我希望在此情況下，我們得到可能是最好的交易。 | I hope we can get the best deal possible under the circumstances.<br>同 I hope we can get the best deal possible in these circumstances. |
| 或者，我們會作出一些讓步。 | Maybe we can make some concessions. |
| 我們正尋求最佳辦法達成決議。 | We're going to find out the best way to resolve it. |
| 雙方妥協是無可避免的。 | Compromises on both sides are inevitable. |
| 彼此分歧縮窄。 | The gap between us narrows. |

# 應對分歧（對外）

196.mp3

| | |
|---|---|
| 如果我沒有誤會你的意思，你的提議跟之前完全一樣。 | If I didn't get you wrong, your proposals are exactly the same as before. |
| 我聽見了你說的話，但是你根本沒有減低開價。 | I've heard what you said, but you didn't lower the offer at all. |
| 很難接受你的條件。 | It's hard to accept your terms. |
| 你的條件很難接受。 | Your terms are unacceptable. |
| 我們不能接受你那樣的條件。 | We're not able to accept your terms like that. |
| 它們不是對我方有利的條件。 | They are not favourable terms for us. |
| 我認為，這不是可以讓人首肯的條件。 | I think it isn't an agreeable term. |
| 你仍然堅持。 | You still insist. |
| 如果你仍然採取固有立場，是無補於事的。 | It doesn't help if you still take a firm stand. |

It doesn't help if you......
如果你……，是無補於事的。
It doesn't help if you urge 15-day payment.
如果你堅持 15 日付款期，是無補於事的。
It doesn't help if you don't think about the rise in cost.
如果你不考慮到成本上漲，是無補於事的。

197.mp3

| | |
|---|---|
| 如果你不放棄原來的開價，我們無法有進展。 | We can't make any progress if you don't give up the original offer.<br>同 We can't make any progress if you don't abandon the original offer. |
| 你能夠使預定日期更有彈性嗎？ | Can you make the schedule more flexible? |
| 我相信有很多可能的解決方法。 | I believe there are many possible solutions. |
| 我要把我的想法告訴你。 | I'll show our cards on the table.<br>同 I'll put our cards on the table. |
| 我將要説明我的想法。 | I'm going to explain what I think. |
| 這是我們要的。 | That's what we want. |
| 這是我們能夠開的價錢。 | This is what we can offer. |
| 那是我們能夠接受的日期。 | That's the date we can accept. |
| 我們不能推延那項活動。 | We can't delay the event. |
| 你知道，農曆新年跟聖誕節一樣重要的。 | You know Chinese New Year is as important as Christmas. |
| 如果那場表演不能在假期舉行，是沒有意義的。 | It's pointless if the show can't take place during the holidays.<br>類 It's pointless if the show can't take place during the festive days.<br>如果那場表演不能在節日舉行，是沒有意義的。 |
| 在聖誕節，它會吸引很多觀眾。 | It will draw a lot of audience at Christmas. |

198.mp3

| | |
|---|---|
| 請你明白，我們無法接受往後的日子。 | Please understand that we can't accept a later date. |
| | Please understand that......<br>請你明白，……。<br>Please understand that it's not a good price.<br>請你明白，這不是好價錢。<br>Please understand that it's not what we expected.<br>請你明白，這不是我們期待的。 |
| 請別延遲。 | No more delay please. |
| 我們要求早上八點那麼早接收場地。 | We request to have the venue as early as 8 am. |
| 九點鐘太遲了。 | 9 am is too late. |
| 我們需要三小時安裝佈景。 | We need 3 hours to set the backdrop. |
| | We need......to......<br>我們需要……。<br>We need a working day to handle the invoice.<br>我們需要一個工作天來處理發票。<br>We need an hour to get it prepared.<br>我們需要一個小時來預備它。 |
| 如果九點鐘是唯一選擇，我們不能在兩點正交還場地。 | If 9 am is the only option, we can't return the venue at 2 pm. |
| 需要多於一個小時來清理場地。 | It takes more than an hour to clear up the place. |
| 為甚麼你不問下一個使用者晚一點接收場地呢？ | Why don't you ask the next user to get it later? |

199.mp3

| | |
|---|---|
| 你可否延長一小時？ | Can you extend one hour? |
| 這不公平。 | It's not fair. |
| 我們給的是同樣價錢。 | We pay the same price. |
| 除非最後一小時是免費，我們不會接受。 | We won't accept it unless the last hour is free.<br>磋商前，蒐集同行資料，在必要時，提出對方的不公平作法，然後乘機爭取更多好處。 |
| 如果我們租用你們立體音響裝置，你們會打更多折嗎？ | Can you offer more discounts if we rent your stereo? |
| 這得要看你訂單的數量。 | It depends on the quantity you'll order.<br>It depends on......<br>這得要看⋯⋯。<br>It depends on how long your fashion show will be.<br>這得要看你的時裝秀表演多久。<br>It depends on which brand you'll choose.<br>這得要看你選哪個品牌了。 |
| 讓我看看月曆。 | Let me check out the calendar. |
| 我要說，這個數字不能縮小彼此的差距。 | I'd say this number can't bridge the gap between us. |
| 嗯，我來主動縮減差距吧。 | Well, I take the initiative to bridge the price gap. |
| 你能否減低 5% 來縮減差距嗎？ | Can you lower 5% to bridge the gap? |
| 4% 如何？ | What about 4%? |

# 達成協議（對外）

200.mp3

| | |
|---|---|
| 你的還價聽起來蠻吸引的。 | Your counteroffer sounds attractive. |
| 這聽來不錯。 | That sounds good to us. |
| 你現在既然減了2%，我也同意增加數量。 | Now that you cut 2% and we also agree to increase the quantity. |
| 好吧，我們同意把表演減至兩小時。 | OK, we agree to cut the show to 2 hours. |
| 這是很難的，不過我同意接受它。 | It's hard but I agree to accept it.<br>類 It isn't an easy decision, but I agree to accept it.<br>這是一個不容易的決定，但我同意接受它。 |
| 這項新條件比之前的那項更好。 | This new term is better than the previous one. |
| 條件確定了。 | The conditions were set. |
| 一切已經獲得確定了。 | All things have been set. |
| 現在看來不錯。 | Things look good now. |
| 我們差不多成了。 | We're almost there. |
| 在我們達成協議前，有一項我想你澄清的。 | One more thing I want you to clarify before we conclude. |
| 你可以把這一項條件加進合約裏嗎？ | Can you add this term to the contract? |

201.mp3

| | |
|---|---|
| 我們可以推敲第十二行的句子嗎？ | Can we refine the sentence on line 12? |
| 自今天一大早開始到現在，我們已有很多進展。 | We've come a long way since early this morning. |
| 我們一直都盡力而為。 | We all tried hard all the way. |
| 謝謝你們的讓步。 | Thank you for the concession you made. |
| 謝謝你們使協議達成。 | Thank you for making it happen. |
| 謝謝你的努力。 | Thank you for your hard work. |
| 我理解你們已經很努力。 | I understand you've worked very hard. |
| 其實你明白到，為甚麼我們要堅持那個提議的日子。 | Actually you understood why we had to insist on the proposed date. |
| 對，那是我們中國人的重要假期。 | Yes, it's an important holiday for us Chinese. |
| 雖然我們有不同意見，但是過程平和，對此我要表示感謝。 | I'm grateful for the peaceful process despite our different opinions.<br>連接詞"despite"後必須是名詞，不是句子。 |
| 我知道你已經努力達成它。 | I can tell you've make effort to make it. |
| 曾有不可控制的因素，不過我們已經移除了。 | There were some uncontrollable factors but we've removed them. |

202.mp3

| | |
|---|---|
| 現在來結束它吧。 | Let's close it now. |
| 我們消除了分歧。 | We've closed the gap. |
| 哎呀，差距沒有了！ | Gosh, the gap is gone! |
| 我現在很滿意達成這項交易。 | I'm now satisfied to do the deal. |
| 我滿意這協議。 | I'm satisfied with the deal. |
| 我們滿意這決議。 | I'm pleased with the resolution. |
| 我們能達成協議嗎？ | Can we conclude an agreement? |
| 你已經使之達成。 | You've brought it to an end. |
| 我們終於解決了矛盾。 | We finally settled the conflict. |
| 你最終跟我們妥協。 | You finally came to terms with us. |
| 我希望從此我們會有長期的合作關係。 | I hope we'll have a long term relationship from now on. |
| 我們公平地解決了大家矛盾的利益。 | We've fairly resolved our conflicting interests. |
| 我相信延長的磋商沒有破壞大家的關係。 | I believe the extended negotiation didn't damage our relationship. |

# 慶祝合作（對外）

203.mp3

| | |
|---|---|
| 我為這個結果感到驚訝。 | I'm amazed at the result. |
| 這是切合實際的協議。 | It was a sensible agreement. |
| 我們搞定了！ | We've made it! |
| 我們克服了所有障礙。 | We've overcome all the obstacles. |
| 能夠這樣結束真好。 | That's so nice to close it like that. |
| 我們現在是業務夥伴了。 | We're business partners now. |
| 我希望從此以後我們將會是好拍檔。 | I hope we'll be good partners from now on. |
| 好事陸續來！ | Good things will come our way! |
| 我們都贏了！ | We carried the day!<br>俗語“carried the day”的意思是勝利或成功。 |
| 我不能想像我們可以忍受那樣漫長的過程。 | I can't imagine that we can stand the long process like that. |
| 我們全都盡力了。 | We all have tried our best. |
| 我們不會忘記今天發生的事情。 | We won't forget what's happened today. |
| 這可能是我一生中最長的談判。 | It might be the longest negotiation I had in life. |

204.mp3

| | |
|---|---|
| 叫人無法忘記。 | It was unforgettable. |
| 今天很漫長。 | It was a long day. |
| 我們應該慶祝談判成功。 | We should celebrate for the success. |
| 你現在有時間嗎？ | Do you have time now? |
| 你現在要離開嗎？ | Do you need to leave now? |
| 樓下有一家不錯的咖啡室。 | There's a very nice café downstairs. |
| 你有興趣喝一杯咖啡嗎？ | Are you interested in a cup of coffee? |
| 留下來喝咖啡可以嗎？ | Can you stay for a coffee?<br>一般而言，工作時不喝酒的，所以先問對方是否有興趣喝咖啡，比較保險合宜。 |
| 不如大家到外面去喝一杯。 | Let's go somewhere and have a drink. |
| 讓我請客。 | Be my guest. |
| 請不要拒絕我。 | Please don't refuse me. |
| 我們應該吃一頓美味的晚餐。 | We should have a fabulous dinner. |
| 讓我去訂位。 | Let me make a reservation. |
| 你們喜歡吃甚麼？ | What kind of food do you like? |
| 我們想嘗試本地菜。 | We want to try local food. |

# 催促訂單（對外）

205.mp3

| | |
|---|---|
| 你可以加快處理我的訂單嗎？ | Can you please speed up my order? |
| 請跟進我的訂單。 | Please follow up my order. |
| 你現在可以查看我的訂單情況嗎？ | Can you now check the status of my order? |
| 甚麼？你在電腦裏找不到？ | What? You can't find it from your computer? |
| 發生甚麼事？ | What's going on? |
| 有甚麼地方不對勁？ | Is there anything wrong? |
| 有錯誤的時候，為甚麼不打電話告訴我？ | Why didn't you call me when there was a mistake?<br>類 Why didn't you call me when you found a mistake?<br>發現有錯的時候，為甚麼不打電話告訴我？ |
| 如果它沒有存貨，你可以刪除它並繼續處理其他貨品嗎？ | If it's not available, can you delete it and process other items? |
| 你可以處理得更有彈性嗎？ | Can you be more flexible? |
| 你今天會處理嗎？ | Will you handle it today? |
| 我答應了我的顧客，下個星期三送貨。 | I've promised my customers that the goods will arrive on next Wednesday. |
| 他們計劃同一天運送那些貨物。 | They plan to ship the goods on the same day. |

206.mp3

| | |
|---|---|
| 所以我務必確定送貨日期是這個星期五。 | So I have to make sure the delivery date is this Friday. |
| 我明白你忙於處理聖誕定單。 | I understand you're busy handling the Christmas orders. |
| 你上個星期收到我的訂單嗎？ | Did you receive my order last week? |
| 我沒有從你那裏收到任何確認。 | I didn't receive any confirmation from you. |
| 我昨天打電話給你，但你不在。 | I called you yesterday but you were not available. |
| 我想知道，我要等多久。 | I was wondering how long I'd be waiting. |
| 多久那些貨物才到？ | How long until the goods arrive? |
| 托運貨物會在月底前抵達口岸嗎？ | Will the consignment arrive at the port by the end of this month? |
| 送貨方面發生甚麼問題？ | What happened to the delivery? |
| 我們已經付了運費一個月！ | We've paid the freight for a month already! |
| 這就奇怪了。 | It's very strange. |
| 通常沒有那麼長的。 | It usually doesn't take so long. |
| 你收到了信用證了，是嗎？ | You received the letter of credit, right? |

207.mp3

你可以預測甚麼時候我收到貨物？
Can you predict when I can collect the goods?

Can you predict......?
你可以預測……？
Can you predict the delivery date?
你可以預測送貨日期？
Can you predict when the goods will arrive in our country?
你可以預測甚麼時候貨物送到我的國家？

對不起，今早我們的系統發生了問題。
Sorry, our system got a problem this morning.

不可能立即查看它。
It's impossible to check it out right away.

請問你可以等一下嗎？
Can you please wait for a moment please?

你的發票號碼是甚麼？
What's your invoice number?

你肯定銀行發了信用證嗎？
Are you sure your bank has issued the letter of credit?

因為接近聖誕節，有很多投遞。
Because it's getting close to Christmas, there are a lot of deliveries.

聖誕節快來了。
Christmas is around the corner.

你明白，我們的生意有淡旺季之分。
You know our business is seasonal.

我們需要多些時間處理發票和單據的事情。
It takes us more time to handle the invoicing and billing.

Speed up 加快
Check 查看
Follow up 跟進
Handle 處理

# 確認收件（對外）

208.mp3

| | |
|---|---|
| 嗨，萊利，你好嗎？今早我收到它了。 | Hi, Larry, How are you? I got it this morning. |
| 我已經收到你的訂單。 | I've received your order.<br>I've received......<br>我已經收到……。<br>I've received your fax.<br>我已經收到你的傳真。<br>I've received your email.<br>我已經收到你的電郵。 |
| 謝謝你的電郵。 | Thank you for your email. |
| 我打電話來的原因是告訴你我們已經收到它了。 | The reason I'm calling is to tell you that we've received it. |
| 我打電話來是確認收到你的發票。 | I'm calling to confirm the receipt of your invoice. |
| 我看過你的訂單了。 | I saw your order. |
| 我不肯定 236 號產品的質素。 | I'm not sure the quality of product no. 236. |
| 那個數字很模糊。我猜打印機沒有墨了。 | The number is blurred. I guess the printer is running out of ink. |
| 請告訴亨利，我們今天收到他的訂單。 | Please tell Henry that we got his order today. |
| 你真快。三十分鐘前我已經收到它了。 | You were quick. I got it 30 minutes ago. |

209.mp3 

| | |
|---|---|
| 目錄送到我們的辦公室了。 | The catalogue has reached our office. |
| 我已經仔細查看細節了。 | I've examined the details. |
| 你已經收到了。真好。 | You've received it. That's great. |
| 一切都沒問題吧？ | Is everything OK? |
| 整套文件包括一份價目表和一本目錄。 | The package should include a price list and a catalogue. |
| 讓我提醒你一下，價錢修改了。 | Let me remind you that the prices are revised. |
| 價錢改了。 | The prices have been changed. |
| 請注意我們改了產品編號。 | Please notice that we've changed the model number. |
| 這裏有修改。 | There's an adjustment. |
| 你注意到修改？ | Did you notice the correction? |
| 你看到不同的地方？ | Can you see the difference? |
| 如你要求，我們以另一型號換了它。 | It was replaced by another model as you requested. |
| 我們只有 100 件。這是為甚麼數量不是 120。 | We only have 100 pieces. That's why it wasn't 120. |
| 我們會在下星期送另外 20 件。 | We will send you another 20 pieces next week. |

210.mp3

| | |
|---|---|
| 到時候我們另發新的發票。 | And we'll issue another invoice by then. |
| 上個星期我們已經寄出那收據了。 | We sent out the receipt last week. |
| 如果你下星期還收不到，請再來電。 | If you don't receive it next week, please call me again. |
| 通常要一個星期多才送到收信人那裏。 | It usually takes a week or so to reach a recipient. |
| 對，我們已經收到你的付款，同一天也發了收據。 | Yes, we've received your payment and issue the receipt on the same day. |
| 我們取消了那張收據，會發新的一張。 | I'll cancel the receipt and issue a new one. |
| 你可以在取消收據確認信上簽名嗎？ | Can you sign the cancellation of the receipt? |
| 那貨品賣光了，有貨的時候我們會打電話給你。 | The item is sold out and we will call you when it is available. |
| 你介意再寄來嗎？ | Would you mind sending it again? |
| 謝謝你們快速的送貨，但我找不到一些貨物。 | Thank you for your fast delivery, but I can't find some products. |
| 發票跟你送來的不一樣。 | The invoice doesn't match what you delivered. |

211.mp3

| | |
|---|---|
| 有些地方不妥。你們輸入一項貨品時出錯了。 | There's something wrong. You made a mistake in entering an item. |
| 我發覺數目錯了。 | I found out the quantity was wrong. |
| 請問你可以調整它嗎？ | Would you please adjust it? |
| 你調整了它後，給我一通電話可以嗎？ | Will you call me back after you've adjusted it? |
| 我等你的傳真。 | I'll wait for your fax. |
| 我記得我們沒有訂這個。 | I remember we didn't order this. |
| 你會傳真來一張新的發票嗎？ | Will you fax me a new invoice?<br>Will you fax me......?<br>你會傳真來……？<br>Will you fax me a corrected price list?<br>你會傳真來一份改正了的價目表嗎？<br>Will you fax me a revised order?<br>你會傳真來一份調整過的訂單嗎？ |
| 這跟我們的訂單有出入。 | This is different from our order. |
| 發票上的價錢比你告訴我的貴。 | The price shown on the invoice is higher than the one you told me. |
| 顯示的價錢是140元，這是不可能的。 | The price shown is $140, which is impossible. |
| 我們訂購了四打，但是送來只有20件。 | We ordered 4 dozens of it but there are 20 pieces only. |

# 報價還款（對外）

212.mp3

| | |
|---|---|
| 我想知道產品的價格。 | I'd like to know the price of a product. |
| 我對新產品系列有興趣。你可以告訴我價錢嗎？ | I'm interested in the new product line. Can you tell me the prices? |
| 大量訂購價錢如何？ | What is the price for a bulk order? |
| 你們有最新的價目表嗎？ | Do you have an updated price list? |
| 這是固定的價格嗎？ | Is it a fixed price? |
| 你們會打折嗎？ | Would you offer an discount? |
| 我是出口商，想知道你們的產品價格。 | I'm an exporter and would like to know the prices of your products. |
| 我們有很多種產品。 | We have a wide range of products. |
| 請問你可否告訴我，你在找哪類產品嗎？ | Can you please tell me what kind of products you are looking for? |
| 你對哪種產品有興趣？ | What types of goods are you interested? |
| 我們賣很多品牌。 | We sell a lot of brands. |
| 有些產品比其他的便宜。 | Some of them are cheaper than others. |
| 我會推介 A 品牌，它是高檔品。 | I'd recommend Brand A, which are high-end products. |

213.mp3

| | |
|---|---|
| 我相信你的顧客會想要更便宜的耐用貨品。 | I believe your customers would prefer some durable goods at lower prices. |
| 它定價 50 元。 | It is priced at $50. |
| 如果你付現金，我們給你九五折。 | We'd offer a 5% discount if you pay in cash. |
| 如果我們付現金，會更便宜嗎？ | Would it be cheaper if we pay cash? |
| 付款方式是怎樣？ | What about the payment method? |
| 請以支票付款。 | Please make payment by cheque.<br>支票在英國和加拿大是 "cheque"，美國是 "check"。 |
| 收貨後 30 天必須付款。 | Payment is required within 30 days from the receipt of goods.<br>Payment is required with 30 days from......<br>……30 天必須付款。<br>Payment is required with 30 days from the invoice date.<br>發票日期起 30 天必須付款。<br>Payment is required with 30 days from the date of shipment.<br>送貨起 30 天後必須付款。 |
| 發票日期 30 後到期還款。 | Payment is due 30 days from the date of the invoice. |
| 我們一送貨便向你發出發票。 | You'll be invoiced when we ship the goods. |
| 30 天後我們會發帳單。 | You'll be billed after 30 days. |
| 我們有提早還款的優惠。 | There's an incentive for those who pay early. |

## 相關生字

| | |
|---|---|
| Exporter | 出口商 |
| Importer | 入口商 |
| Buyer | 買家 |
| Distributor | 分銷商 |
| Seller | 賣家 |
| Supplier | 供應商 |
| Manufacturer | 製造商 |
| Producer | 生產商 |
| A letter of credit | 信用證 |
| A bill of lading | 提貨單 |
| Proof of payment | 付款證明 |
| Payment | 付款／還款 |
| Consignment | 托運貨物 |
| Trade fair | 展銷會 |
| Terms of sale | 售貨條例 |
| Invoice | 發票 |
| Bill | 帳單 |
| Receipt | 收據 |
| Price list | 價目表 |

## 寸土必爭

經商往來一定會有討價還價或磋商合作的機會。無論自己是否佔上風，必須預先做好資料蒐集的工夫，不要給人家有「你是吳下阿蒙，可以被欺負」的印象。跟國外商家做生意，最好先打聽在他們的國家裏做生意的文化和行情，尤其是如何計算還貨款的日期；不同國家或公司對「30天還款期」（“Net 30 days” settlement）有不同詮釋。一些是從送貨當天起計算，另一些或是從送貨該月的月底才開始還款期。譬如説，送貨日是 3 月 8 日，第一種計算方法是 4 月 8 日還款，後者是 4 月 30 日。在磋商的過程，別只管説出自己的要求或條件，記得要讓對方説個明白，你自己也要聽清楚，如果你身邊有詮譯員，趁詮譯員翻譯的時候（假設你聽懂對方的意思），暗自再盤算自己的底線，思考如何作出一些讓步，來換取更大的利益。

# Chapter 8

# 營銷宣傳

# 調查目的（一般）

216.mp3

| | |
|---|---|
| 市場調查可幫助我們預測市場潮流。 | Market research can help us predict market trends.<br>Market research can help us......<br>市場調查可幫助我們……<br>Market research can help us identify potential customers.<br>市場調查可幫助我們找出潛在的顧客。<br>Market research can help us design a new product.<br>市場調查可幫助我們設計新產品。 |
| 我們會集中在年齡介乎 20 和 30 之間的人。 | We'll focus on people aged between 20 and 30.<br>We'll focus on......<br>我們會集中在……<br>We'll focus on their preference in colour.<br>我們會集中在他們對顏色的偏好。<br>We'll focus on drinking habit.<br>我們會集中在飲酒習慣。 |
| 產品設計將會是我們所關注的。 | Product design will be our concern. |
| 它也被構思去研究價格範圍。 | It's also designed to look into the price range. |
| 我們關注他們的購買習慣。 | We're concerned about their buying habits.<br>類 We're concerned about their shopping behaviour.<br>我們關注他們的購物行為。 |
| 我們想找出他們喜歡在哪裏買我們的產品。 | We'd like to find out where they like to buy our products. |
| 我們要確定我們的產品能接觸目標顧客。 | We have to make sure that our products reach target people. |

217.mp3

| | |
|---|---|
| 我們會派他們其中的三個人到商場觀察那裏的人。 | We'll assign three of them to observe people in the mall. |
| 保羅會瀏覽互聯網做研究，分析我們的競爭者。 | Paul will do the internet research to analyze our competitors. |
| 你可否提議一些關於市場研究的網站嗎？ | Can you suggest some helpful websites about market research? |
| 我預期這項市場研究會用上三個月。 | I expect the market research will take up three months. |
| 研究範圍會覆蓋旅遊區。 | The research will cover the tourism district. |
| 問卷在下個星期預備好。 | The questionnaire will be ready next week. |
| 我想見營業經理，為了更了解我們的客戶。 | I'd like to meet the sales manager in order to understand more about our clients. |
| 對於我們主要競爭對手的服務，我們也會想分析他們的反應。 | We will also analyze their responses to the services provided by our major competitors. |

# 草擬問卷（一般）

218.mp3

| | |
|---|---|
| 我會寫一個包括有15條問題的問卷。 | I'll write a questionnaire that consists of 15 questions. |
| 我希望這是一個15分鐘的電話訪問。 | I hope that it's a 15-minute phone interview. |
| 我們會在商場進行面對面的訪問。 | We'll conduct a face-to-face interview in the mall. |
| 一份有20條問題。 | It will be a set of 20 questions. |
| 800人會透過電話接受訪問。 | 800 people will be asked over the phone. |
| 如果我們提供利誘的話，他們拒絕的機會低一些。 | There'll be less chance they'll refuse if we offer an incentive. |
| 我們應該寄贈券給他們來表達謝意嗎？ | Should we send them a couple to express our gratitude? |
| 我也會設計一些附加到電郵的電子贈券。 | I may also design an e-coupon attached in emails. |
| 我們可以給他們一個贈券號碼。 | We may give them a coupon code. |
| 他們可在網上換禮物。 | They may redeem a gift online. |
| 大家來草擬調查的概要。 | Let's draft an outline of the survey. |

219.mp3

| | |
|---|---|
| 人口統計的資料也包括在內。 | Demographic data has to be included. |
| 我們不會記下受訪者的名字。 | We don't record any name of the interviewees. |
| 100 人會被訪問。 | 100 people will be interviewed. |
| 住在市內最少三年是其中的一個要求。 | Living in the town at least 3 years is one of the criteria. |
| 提醒訪問員，他們不要引導受訪人回答。 | Remind the interviewers that they're not supposed to lead them to answer. |
| 訪問員要求讀出完全一樣的文字。 | Interviewers are required to read out the exact words. |
| 盡管受訪者不明白，他們也不應該用自己的意思解釋問題。 | They should not interpret the questions when the interviewees don't understand. |
| 我們計劃僱用一些兼職訪問員。 | We're planning to hire some part-time interviewers.<br>同 We're planning to recruit some part-time interviewers. |
| 我們應該問關於我們的品牌形象的問題。 | We should ask about the image of our brand. |
| 我們該把多少問題包括在問卷裏？ | How many questions should we include in the questionnaire? |
| 將會有選擇題。 | There'll be multiple choice questions. |

| | |
|---|---|
| 問題應該是直接的。 | Questions should be straightforward.<br>類 Questions should be simple.<br>問題應該是簡單的。 |
| 別問複雜的問題。 | Don't ask complicated questions. |
| 他們會誤解複雜問題。 | They'd misunderstand complicated questions. |
| 開放式問題會給我們更多想法。 | Open questions may give us more ideas. |
| 別強迫他們回答所有問題。 | Don't force them to answer all the questions. |
| 別使他們對這項調查反感。 | Don't make them feel bad about the survey. |
| 訪問員的聲線應該是友善愉快的。 | The interviewers should sound friendly and cheerful. |
| 我們將提供一些訓練給訪問員。 | We'll provide some training for the interviewers. |
| 有經驗的訪問員比較好。 | Experienced interviewers would be preferred. |

Open question 開放式問題
Simple 簡單
Complicated 複雜
Friendly 友善
Multiple choice 選擇題
Straightforward 直接
Cheerful 愉快

# 電話調查（對外）

221.mp3

| | |
|---|---|
| 嗨，這是 ABC 市場研究機構。今天你好嗎？ | Hi, this is ABC Market Research Institute. How are you today? |
| 我的名字是加利，市場研究員。 | My name is Gary, a marketing researcher. |
| 我是代表 ABC 市場研究機構進行調查。 | I'm carrying out a survey on behalf of ABC Market Research Institute. |
| 我們想了解你的時裝品味。 | We'd like to understand your fashion taste. |
| 研究目的是多了解你購買雜貨的習慣。 | The purpose of the research is to know more about your grocery shopping.<br>調查員訪問首訪對象時，不要用市場學的專門用語，以免他們聽不懂你的來意。 |
| 這是關於你對娛樂表演的觀感。 | It's about your view on entertainment shows.<br>It's about......<br>這是關於……<br>It's about your shopping preference.<br>這是關於你的購物偏好。<br>It's about your dining experience.<br>這是關於你外出進餐的經驗。 |
| 你能否抽出 15 分鐘來回答我們的問題？ | Would you be able to spare 15 minutes of your time to answer our questions? |
| 你可以回答我一些問題嗎？ | Would you answer me some questions? |
| 你現在可以給我幾分鐘嗎？ | Can you spare me a few minutes now?<br>同 Can you spare me a couple minutes now? |

222.mp3

| | |
|---|---|
| 我想跟你進行電話訪問。 | We'd like to conduct a phone interview with you.<br>雖然本節設計為電話調查，其實也適用於街頭訪問。 |
| 這不會很長。 | It won't take long. |
| 我會很快完成。 | I'll be quick. |
| 我們估計 15 分鐘會完成。 | We estimate it'll finish in 15 minutes. |
| 如果我再打電話來，甚麼時候方便你？ | What time is good for you if I call back?<br>同 What time is convenient for you if I call back? |
| 也許明天我再來電。 | Maybe I'll call you again tomorrow. |
| 我可以明天晚上 9 點前打電話給你？ | Can I call you in the evening before 9 tomorrow? |
| 對不起，打擾你。 | Sorry for bothering you. |
| 首先，我想問一些關於你的基本資料。 | First of all, I'll ask you some basic information about you. |
| 我會問一條多項選擇題。 | I'll ask you a multiple choices question. |
| 當你聽到對的答案，請説是。 | When you hear the right answer, please say yes. |
| 你不用等我讀出所有選擇。 | You don't need to wait until I've read out all the choices. |
| 這樣可以省下你的時間。 | It may save your time. |

223.mp3

| | |
|---|---|
| 來開始吧。 | Let's get started. |
| 你的年齡範圍是甚麼？ | What's your age range? |
| 你住在哪個地區？ | In which area are you living? |
| 你的職業是甚麼？ | What is your job? |
| 你在醫院工作。我把你放在醫護界別吧。 | You're working in a hospital. I'll put you in the healthcare category then. |
| 請問你可以告訴我你的月薪範圍？ | Can you please tell me the range of your monthly salary? |
| 你覺得回答它感到不舒服。好的，我們跳過它吧。 | You don't feel comfortable answering it. OK, let's skip it. |
| 沒問題。你可以拒絕回答任何問題。 | That's fine. You may refuse to answer any questions. |
| 你不想回答的時候，請隨便告訴我。 | Please feel free to tell me when you don't want to answer. |
| 家庭收入如何呢？ | What about your household income? |
| 粗略估計就是行了。 | Just a rough estimate would be fine. |

一些敏感的問題，例如涉及經濟收入的，受訪對象不想回答的話，你要立即解釋，他們可以拒絕回答，以免他們終止整個調查訪問。

224.mp3

| | |
|---|---|
| 你寧願到哪裏買上班裙子？百貨公司、商場、網上商店…… | Where do you prefer to buy office skirts? Department stores, malls, online stores...... |
| 我想知道你多久去超級市場一次。 | I wonder how often you go to the supermarket. |
| 你多久買一雙鞋子？ | How often do you buy a pair of shoes?<br>How often do you......<br>你多久……？<br>How often do you go to the bank?<br>你多久去一次那間銀行？<br>How often do you see a movie?<br>你多久看一次電影？ |
| 你曾否退回貨物給零售商嗎？ | Did you ever return merchandise to a retailer? |
| 你可以描述那次經驗嗎？ | How would you describe the experience? |
| 那是愉快、樂於助人、中立、糟糕或不愉快？ | Was it pleasant, helpful, neutral, bad or unpleasant? |
| 對於那次修整服務你有多滿意？ | How satisfied were you with the repairing services? |
| 以下那些形容詞最可以描述你的經驗？ | Which of the following adjectives best describe your experience? |
| 你覺得那顧客服務有甚麼感覺？ | How do you feel about the customer service? |

225.mp3

| | |
|---|---|
| 非常多謝你的參與。 | Thank you very much for your participation.<br>Thank you very much for.<br>非常多謝你的……。<br>Thank you very much for your cooperation.<br>非常多謝你的合作。<br>Thank you very much for your time.<br>非常多謝你的時間。 |
| 為表達我們的感謝，我們送你一張免費贈券。 | To express our gratitude, we'll offer you a complimentary coupon. |
| 我這就給你一張贈券。 | I'm going to give you a coupon now.<br>Please go to our website: www.abcresearch.com.<br>請到我們的網站：www.abcresearch.com。 |
| 按一下「換領獎品」圖像。 | Click the "Redeem gift" icon. |
| 你鍵入那個號碼，這就是你的了。 | You enter the code in the box and there you are. |
| 你可以把你的電郵地址告訴我，那麼我可以把它寄給你？ | Would you give me your email address so that we may send it to you? |
| 如果還有新的研究，我可以再打電話給你嗎？ | Can I call you again if there's a new research? |
| 沒關係，我們不會再聯絡你。 | It doesn't matter. We won't contact you again. |
| 我們不會把你的資料向第三者揭露。 | We won't disclose your data to a third party for sure. |

# 廣告宣傳（一般）

226.mp3

| | |
|---|---|
| 大家來着手我們的廣告活動吧。 | Let's get start our advertising campaign. |
| 大家來討論我們要用那種媒體。 | Let's discuss which media we'll use. |
| 那種形象我們應該建立？ | What kind of images should we establish?<br>同 What kind of images should we build up? |
| 我們可以決定那將會是哪類廣告？ | Can we decide which type of advertising it will be? |
| 資訊式廣告可以幫助我們的潛在消費者更認識那產品。 | Informative advertising may help our potential consumers know the product better. |
| 我希望它那讓觀眾知道我們的新服務。 | I hope it may inform the audience about our new services. |
| 我希望這會令人相信。 | I hope it'll be convincing. |
| 它應該是具説服力的。 | It should be persuasive. |
| 我們應該用模特兒嗎？ | Shall we use models? |
| 用名人的話，成本高。 | It'll cost a lot to use a celebrity.<br>同 It'll cost a lot to use famous people. |
| 那麼廣告音樂如何呢？ | What about jingles? |
| 誰作曲？ | Who will compose it? |

227.mp3

| | |
|---|---|
| 我們的品牌一向是高人一等和奢侈的象徵。 | Our brand is always a symbol of class and luxury.<br>Our brand is always a symbol of [noun].<br>我們的品牌一向是（名詞）的象徵。<br>Our brand is always a symbol of passion and energy.<br>我們的品牌一向是激情和能量的象徵。<br>Our brand is always a symbol of elegance.<br>我們的品牌一向是優雅的象徵。 |
| 我們把卡通人物用在產品上。 | We'll associate a cartoon figure with our product. |
| 我們已經把我們的產品定位在細分的市場裏。 | We have positioned our product in a market segment. |
| 免費樣本會是我們下一個花招。 | Giveaway will be our next gimmick. |
| 我們想突出一個充滿活力的形象。 | We'd like to project an energetic image.<br>We'd like to project an [adjective] image.<br>我們想突出一個（形容詞）的形象。<br>We'd like to project a young and vivid image.<br>我們想突出一個年輕和朝氣的形象。<br>We'd like to project a mysterious image.<br>我們想突出一個神祕的形象。 |
| 對於口號，我沒有頭緒。 | I have no idea of our slogan. |
| 口號應該是又短又簡單。 | A slogan should be short and simple. |
| 阿健會給我們看他的作品。 | Ken will show us his portfolio. |
| 他是產品攝影師。 | He's a product photographer. |

228.mp3

| | |
|---|---|
| 廣告公司會派一位代表在今個下午來匯報。 | The advertising agency will send a representative to give us a presentation this afternoon.<br>同 The ad agency will send a rep to give us a presentation this afternoon. |
| 這是那拍攝程序的記事板。 | This is the storyboard. |
| 它顯示電視廣告的程序。 | It shows the sequence of the TV commercial. |
| 它從一位模特兒的特寫開始。 | It'll start with a close-up of a model. |
| 我們希望它給觀眾震撼的效果。 | We hope it'll give the audience a stunning effect. |
| 我相信它會給人留下深刻印象。 | I believe it'll stun the people. |
| 消費者或許會想知道，他們如何能更好看。 | Consumers may wonder how they can look better. |
| 這肯定會吸引年輕人。 | It'll appeal to youngsters for sure. |
| 他們會相信，這產品會改善他們的外觀。 | They'll believe that the product can help them look better.<br>They'll believe that the product can......<br>他們會相信，這產品會……<br>They'll believe that the product can draw more attention to them.<br>他們會相信，這產品會把更多目光投到他們身上。<br>They'll believe that the product can boost their energy.<br>他們會相信，這產品會提升他們的活力。 |
| 這照片給我浪漫的感覺。 | The picture gave me a sense of romance. |

229.mp3

| | |
|---|---|
| 它產生浪漫的情懷。 | It produced a romantic mood. |
| 這正是我們想表達的。 | That's exactly what we want to convey.<br>類 That's exactly what we want to deliver.<br>這正是我們想傳遞的。 |
| 但我想知道這元素會不會說服到人。 | But I wonder if this element will persuade people. |
| 有些人為必會相信這一套。 | Some people may not buy this idea. |
| 這視乎他們如何詮釋。 | It depends on how they interpret. |
| 我們已經預放給一群 20 人看。 | We've show the preview to a group of 20 people. |
| 他們給予正面的反應。 | They gave us positive responses. |
| 也許我們會調整故事的連貫。 | Maybe we'll fine-tune the flow of the story. |
| 當然，我們會稍為調整那首廣告音樂。 | Of course, we may make some adjustment on the jingles. |
| 你寧願以出名的歌手來唱這首歌。 | You'd prefer a famous pop singer to sing the song. |
| 其實我們已經跟他的經理人商討了。 | Actually we've negotiated with his agency. |
| 他們要求的價錢太高。 | They asked for too high a price. |

# 產品描述（對外）

230.mp3

| | |
|---|---|
| 這是極好的產品。 | It's a great product. |
| 它將會以合理的價格出售。 | It will be sold at a reasonable price. |
| 它的價錢讓人負擔得起。 | Its price is affordable. |
| 它是用堅固木材製成的。 | It's made of sturdy wood.<br>It's made of......<br>它是用……製成的。<br>It's made of titanium.<br>它是用鈦金屬製成的。<br>It's made of recycled paper.<br>它是用循環再用紙製成的。 |
| 我們採用特別物料。 | We used special materials. |
| 這包裝獨特迷人。 | The packaging is glamorous. |
| 我們只採用新鮮的材料。 | We only use fresh ingredients. |
| 加多一層表層，增強它的堅固。 | An additional coating enhances its sturdiness. |
| 很難弄碎這塑料。 | It's hard to break the plastic. |
| 那外層也阻擋紫外線。 | The coating may block UV rays as well. |
| 95% 的材料是有機的。 | 95% of the ingredients are organic. |
| 它是獲得認證的有機產品。 | It is a certified organic product. |
| 我們給它獲得 ISO 認證了。 | We got ISO certification for it. |

231.mp3

| | |
|---|---|
| 生產部投放了很多新意念在它的設計裏。 | The production department has put a lot of new ideas in its design. |
| 市場中不可能有像它的產品。 | There's unlikely a product like it in the market.<br>類 There's unlikely a similar product in the market.<br>市場中不可能有類似的產品。 |
| 我們發明了新的科技來縮小它的體積。 | We invented a new technology to reduce its size. |
| 它的重量是難以置信的輕。 | Its weight is incredibly light. |
| 這是便於攜帶。 | It's convenient to carry it. |
| 這是非常適合馬不停蹄的日子。 | It's great for on-the-go days. |
| 他們會愛它嬌小的體積。 | They will love its handy size. |
| 流線形設計很吸引人。 | The streamlined design is attractive. |
| 這光亮的蓋面給人專業的感覺。 | The sleek cover looks professional. |
| 紅色配合我們的熱情形象。 | The red colour marches our passionate image. |
| 這鮮豔奪目的顏色給我們夏天的感覺。 | The vivid colours give us a summerly feel. |
| 這絕對是跟之前的型號不一樣。 | It's absolutely different from the previous model. |

# 籌備參展（一般）

232.mp3

| | |
|---|---|
| 我們申請了一個展銷攤位。 | We've apply for a booth. |
| 那裏會有 350 個展銷攤位。 | There'll be 350 booths. |
| 在展覽大堂中，他們會設 350 個展銷攤位。 | In the exhibition hall, they'll set 350 booths. |
| 這是一項大型活動。 | It'll be a big event. |
| 我認為我們不應該錯過宣傳我們的機會。 | I don't think we should miss the chance to promote ourselves. |
| 將會有很多從內地來的代表。 | There'll be a lot of delegate coming from the mainland. |
| 小冊子會重印為簡體字。 | The brochure will be reprinted in simplified Chinese characters. |
| 我們應該在三月底前接觸策劃人。 | We should contact the planner by the end of March. |
| 主辦單位向我們發出了邀請。 | The organizer sent us an invitation.<br>類 The planner has invited us.<br>主辦單位邀請了我們。 |
| 必須查看他們的設施。 | It's necessary to check their facilities. |
| 請你要求他們把平面圖傳真給我們。 | Please ask them to fax the floor plan to us. |
| 沒有平面圖，很難選擇展銷攤位。 | It's hard to choose a booth without a floor plan. |

233.mp3

| | |
|---|---|
| 我們可以參觀會場嗎？ | Can we visit the venue? |
| 你可以問主辦單位讓我們參觀會場嗎？ | Can you ask the organizer to let us visit the venue? |
| 要確定地點方便。 | Make sure the location is convenient.<br>類 Make sure the location is accessible.<br>要確定地點容易到達。 |
| 嘗試找一個接近入口的展銷攤位。 | Try to look for a booth close to the entrance. |
| 我們可以免費用他們的會議室？ | Can we use their meeting rooms free of charge? |
| 我們需要印 300 份目錄。 | We need to print 300 catalogues. |
| 我們預期五天內分發 500 份目錄。 | We expect to distribute 500 catalogues in five days. |
| 我們會派發 200 份免費試用品。 | We'll give out 200 free samples. |
| 我們應該租賃一些燈箱來宣傳我們的展銷攤位嗎？ | Should we rent some lightboxes to promote our booth? |
| 我把大家分成兩更輪班。 | I'll split us in 2 shifts. |
| 他們只提供一個免費車位給每位參展商。 | They'll provide one free parking spot only to each exhibitor. |

234.mp3

| | |
|---|---|
| 我會打電話給活動籌劃經理，多問一些細節。 | I'll call the event manager to ask for more details. |
| 我們定目標要招呼 200 名代表。 | Our target is to accommodate 200 delegates. |
| 我們的行政總裁會在第二天主持一個論壇。 | Our CEO will host a forum on day 2. |
| 歡迎來到我們的攤位。 | Welcome to our booth. |
| 我是 ABC 公司的營業代表。 | I'm the sales rep of ABC Company. |
| 我很高興向你介紹我們的新產品。 | I'm glad to introduce our new products to you. |
| 讓我示範怎麼用這東西。 | Let me show you how to use it. |
| 歡迎到我們的陳列室。 | Welcome to our showroom! |
| 這是你第一次來嗎？ | Is it your first time here? |
| 讓我向你介紹我們的最新型號。 | Let me show you our latest model.<br>Let me show you......<br>讓我向你介紹／展示／給你看……。<br>Let me show you our fitness club.<br>讓我向你展示我們的健美中心。<br>Let me show you the brochure.<br>讓我給你看看這小冊子。 |
| 你在找哪種產品？ | Which product are you looking for? |

235.mp3

| | |
|---|---|
| 它是為今季而製造的。 | It was manufactured for this season. |
| 你在找最新的。 | You're looking for the latest one. |
| 你真曉得我們的產品。 | You're on the ball!<br>俗語“on the ball”是用來讚別人對一些所知甚豐和很能幹。遇上一些對產品頗有研究的顧客，可以這樣來讚賞對方。 |
| 這就是我們的目錄。 | Here you go. This is our catalogue. |
| 請參考我們的購物指南。 | Please refer to our buying guide. |
| 讓我打開到第10頁。 | Let me turn to page 10. |
| 你可以在這一頁看到你想要的型號。 | You may see the models you want on this page. |
| 讓我告訴你一些特點。 | Let me tell you the features. |
| 我們有三間寬敞的排舞室。 | We have 3 spacious studios. |
| 休憩室裏面有零食部。 | There's a snack bar in the resting area. |
| 我們的老師很優秀。 | Our teachers are excellent.<br>......are excellent.<br>……很優秀。<br>Our consultants are excellent.<br>我們的顧問是很優秀。<br>Our designers are excellent.<br>我們的設計師很優秀。 |
| 你想現在見他們嗎？ | Do you want to meet them now? |

236.mp3

| | |
|---|---|
| 跟他們其中一位談談嗎？ | Do you want to talk to one of them? |
| 他們可以解答你更深入的問題。 | They may answer your more in-depth questions. |
| 他們可以解釋為甚麼我們採用一個不同的系統。 | They can explain why we adopted a different system.<br>同 They can explain why we used a different system. |
| 我們樂意讓你認識到我們的服務。 | We're happy to let you know about our service. |
| 請隨便試用這些手提電腦。 | Please feel free to try to use the laptops. |
| 你可以在本週內參加一堂免費的舞蹈班。 | You may join in a free dance class within this week.<br>同 You may join in a complimentary dance class within this week. |
| 你覺得我介紹的這件產品如何？ | How do you think about the product I recommend? |
| 我們以這打破常規的設計為榮。 | We're proud of the bend-the-rules design. |
| 如果你想找價錢實惠的，可考慮這個。 | If price is your concern, you may consider that one. |
| 我想解釋我們用來製造它的新技術。 | I'd like to explain our new technology used in making it. |

Showroom 陳列室
Excellent 優秀的／出色的
Latest 最新的

# 籌備展銷（一般）

237.mp3

| | |
|---|---|
| 我正草擬一份新聞稿。 | I'm drafting a press release. |
| 我們會發出一份新聞稿。 | We will issue a press release. |
| 那份新聞稿已經傳真給傳媒了。 | The press release has been faxed to the media. |
| 我把那份新聞稿翻譯成中文了。 | I've translated the press release in Chinese. |
| 我可以看一遍新聞稿嗎？ | Can I go over the press release? |
| 我打電話給記者。 | I'll call the reporters. |
| 努力勸他們來。 | Try to persuade them to come. |
| 我們會預備紀念品給顧客和記者。 | We'll prepare souvenirs for customers and reporters. |
| 我們將會邀請一位電影明星。 | We're going to invite a movie star. |
| 一位超級名模來出席開幕禮。 | A supermodel will attend the opening.<br>同 A supermodel will attend the kick-off. |
| 告訴他們，我們在下午 1:30 開始活動。 | Tell them we'll start the event at 1:30pm. |
| 展銷會會在 10 點開始。 | The show will start at 10. |

| | |
|---|---|
| 我們會在商場設一個促銷攤位。 | We'll set a booth in the mall. |
| 我們送甚麼贈品給當日入會的人呢？ | What incentives can we offer to those who join the membership that day? |
| 我們鎖定學生為目標。 | We'll target at students. |
| 大家來設計一塊橫額。 | Let's design a banner. |
| 我們會懸掛一個大標牌在商場的入口。 | We'll hang a huge sign at the entrance to the mall. |
| 上次我們在哪裏印海報？ | Where did we print the posters last time? |
| 或者我們要聘請一位平面設計師。 | Maybe we need to hire a graphic designer. |

Press release 新聞稿
Poster 海報
Mall 商場
Banner 橫幅
Sign 標牌

# 商場促銷（對外）

239.mp3

| | |
|---|---|
| 嗨，你是學生嗎？ | Hi, are you a student? |
| | Hi, are you......?<br>嗨，你是……嗎？<br>Hi, are you an office lady?<br>嗨，妳在辦公室上班嗎？<br>Hi, are you a mother?<br>嗨，你是母親嗎？ |
| 你今天可以省 100 元！ | You may save $100 today! |
| 你想省 200 嗎？ | Do you want to save $200? |
| 你聽過我們的品牌嗎？ | Have you ever heard about our brand? |
| | Have you ever......?<br>你（動詞）過……嗎？<br>Have you ever tried hot yoga?<br>你試過高溫瑜伽嗎？<br>Have you ever used our skin products?<br>你用過我們的護膚品嗎？ |
| 你想要一堂免費化妝班嗎？ | Do you want a free makeup lesson? |
| 我們給你一套試用品！ | We're offering you a sample set! |
| | 在商場促銷，消費者匆忙經過，第一句話最好簡短些，讓他們清楚聽見你們提供的「好處」。 |
| 來看看我們瑜伽班的詳細內容。 | Come see the details of our yoga classes. |
| 如果你今天加入我們的健美中心，你可以多享八五折。 | If you join our fitness club today, you may enjoy an extra 15% discount. |
| 我們只想首 30 名顧客打折。 | We only offer the discount to the first 30 customers. |

240.mp3

| | |
|---|---|
| 明天我們不在這裏了。 | We won't be here tomorrow. |
| 這是我們在這裏的最後一天。 | It's the last day we're here. |
| 別錯過機會！ | Don't miss the chance!<br>類 Don't miss out!<br>別錯過！ |
| 今天是我們顧客感謝日！ | Today is our Customer Appreciation Day! |
| 請停下腳步進來，我們有化妝示範、即場抽獎和折扣！ | Please stop in for makeup demos, door prizes and discount! |
| 促銷活動不會很長。 | This promotional campaign won't last long. |
| 你買第二件的話半價。 | You may buy one get the second one 50% off. |
| 這是真的很便宜的產品。 | It's a real bargain. |
| 我們也送你一套禮物。 | We also give you a gift set. |

Promotional campaign 促銷活動　　Bargain 便宜貨
Gift set 禮物套裝

# 熱線服務（對外）

241.mp3

| | |
|---|---|
| 嗨，ABC顧客服務熱線。這是馬克。我可以怎樣幫到你？ | Hi, ABC customer service hotline. Mark's speaking. How can I help you? |
| 我明白。你在三天前買的。 | I see. You bought it 3 days ago. |
| 而它現在不操作了。 | And it doesn't work now. |
| 你有收據嗎？ | Do you have the receipt? |
| 你有保證卡嗎？ | Do you have the warranty card?<br>類 Did you keep the warranty card?<br>你有保留保證卡嗎？ |
| 你有把登記表格寄回給我們嗎？ | Did you send us back the registration form? |
| 你有在線上登記嗎？ | Did you register online? |
| 你收到我們給你的保證編號嗎？ | Did you get the warranty code from us? |
| 讓我查看你的名字是否在我們的名單上。 | Let me check if your name is on our list. |
| 這會用上好幾分鐘。 | It may take a few minutes. |
| 請別掛線。 | Please don't hang up the line. |
| 嗨，謝謝你的等候。 | Hi, thank you for holding.<br>類 Hi, thank you for your patience.<br>嗨，謝謝你的忍耐。 |

242.mp3

| | |
|---|---|
| 我在資料庫中找到你的名字。 | I've found your name in our database. |
| 因為你遺失保證卡，你可否告訴我，你的電話號碼來證實身份？ | Since you lost the warranty card, can you tell me your home phone number to verify? |
| 請問你的地址？ | And your address please? |
| 我們的技術員在三個工作天內將會到你府上。 | Our technician will go to your home within 3 business days. |
| 請注意，我們會收取 50 元檢驗費。 | Please note that we'll charge you $50 as an inspection fee. |
| 就算我們不修理任何零件，也收取這筆費用。 | We'll charge you the fee even if we don't fix anything. |
| 這是用來彌補人工成本。 | It's to cover the labour cost. |
| 聽起來我們可能要更換軸承，這要 100 元。 | It sounds that we may replace the bearing, which costs $100. |
| 我們的職員不會在當日收那筆費用。 | Our staff won't take the fee on the spot. |
| 檢驗後，那筆收費會在下個月的帳單顯示。 | The fee will be shown on the bill next month after inspection. |
| 你還想要我們的服務嗎？ | Do you still want our service? |

243.mp3

| | |
|---|---|
| 甚麼時間方便你呢？ | What time is good for you? |
| 你寧願晚上？ | You prefer the evening? |
| 星期二晚上 6 至 8 點鐘如何？ | What about 6 to 8 pm on Tuesday? |
| 技術員會在來到府上前，給你一通電話。 | The technician will give you a call before he comes. |
| 請你來我們的顧客服務中心。 | Please come to our customer service centre. |
| 我們會檢查，如果可以的話便立即維修。 | We may check it and repair it right away if we can. |
| 請記得帶收據來。 | Please remember to bring along the receipt.<br>Please remember to bring along......<br>請記得帶……來。<br>Please remember to bring along the package box.<br>請記得帶包裝箱來。<br>Please remember to bring along your membership card.<br>請記得帶會員證來。 |
| 我們的營業時間由 9 至 8 點鐘。 | Our business hour is from 9 to 8. |
| 我們也在星期日開門。 | We're open on Sundays as well. |
| 我們沒辦法確定你要等多久。 | I can't tell how long the wait will be. |
| 我們不接受電話預約。 | We don't set up an appointment over the phone. |

# 面對面服務（對外）

244.mp3

| | |
|---|---|
| 請坐。 | Please take a seat. |
| 有甚麼問題？ | What's the problem? |
| 我可以看看嗎？ | Can I have a look? |
| 甚麼時候開始不妥的？ | When did it start to happen? |
| 曾經發生過嗎？ | Has it happened before? |
| 你聽見甚麼聲音？ | What sound did you hear? |
| 有奇怪嗶嗶聲。 | There was a strange beep sound. |
| 沒有訊號。 | There's no signal. |
| 完全沒有反應。 | It doesn't respond at all. |
| 現在我除掉電池。 | Now I'm removing the battery. |
| 我想，問題是由於這塊電池引起的。 | I think the problem was caused by the battery. |
| 你充電多久？ | How long did you charge the battery for? |
| 可能有水跑進裝置裏去。 | Maybe water got into the device. |
| 你介意把它留下來一個星期嗎？ | Do you mind leaving it to us for a week? |
| 通常需要三天。 | Usually it takes 3 days. |

# 介紹產品（對外）

245.mp3

| | |
|---|---|
| 這是最新的型號。 | This is the latest model. |
| 這是非常新的。 | It's very new. |
| 這條產品系列是最新的。 | The product line is up-to-date. |
| 它有很多新特點。 | It's got a lot of new features. |
| 我們的產品以天然材料而聞名。 | Our products are well-known for natural ingredients. |
| 這是我們研發來滿足消費者需要的新產品。 | It's a new product we developed to cater consumers' needs.<br>It's a new product we developed to......<br>這是我們研發來……的新產品。<br>It's a new product we developed to suit consumers' busy life.<br>這是我們研發來適合消費者忙碌生活的新產品。<br>It's a new product we developed to adapt to consumers' tastes.<br>這是我們研發來遷就消費者品味的新產品。 |
| 它們是高品質的產品。 | They are high-quality products. |
| 我們用的物料是不含化學品的。 | The material we used is chemical-free.<br>The material we used is......-free.<br>我們用的物料是不含……的。<br>The material we used is BPA-free.<br>我們用的物料是不含雙酚 A 的。<br>The material we used is fragrance-free.<br>我們用的物料是不含化學品的。 |
| 每天用它最理想。 | It's perfect for daily use. |

246.mp3

| | |
|---|---|
| 這是特別調配，以減低過敏的風險。 | It's formulated to minimize the risk of allergy. |
| 加了很多功能進去。 | More functions are added to it. |
| 它比之前用電更少。 | It uses less power than before. |
| 這時髦外觀很吸引人。 | The chic look is appealing. |

The...... look is appealing.
這……外觀很吸引人。
The fashionable look is appealing.
這時尚外觀很吸引人。
The stylish look is appealing.
這具格調的外觀很吸引人的。

| | |
|---|---|
| 我們把它的設計變得更完善。 | We have refined its design. |
| 這跟前一款型號不一樣。 | It's different from the previous model. |
| 它附有一些配件。 | It comes with some add-ons. |
| 配件需另行購買。 | Accessories are optional. |
| 這是一位國際知名的藝術家設計它的。 | It's designed by an internationally famous artist. |
| 這小巧體積可適合大部分工作檯。 | Its compact size may fit into most of the workstations. |

Its...... size may fit into most of the......
這……體積可適合大部分……。
Its portable size may fit into most ladies' purses.
這便攜的體積可適合大部分女士的小包包。
Its tiny size may fit into most students' backpack.
這極小的體積可適合大部分學生的背包。

247.mp3

| | |
|---|---|
| 大部分組件在德國裝配。 | Most of the components are assembled in Germany. |
| 這是專利設計。 | It's a patented design. |
| 我們已經為這創新的產品申請特許證。 | We've licensed this innovative product. |
| 這玩具通過了美國的安全測試。 | This toy has passed safety tests in the US. |
| 我們用的物料通過食物安全測試。 | The material we used has passed the food safety. |
| 我們不進行任何的動物測試。 | We don't conduct any animal testing. |
| 不像其他產品，它只有精華油，不含香料。 | Unlike other products, it doesn't contain any perfume but essential oils. |
| 我們用韌度強的塑料取代它。 | We've replaced it by strong plastic. |
| 它看來易碎，其實很堅固的。 | It looks delicate but actually it's strong. |
| 它豪華的外表讓人感到它很昂貴。 | Its gorgeous look makes it look expensive. |
| 這是優雅奢侈的太陽鏡，採用鉻金屬製造。 | It's a pair of posh sunglasses made of chrome. |
| 這是物超所值。 | It's an unbelievable value for money. |

### 相關生字

| | | | |
|---|---|---|---|
| Market research | 市場調查 | Animal test | 動物測試 |
| Phone interview | 電話訪問 | ISO certification | 「國際標準組織」認證 |
| Street interview | 街頭訪問 | Door prizes | 即場抽獎 |
| Questionnaire | 問卷 | Discount | 折扣 |
| Materials | 物料 | Raffles | 獎券 |
| Ingredient | 材料 | Lucky draw | 幸運抽獎 |
| Patent | 專利 | Food tasting | 試食 |
| Gadget | 小器材／小玩意兒 | Product sample | 試用品 |
| Component | 組件 | Workshop | 工作坊 |
| Striking | 令人印象深刻 | Forum | 論壇 |
| Safety test | 安全測試 | | |

### 行銷秘訣

促銷活動中，行銷商當然是以推廣自己的產品或服務為首要目標。他們既要突出產品或服務的優點，但是用語又要避免過份誇張或言過其實。因為，一些消費者不喜歡花言巧語，不容易就此被說服。而且，如果他們用過那些產品後，發覺跟推銷的內容有出入的話，更是影響商譽，甚至推銷員也遭投訴。讀者想多學有關推廣用的生字或慣用語，建議你們多瀏覽一些國際品牌或集團的網站，參考他們對產品的描述（Product description）。他們多聘用出色的廣告撰稿員，行文用字必定值得讓大家學習。為了吸引途人參觀你的展銷攤位，句子最好保持簡短，讓他們在一兩秒之間收到你的宣傳信息，可以的話，也提出一些免費的優惠，例如：如果是賣按摩乳液的，可以大聲說：“Free massage!”只要是有人走過來表示有興趣，推銷員便立即把樣本（Product sample）塗在對方的手背，一邊替他們按摩，一邊用適當的描述來推介產品的優點。

# Chapter 9

# 危機應對

# 聆聽投訴（對外）

250.mp3

| | |
|---|---|
| 我們注意到你對我們產品的關注。 | We noted your concern about our product. |
| 我們可以做甚麼幫到這件事？ | Is there any way we can help with this? |
| 我今天可以為你做甚麼？ | What can I do for you today? |
| 可以給我回覆的電話號碼，以防萬一斷線？ | May I have your call-back number in case it's disconnected? |
| 可否把戶口號碼告訴我？ | May I have your account number?<br>May I have your...... number?<br>可否把……號碼告訴我？<br>May I have your warranty number?<br>可否把保養號碼告訴我？<br>May I have your receipt number?<br>可否把收據號碼告訴我？ |
| 謝謝，你是鍾斯女士嗎？ | Thank you, is this Ms Jones? |
| 你想我做甚麼呢？ | What would you like me to do? |
| 有甚麼地方看來有問題？ | What seems to be the problem? |
| 您能夠讓我知道發生甚麼事情？ | Could you let me know what's going on? |
| 聽見這件事很抱歉。 | I'm sorry to hear that. |
| 你可以告訴我為甚麼想找經理？ | Can you tell me why you wanted to talk to a manger? |

251.mp3

| | |
|---|---|
| 你有保留收據嗎？ | Do you keep the receipt? |
| 你手上有收據嗎？ | Do you have the receipt at hand? |
| 你有購物證明，例如收據？ | Do you have proof of purchase such as a receipt? |
| 可以把收據號碼給我嗎？ | Can you give me the receipt number? |
| 你是戶口持有人嗎？ | Are you the account holder? |
| 請讓我核實你的身份。 | Let me verify your identity. |
| 你的生日日期是何時？ | What's your birth date? |
| 你可以把聯絡地址給我？ | Can you tell me your contact address? |
| 你在底部看到序號嗎？ | Can you see the serial number on the bottom? |
| 它應該印在那裏。 | It should be printed there. |
| 它是 10 位數字。 | It's a 10-digit number. |
| 首先，移除電池。 | First of all, remove the battery. |
| 清楚看到嗎？ | Is it clear to read? |
| 讓我問你幾個問題。 | Let me ask you a few questions. |
| 看看我能不能給你方便？ | Let's see if I can accommodate you. |

252.mp3

| | |
|---|---|
| 讓我看今天可為你做到甚麼。 | Let me see what I can do for you today. |
| 你説我們忘記你的訂單。 | You said that we misplaced your order.<br>You said that we misplaced your order.<br>你説我們……你的訂單。<br>You said that we overlooked your order.<br>你説我們遺漏你的訂單。<br>You said that we ignored your order.<br>你説我們沒有理會你的訂單。 |
| 你發覺有一項產品不達我們一向的標準。 | You found that there's an item under our usual standard. |
| 服務質素比以前差。 | The quality of service was worse than before. |
| 我們的顧客服務每下愈況。 | Our customer service keeps getting worse. |
| 沒有人為你服務，直到你要找經理。 | No one came to serve you until you looked for the manager. |
| 他們沒有耐性把細節告訴你。 | They were not patient enough to tell you the details. |
| 他拒絕示範怎樣操作它。 | He refused to demonstrate how to operate it. |
| 你無法使用我們的服務台。 | You were unable to access our help desk. |
| 你為了延遲送貨而不高興。 | You're not happy with the delayed delivery. |
| 你這個禮拜沒有收到任何東西。 | You didn't receive anything this week.<br>複述投訴內容，讓對方覺得你認真聽他的説話。 |

# 找出不滿的原因（對外）

253.mp3

| | |
|---|---|
| 你不滿意我們的顧客服務。 | You're not satisfied with our customer service. |
| 你記得日期和時間嗎？ | Do you remember the day and time? |
| 何時發生的？ | When did it happen?<br>同 When did it take place? |
| 你記得那天誰為你服務？ | Do you remember who serve you that day? |
| 誰接聽你的電話？ | Who picked up your call? |
| 誰處理你上次的來電？ | Who handled your last call? |
| 對話內容是甚麼？ | What's the content of the conversation? |
| 你覺得我們的代表怎樣冒犯你？ | How did you find that our representative offended you? |
| 你可以描述他說了甚麼？ | Can you describe what he said? |
| 讓我肯定我明白這些…… | Let me make sure I've got this right then...... |
| 你看到買回來的貨品有問題。 | You've seen the fault in an item you bought. |
| 你覺得他不在乎。 | You felt that he didn't care.<br>You felt that he......<br>你覺得他……<br>You felt that he wasn't responsible.<br>你覺得他不負責任。<br>You felt that he didn't want to answer your basic questions.<br>你覺得他沒有回答你基本的問題。 |

254.mp3 

| | |
|---|---|
| 她沒有回答你任何問題。 | She didn't answer any of your questions. |
| 那件產品未如你想應有的質素。 | The product doesn't work as you thought it should. |
| 我們的員工沒有做到承諾。 | Our staff didn't make good on a promise. |
| 他忽略你的要求。 | He ignored your request. |
| 他重複了你的訂單。 | He duplicated your order. |
| 你不滿意他草率的態度。 | You're not satisfied with his careless manner.<br>You're not satisfied with his...... manner.<br>你不滿意他……的態度。<br>You're not satisfied with his rude manner.<br>你不滿意他粗魯的態度。<br>You're not satisfied with his sloppy manner.<br>你不滿意他馬虎的態度。 |
| 下載遊戲很慢。 | The games are slow to download. |
| 沒有網上服務。 | The online services are not available. |
| 你為此而不愉快。 | You're unhappy with this. |
| 你有接通困難。 | You are experiencing connecting problems.<br>同 You are experiencing linking problems.<br>你有接通困難。 |
| 以你的觀點，每個在這裏工作的人都態度不佳。 | From your perspective, everyone who works here has a bad attitude. |
| 你受到勢利的態度對待。 | You got a hit of the snobby attitude. |

255.mp3

| | |
|---|---|
| 你有兩次被自大的態度對待。 | You got serious snotty attitude both times. |
| 所以你想我們退款。 | So you want money back. |
| 你現在要求換貨。 | You're asking to exchange the product. |
| 你想退貨。 | You want to return it. |
| 你想我們修理一下。 | You'd like us to do some repair. |
| 我們的服務並沒有達到你的期望。 | You expected something from us that didn't occur. |
| 營業人員沒有提供配合你需要的產品。 | The sale person didn't match the product with your need. |
| 他沒有尊重你。 | He didn't treat you with respect. |

He didn't treat you with......
他沒有……你。
He didn't treat you with care.
他沒有關注你。
He didn't treat you with understanding.
他沒有理解你。

| | |
|---|---|
| 她沒有給予專業意見。 | She didn't give professional advice. |
| 你無法相信，我們的職員會那樣做。 | You can't believe that our staff would act the way they do. |
| 你不會再光臨。 | You will never revisit. |
| 那件產品不符合你的要求。 | The product didn't meet your requirement. |

# 道歉與認同對方感受（對外）

256.mp3

| | |
|---|---|
| 我或許搞錯。 | I might be wrong. |
| 很抱歉，你那麼失望。 | I'm sorry that you're so frustrated. |
| 對不起，這似乎肯定有錯。 | I'm sorry there certainly seems to be a mistake. |
| 我為那瑕疵道歉。 | I apologise for the defect. |
| 我為曾發生的事情而道歉。 | I'd like to apologize for what happened. |
| 對不起，你沒有如期收到那件產品。 | I'm sorry that you haven't received the product as promised. |
| 我為錯失向顧客提供更佳服務而道歉。 | I apologize for the missed opportunity to serve the customer better. |
| 請接受我的個人道歉。 | Please accept my personal apology. |
| 我為你使人遺憾的經驗致歉。 | My apology for your unfortunate experience. |

My apology for......
我為……致歉。
My apology for inconvenience.
我為不便之處致歉。
My apology for the inappropriate behaviour.
我為不適當的行為致歉。

| | |
|---|---|
| 很抱歉，你今天要打電話來。 | I'm sorry that you had to make this call today. |
| 我為你感到失望抱歉。 | I'm sorry for any frustration you may have experienced. |

257.mp3

| | |
|---|---|
| 這個誤會帶給你不便，很抱歉。 | I'm sorry for any inconvenience this misunderstanding may have caused you. |
| 很抱歉，我為你遭遇的問題感到難受。 | I'm sorry, I feel awful about your problem. |
| 我為這個誤會感到抱歉。 | I'm sorry for the misunderstanding. |
| 我們認真為中斷的網上服務而致歉。 | We sincerely apologize that the internet were disrupted. |
| 我想再次為不便之處致歉。 | I'd like to apologize again for the inconvenience. |
| 關於這場誤會，非常抱歉。 | I'm terribly sorry about the misunderstanding. |
| 我明白你很失望。 | I understand your frustration.<br>道歉後，立即表示理解的感受，容易讓對方紓緩情緒。 |
| 我明白你在説甚麼。 | I understand what you're saying. |
| 可想而知你對這件事的感受。 | I can appreciate how you feel about that. |
| 我知道你有合理理由而苦惱。 | I can tell that you have a legitimate reason for being upset. |
| 我可以理解你很憤怒。 | I can understand that you're angry. |
| 這一定真的糟透了。 | It must have been really awful. |
| 糟了，一定令人煩惱。 | Gosh, that must be annoying. |

# 表示跟進（對外）

258.mp3

| | |
|---|---|
| 我會很快解決它。 | I'll fix it quickly. |
| 我會解決它。 | I'm going to fix it. |
| 我們致力快速回應。 | We strive to respond promptly. |
| 這將會正確地辦妥。 | It will be done properly. |
| 我會改正這件事。 | I'm going to make this right. |
| 我仍然在處理這個問題。 | I'm still working on the problem. |
| 希望很快解決到它。 | Hopefully it will be fixed soon. |
| 我們能夠做甚麼讓你感到愉快？ | What can we do to keep you happy? |
| 你預期我們怎樣處理這件事情？ | What do you expect us to do with this? |
| 我們會努力改正這個狀況。 | We'll make effort to correct the situation. |
| 我們馬不停蹄恢復服務。 | We're working around the clock to resume the service.<br>類 We're working around the clock to continue the service.<br>我們會馬不停蹄繼續服務。 |
| 需要三個工作天才能回覆你有何解決辦法。 | It'll take 3 business days to get back to you with a resolution. |
| 我們會盡力而為。 | We'll do everything we can. |

259.mp3

| | |
|---|---|
| 我們會逐步地解決它。 | We'll take steps to solve it. |
| 我們儘快即時解決。 | We'll make immediate relief as soon as possible. |
| 我們正進行發出訊號。 | We're making progress of sending the signals. |
| 我們會做到最好來解決問題。 | We'll try our best to solve the problem. |
| 我會負責這件事。 | I'll take ownership of the issue. |
| 我是幫助你的。 | I'm here to help you. |
| 我想知道你的問題多一些。 | I'm interested in your concern. |
| 對，你有權覺得苦惱。 | Yes, you have a right to be upset. |
| 我會在兩天內給你消息。 | I'll update you in 2 days. |
| 只要糾正好，我就立即聯絡你。 | I'll get back to you once it's been remedied. |
| 讓我解釋我會採取的步驟。 | Let me explain the steps I'll take. |
| 我會查清楚這件事。 | I'll check on that. |
| 我們不會漠視這件事。 | We won't disregard this. |
| 我答應跟進你。 | I promise to follow up with you. |
| 我知道你想得到正面的結果。 | I know what you want is a positive outcome. |

# 解決及道謝（對外）

260.mp3

| | |
|---|---|
| 對不起，我不能那樣做。 | I'm sorry. I can't do that. |
| 我可以這樣做。 | I can do this. |
| 我們可以換它。 | We may replace it. |
| 我們可以換類似的型號給你嗎？ | Can we replace with a similar model? |
| 我們想送你一張獎券。 | We'd like to offer you a gift voucher. |
| 這款型號暫時缺貨。 | This model isn't available at the moment. |
| 沒有完全一樣的貨品。 | An exact replacement isn't available. |
| 我們很抱歉，你這個電話有問題。 | We're sorry that you've had a problem with the phone. |
| 你可以把那隻手錶帶來？ | Could you bring in your watch? |
| 我們的技術員會檢查裝置。 | Our technician will check the settings. |
| 我們樂於為你安排退款。 | We're happy to arrange a refund for you. |
| 你想退款，對嗎？ | You want a refund, right? |
| 需要一個星期完成這類報告。 | It takes about a week to make a report of this sort. |

261.mp3

| | |
|---|---|
| 我們為你下次購物提供折扣。 | We'll offer you money off on their next purchase. |
| 為了補償，我想送你 $100 禮券。 | I'd like to make amends with a $100 gift certificate. |
| 這是不是可接受的解決方法？ | Is it an acceptable solution? |
| 你滿意這個解決方法嗎？ | Are you satisfied with the solution? |
| 你的回應可改善我們的業務。 | Your feedback can improve our business. |
| 我明白你的投訴有理。 | I see there's a good reason for the complaint. |
| 我保證，顧客贏得正確對待。 | We assure that customers deserve to be treated right. |
| 保養只包含製造商的缺失。 | The warranty only covers manufacturer defects. |
| 你沒有延長了的保養期。 | You don't have an extended warranty. |
| 你不可藉保養期來免費修理它。 | You can't get it fixed under warranty. |
| 這是為甚麼我們不能為你提供免費保養服務。 | That's why we can't cover you under the warranty. |
| 我很高興你現在明白。 | I'm glad you understand now. |
| 我們努力保持讓你滿意。 | We strive to keep you satisfied. |

# 經理詢問及指示（對下）

262.mp3

| | |
|---|---|
| 有甚麼問題？ | What's the problem? |
| 你認為他是真正要投訴的顧客嗎？ | Do you think he's a real complainer? |
| 我們的服務有不妥的地方嗎？ | Is there something wrong in our service? |
| 他覺得我們的產品真的有問題嗎？ | Did he have a genuine issue with our product? |
| 他是不是只想得好處的投訴者？ | Is he just a fake complainer? |
| 他只想抱怨一番罷了？ | Does he want to moan only? |
| 他是不是想找免費的好處？ | Is he after something for free? |
| 他可能作假來得到一些好處？ | He may be making a false claim to get some bonus. |
| 她可能為了某一場合穿了它，然後退貨。 | She may wear it for an occasion and then return it. |
| 這些人喜歡對質。 | These folks enjoy confrontation. |
| 他的投訴似乎不是有效的投訴。 | He seems not to have a valid complaint. |

經理聽了下屬匯報後，憑經驗決定那些投訴人是不是真的發現問題而投訴，還是為了得到公司息事寧人而送出的免費優惠。

| | |
|---|---|
| 或者他心情不好。 | Maybe he's in a bad mood. |

263.mp3

| | |
|---|---|
| 你要避免採取戒備姿態。 | You have to resist getting defensive. |
| 再謹慎問他來決定因由。 | Ask him carefully again to determine the cause. |
| 別打斷他，就算你明知道他要説甚麼。 | Don't interrupt him even if you think you know what he's going to say. |
| 表現得你正在聆聽。 | Show him that you're listening. |
| 讓他講完整件事。 | Let him tell you the whole story. |
| 讓他宣洩感受。 | Let her vent her feelings. |
| 讓他覺得你在留心聽他説甚麼。 | Make him feel like you pay attention to what he's said. |
| 易地而處。 | Put yourself in his shoes. |
| | "Put yourself in one's shoes" 是俗語，意思是以別人的角度去看事情。 |
| 當你見他的時候，要表現得很專心。 | When you meet him, demonstrate attention. |
| 當你聽他説話的時候，保持眼神接觸。 | Keep eye contact while you're listening to him. |
| 之後，你可以評估如何做。 | After that, you may assess what to do. |
| 大家來正確評估這個情況。 | Let's make the proper assessment of the situation. |
| 承認你忽略了。 | Admit that you neglected. |

264.mp3

| | |
|---|---|
| 別說對不起，因為她明顯在撈免費的好處。 | Don't say sorry because obviously she's after something for free. |
| 你獲得所有事實前，不應該承認錯誤。 | You shouldn't admit fault until you get all the facts. |
| 只說「對不起」來道歉不合符他的標準。 | Apologise by saying sorry it isn't up to his standard. |
| 道歉看來真誠是很重要的。 | It is essential that the apology appears genuine. |
| 道歉應該表現出我們的確在乎顧客。 | An apology should show that we care about the customer. |
| 道歉後要表示理解。 | Express empathy after an apology. |
| 你有錯。 | You're at fault. |
| 別以為顧客針對個人。 | Don't take the customer personally. |
| 讓我們想出賠償。 | Let's figure out compensation. |
| 給他公平的賠償。 | Offer him fair compensation. |
| 別給任何賠償。 | Do not offer any compensation. |
| 給他 $100 贈券。 | Offer him a $100 coupon. |

Offer him......
給他……。
Offer him a replacement.
給他替換貨品。
Offer him discounts.
給他打折。

265.mp3

| | |
|---|---|
| 給他打九折作為道歉。 | Offer a 10% discount as an apology. |
| 給他退款。 | Provide him a refund. |
| 為遲了送貨而道歉。 | Apologize for the late delivery. |
| 全權負責這個問題。 | Take ownership of the problem. |
| 向她提供以公司政策為根據的解決方案。 | Offer a company-based policy solution to her. |
| 我們不會送太多免費禮物。 | We won't give a lot of freebies away. |
| 這樣做會幫助肯定他會再來光顧。 | It may help to ensure that he'll return to us. |
| 我明白有些人喜歡吹毛求疵。 | I understand that some people like to pick faults. |
| 告訴他你確保這不會再發生。 | Tell him that you're sure it won't happen again. |
| 記得記錄他說過甚麼。 | Remember to record what he said. |
| 對話時，做筆記。 | Take notes during the conversation. |
| 記下通電時說的重要事情。 | Jot down important things being said during the call. |
| 保存相關文件記錄。 | Keep the documentation. |
| 如果他再投訴，文件記錄可證明你是對的。 | The documentation may back you up if he complains again. |

# 向經理解釋及匯報（對上）

266.mp3

| | |
|---|---|
| 有一位顧客投訴。 | A customer made a complaint. |
| 我的客戶提出嚴正的投訴。 | My client lodged a serious complaint. |
| 我們沒有準時退貨。 | We didn't return the product in good time. |
| 他投訴那些食物。 | He was complaining about the food. |
| 他因為延誤而不高興。 | He was not happy about the delay. |
| 我們誤了限期。 | We missed the deadline. |
| 我們的營業職員搞亂了他的訂單。 | Our sale staff mixed up his order. |
| 他想要退款。 | He wants a refund. |
| 她為我們引起的不便而要求賠償。 | She requested compensation for the inconvenience we caused. |
| 那位顧客投訴產品壞了。 | The customer complained that the product has broken. |
| 有一位顧客因有問題來找我。 | A customer came to me with a problem. |
| 那產品有問題。 | There was a problem with the product. |
| 他想來辦公室當面談。 | He'd like to come to the office and talk in person. |
| 那麼我們無法有效率地解決這個情況。 | So we can't resolve the situation effectively. |

🎧 267.mp3

| | |
|---|---|
| 如何應付只想得好處的投訴者？ | How to deal with the fake complainer? |
| 這是很難處理的個案。 | This is a tough one. |
| 他起來很生氣。 | He sounds angry. |
| 很難應付他。 | It's difficult to deal with him. |
| 他想換取很多好處。 | He wants a lot in return. |
| 他拒絕付帳單。 | He refused to pay the bill. |
| 他堅持説，這是我們的錯。 | He persisted in saying that it's our fault. |
| 他以合理的態度投訴。 | He complained in a reasonable manner. |
| 在我看來，他想得到一些我們不該給的東西。 | It seems to me that he wants to get something that he's not entitled to be given. |
| 我可以做甚麼來糾正它？ | What can I do to make things right? |
| 你對這個個案有甚麼意見？ | What are your opinions on this case? |
| 如果你收到這個投訴，你會怎樣反應？ | How would you have responded if you received this complaint? |
| 他從不滿意。 | He's never satisfied. |
| 他一味説有不妥當的地方。 | He just kept saying there's something wrong. |

268.mp3

| | |
|---|---|
| 他不欣賞我們解決它的努力。 | He didn't appreciate our effort to resolve it. |
| 她聲稱，我們沒有採取行動跟進。 | She claimed that we didn't take any action to follow up. |
| 她沒有等候我的回應就大聲嚷道。 | She yelled and didn't wait for my response. |
| 我嘗試讓他發洩心裏的沮喪。 | I tried to allow him to get his frustration out.<br>同 I tried to allow him to vent his frustration. |
| 我告訴了他，我明白他的失望。 | I've told him that I understood his frustrations. |
| 他對我大聲嚷叫。 | He was yelling at me. |
| 她打電話進來大叫。 | She called in screaming. |
| 他很難滿足。 | He's difficult to satisfy. |
| 我嘗試殷勤。 | I've tried to be courteous. |
| 我問了一些基本的問題。 | I asked some basic questions. |
| 我問了他去看看，它是不是正確接駁了數據機。 | I've asked to check if it was properly connected to the modem. |
| 他提及，他甚麼也沒有做，只是開機而已。 | He mentioned he didn't do anything other than turn it on. |
| 我請他告訴我，他用甚麼來開它。 | I asked him to tell me what he used to open it. |

269.mp3

| | |
|---|---|
| 我的即時反應是叫他找收據。 | My immediate response was that I asked him to look for the receipt. |
| | My immediate response was that......<br>我即時反應是……。<br>My immediate response was that I said sorry.<br>我即時反應是我說對不起。<br>My immediate response was that I explained the procedures.<br>我即時反應是我解釋程序。 |
| 根據他說，他只是切斷它。 | According to him, all he did was disconnect it. |
| 我讓他重複又重複同樣的說話。 | I let him repeat the same thing over and over again. |
| 對，我明天回覆。 | Yes, I'll call back tomorrow. |
| 我不能直接解決問題。 | I can't solve the problem directly. |
| 我花了時間解釋他如何容易改計劃。 | I took the time to explain how he may change the plan easily. |
| | I took the time to explain how he may......<br>我花了時間解釋他如何……。<br>I took the time to explain how he may retrieve the information.<br>我花了時間解釋他如何擷取資訊。<br>I took the time to explain how he may install the software.<br>我花了時間解釋他如何裝置軟件。 |
| 我以專業態度陳述事實。 | I stated the facts in a professional manner. |
| 我以正面的反應回應了。 | I've responded with a positive response. |

# 向同事投訴（一般）

270.mp3

| | |
|---|---|
| 你有時間嗎？ | Do you have time? |
| 我想討論我們的工作。 | I'd like to discuss our work. |
| 你何時有些時間談？ | When do you have some time to talk? |
| 為了某些原因，我為你感到難過。 | For some reason, I'm kind of upset with you. |
| 我的目標是進行解決問題的討論。 | It's my goal to have problem-solving discussions.<br>It's my gaol to......<br>我的目標是……。<br>It's my goal to look for a productive solution.<br>我的目標是尋找富成效的解決方案。<br>It's my goal to create a way we can work better.<br>我的目標是想出我們能做得更好的方法。 |
| 你把最後一分鐘的工作丟給我。 | You dump last-minute work on me. |
| 你本來可以避免這樣做。 | You could've avoided doing so. |
| 你在幾乎傍晚時才把它發出來。 | You don't assign it out until late afternoon. |
| 與你一起工作令我不好過。 | I am having a hard time working with you. |
| 你屢次早走。 | You leave early frequently. |
| 你在項目最後的幾個星期放假。 | You took days off during the last few weeks of the project. |

271.mp3

| | |
|---|---|
| 你經常丟下我一個人工作。 | You often leave me to work alone. |
| 你濫用彈性工作時間。 | You abuse flextime. |
| 你在最後一分鐘改變你的計劃表。 | You changed your schedule at the last minute. |
| 你喜歡來來去去，沒有謹守崗位。 | You come and go as you please. |
| 你搞糟我的工作安排。 | It is screwing up my work schedule. |
| 所以我沒法放我該放的假期。 | So I can't take time off that I'm entitled to. |
| 小組其他成員無法制訂計劃。 | The rest of the group can't make plans. |
| 與你一起工作，我不能計劃任何事情。 | I can't make plans when I work with you. |
| 這樣已經三個月了。 | This has been going on for 3 months. |
| 我們可以怎樣做來解決它？ | What can we do to fix it? |
| 我們可以怎樣確保，我準時收到資料？ | How can we be sure that I can get the data on time? |
| 你幾乎每天遲到，令我們感到為難。 | We're having problem with your being late almost every day.<br>同 We're having problem with your arriving in late almost every day. |
| 大部分時間，你都不在。 | Most of the time, you're not here. |

272.mp3

| | |
|---|---|
| 你不在辦公室時，我們就要接你客戶的電話。 | We have to pick up your client's call when you're not in your cubicle. |
| 恐怕你講了太多私人電話。 | I'm afraid that you have too many personal calls. |
| 我們經常不能把電話接通到你的線上。 | We often can't put calls through on your line. |
| 客戶不停煩我，因為你不回覆他們。 | The clients bug me because you don't get back to them. |
| 我無法處理所有客戶。 | I can't take care of all the clients. |
| 解答你所有客戶的問題不是我的工作。 | It's not my job to answer your clients' questions. |
| 他們甚至說，他們不能留口訊給你。 | They even said that they're not able to leave a voice mail message for you. |
| 你的客戶很失望，要用很多時間解釋。 | Your clients are frustrated and it takes a lot of time to explain. |
| 用我的時間來頂替你不公平。 | It's not fair to use my time to cover you like that. |
| 讓我們確認它。 | Let's acknowledge it. |

Let's......it.
讓我們……它。
Let's face it.
讓我們面對它。
Let's fix it.
讓我們解決它。

# 向經理投訴（對上）

273.mp3

| | |
|---|---|
| 有一個理據充分的投訴。 | I had a valid complaint. |
| 我是客觀地評估這項投訴。 | I've evaluated this complaint objectively. |
| 我現在可以在走廊跟你談嗎？ | Can I talk to you in the hallway now? |
| 我今天可以私下見你嗎？只是10分鐘。 | May I meet you in private today? Just 10 minutes. |
| 我已經給他一個解決問題的機會。 | I've given him a chance to fix the problem. |
| 我已經找到問題。 | I've identified a problem. |
| 我跟約翰有問題。 | I have issues with John. |
| 我直接跟她說。 | I've talked to her directly. |
| 他太暴躁，不能聽我說。 | He was too explosive to listen to me.<br>He was too...... to listen to me.<br>他太……，不能聽我說。<br>He was too angry to listen to me.<br>他太憤怒，不能聽我說。<br>He was too defensive to listen to me.<br>他太有戒心，不能聽我說。 |
| 這不是針對人的投訴，這是生意上的問題。 | It's not a personal complaint, but a business problem. |

274.mp3

| | |
|---|---|
| 這不是第一次他忽略我們的要求。 | It's not the first time he ignored my request. |
| 我已經給他機會解釋他對此事的看法。 | I've given him the opportunity to explain his side of the story. |
| 我冷靜着手處理問題。 | I approached the problem with calm. |
| 我想你為此事做些事情。 | I want you to do something about it. |
| 他偷辦公室文具。 | He stole office supplies. |
| 文具也許要鎖上保存。 | The supplies may be kept under lock and key. |
| 很多她的電話傳過來我接。 | There are many of her calls rolling over to me. |
| 他的電話經常接不通。 | His line is always tired up. |
| 他的客戶向我投訴，他們無法收到他的回覆。 | His clients complained to me that they couldn't get his calls back. |
| 我的客戶最後要留言到我的留言信箱，因為我整天接聽他的電話。 | My clients wind up going to my voice mail because I answer his calls during the day. |
| 他打很多私人電話。 | He makes a lot of personal calls. |
| 他的大部份電話是私人的。 | Most of his calls are personal. |
| 你也看到，他經常出席會議遲到。 | As you can see, he often shows up late for meetings. |

275.mp3

| | |
|---|---|
| 他經常喝咖啡休息而不工作。 | He missed work by taking frequent coffee breaks. |
| 他就是漠視限期。 | He just ignored the deadline. |
| 我努力趕限期，但他把工作擱置一旁。 | He put it aside while I worked hard to meet the deadline. |
| 我要趕及限期有困難。 | I've had trouble meeting the deadlines. |
| 他不能跟上項目進度。 | He failed to meet the project schedule. |
| 他在限期後才做工作。 | He just turned in work after the deadline. |
| 他的工作量比其他小組成員少。 | He works less than other group members. |
| 他不合作。 | He's uncooperative. |
| 我很努力嘗試調配工作以迴避她令人煩厭的習慣。 | I've tried very hard to work around her annoying habits. |
| 我主動多做一些工作來幫助他。 | I went out of my way to help him. |
| 他的行為真的很差。 | His behaviour was really bad. |
| 作為他的作業主管，請你儘快妥善處理。 | As his line manager, please sort it as soon as possible. |
| 如果你不理睬，我就找人事部。 | If you ignore it, I'll go to HR. |

276.mp3

| | |
|---|---|
| 我沒有從他那邊收到任何數據。 | I didn't receive any data from him. |
| 他沒有按工作進度把分析傳給我。 | He didn't pass me the analysis on schedule. |
| 我已經把數據交給他，但他說他找不到。 | I've given him the data but he said he couldn't find it. |
| 我會很感激，如果你跟他相談這件事。 | I'd appreciate it if you can talk to her about this. |
| 他對我說關於性的言詞。 | He made sexual remarks to me. |
| 這樣太過份了。 | This was going too far. |
| 我有時候能與他對質，若他公開地表現無禮。 | Sometimes I'm able to confront him when he's openly nasty. |
| 他在幾次場合中騷擾我。 | He has harassed me on a few occasions. |
| 他昨天所做的騷擾令人震驚。 | The harassment he made yesterday was shocking. |
| 我已經告訴他，這是騷擾。 | I've told him that it was harassment. |
| 但他沒有停下來，仍然那樣說話。 | But he didn't stop talking like that. |
| 這是侮辱。 | It was insulting. |
| 我不認為公司可以容忍它。 | I don't think the company can tolerate it. |

# 經理調停（對下）

277.mp3

| | |
|---|---|
| 聽到你有這壓力的情況，很抱歉。 | I'm so sorry to hear about your stressful situation. |
| 我很抱歉你要經歷這件事。 | I'm sorry that you had to go through this. |
| 我會嘗試跟她談。 | I'll try to talk to her. |
| 我會找出事實。 | I'll find out the facts. |
| 我會跟進。 | I'll follow up. |
| 你可以提出更多細節？ | Can you give me more details? |
| 你有證據嗎？ | Do you have any proof? |
| 有其他同事知道嗎？ | Do any other coworkers know that? |
| 你曾經跟他説嗎？ | Have you ever talked to him? |
| 他的反應如何？ | What was his response? |
| 自此他有改善？ | Did he improve since then? |
| 我已經留意到一段時間。 | I've noticed this for some time. |
| 表面來看，這會破壞團隊工作。 | Apparently, that's spoiled the team work. |
| 有沒有你誤解他説話的可能？ | Would it possible that you misunderstood his words? |
| 這個投訴可能牽涉歧視。 | This complaint may involve discrimination. |

278.mp3

| | |
|---|---|
| 請等候，我會調查。 | Please wait and I'll investigate. |
| 希望事情升級到人事部前，我們解決它。 | Hope that we can settle it before things get escalated to HR. |
| 衝突是無可避免的。 | Conflict is inevitable. |
| 爭執發生了。 | A dispute has come up. |
| 讓我們有建設性地處理衝突。 | Let's handle conflicts constructively. |
| 新想法將會被實行。 | New ideas are being implemented. |
| 管理你們兩位是我的職責。 | It's my job to supervise you both. |
| 請坐下來想出解決辦法。 | Let's sit down to come up with a solution. |
| 今天我們設立這調停會議。 | Today we've set up this mediation meeting. |
| 你需要處理你自己的期望。 | You need to manage your own expectations. |
| 請成為彼此支持的團隊成員。 | Please be a supportive team player. |
| 面對這件事吧，我們沒有人喜歡對抗的。 | Let's face it, none of us like confrontation. |
| 這是公司應該運作的方式。 | That's how a company works. |
| 我欣賞你們的周詳考慮。 | I appreciate your discretion. |

# 向下屬傳遞壞消息（對下）

279.mp3

| | |
|---|---|
| 我想討論一個很艱難的題目。 | I want to discuss a difficult topic. |
| 請問你 2 點鐘能到我的辦公室嗎？ | Can you please come to my office at 2? |
| 我不能在電話中討論。 | I can't discuss it over the phone. |
| 需要面對面討論。 | This discussion needs to take place face-to-face. |
| 我有一些重要的事情談。 | I have something very important to talk about. |
| 請坐。 | Please sit down. |
| 你好嗎？ | How are you doing?<br>當下屬進入房間後，先請他坐下再問候一番。 |
| 你已經在這裏工作 3 年了。 | You've been working for 3 years here. |
| 我真的很欣賞你一直為這個項目的付出。 | I really appreciate you've been doing for the project. |
| 讓我坦白跟你説。 | Let me be honest with you. |
| 我不轉彎抹角。 | I don't beat around the bush.<br>俗語 "beat around the bush" 意思是説話繞圈子，即廣東話的「帶人遊花園」。 |
| 我有壞消息説給你聽。 | I have bad news to deliver. |
| 我現在給你壞消息。 | I'm giving you some bad news. |

280.mp3

| | |
|---|---|
| 我真的很抱歉要把這件事告訴你。 | I'm truly sorry to have to tell you this. |
| 管理高層已經給我一份解僱通知書。 | The top management has given me a layoff notice. |
| 他們決定終止你項目經理的職位。 | They've decided to terminate your position as project manager. |
| 你的職位被辭掉，因為你表現不佳。 | Your position is being eliminated because of your poor performance. |

Your position is being eliminated because......
你的職位被辭掉，因為……
Your position is being eliminated because of unethical behaviour.
你的職位被辭掉，因為你的不道德行為。
Your position is being eliminated because of job elimination.
你的職位被辭掉，因為職位流失。
Your position is being eliminated because of corporate layoffs.
你的職位被辭掉，因為公司裁員。

| | |
|---|---|
| 你知道將有合併。 | You know there'll be a merger. |
| 會有收購行動。 | There's an acquisition. |
| 這是由於縮減編制。 | It's due to downsizing. |
| 我們正大幅減省成本。 | We're cutting cost significantly. |
| 我們進行大幅開支削減。 | We engaged in significant spending cuts. |
| 減少員工是最後措施。 | Staff reduction is the final resort. |

281.mp3

| | |
|---|---|
| 這導致辭退你的結果。 | This leads to lay you off. |
| 雖然我們已經為你提供訓練，你仍然無法掌握職位要求的技能。 | Although we have provided you for training, you still can't master skills required for the job. |
| 你的表現並沒有改善。 | You were not able to improve your performance. |
| 這個職位是多餘的。 | This position is redundant. |
| 這跟你的表現無關。 | It's nothing about your performance. |
| 結果，我們要在5月1日終止聘任你。 | As a result, we have to terminate your employment effective as of May 1. |
| 因此，你最後的工作日是4月30日。 | Therefore, your last day will be April 30. |
| 我想你明白，這不是你的錯。 | I want you to know that this is not your fault. |
| 對，你被辭退。 | Yes, you're laid off. |
| 我明白這令人震驚。 | I understand it's shocking. |
| 這是即時生效。 | It's effective immediately. |
| 你被要求立即離開辦公室，這是公司政策。 | This is the company policy that you're asked to leave the office immediately. |

282.mp3

| | |
|---|---|
| 你可以在這個會議後，收拾私人物品。 | You may collect your personal items after this meeting. |
| 我會安排職員護送你。 | I've arranged an escort for you. |
| 一位保安員會護送你。 | A security officer will escort you. |
| 你需要幫助收拾私人物品嗎？ | Do you need help packing up your personal belongings?<br>同 Do you need help packing up your personal effects? |
| 你需要在工作的電腦中擷取個人資料？ | Do you need to retrieve any personal information in your work computer? |
| 請你在離開前把門匙和職員證交給珍妮可以嗎？ | Can you please hand in the door keys and ID badge to Jenny before you leave? |
| 或者，我們可以計劃好如何完成仍在進行的工作。 | Maybe we can plan how to wrap up the work-in-progress. |
| 請隨意告訴我，我可以做甚麼來幫助你離職前的日子。 | Please feel free to tell me what I can help you prepare the final day at work. |
| 這個下午我會把你被辭退的消息電郵給同事。 | I'm going email the news of your layoff to the co-workers this afternoon. |
| 你現在感到很大壓力嗎？ | Are you overwhelmed right now? |

283.mp3

| | |
|---|---|
| 有甚麼我可以做來幫助你預備最後一個月？ | Is there anything I can do to help you get ready for the last month? |
| 我很感謝你的忠心效力。 | I really appreciate your loyalty.<br>I really appreciate......<br>我很感謝你的……<br>I really appreciate your excellent performance.<br>我很感謝你的優越表現。<br>I really appreciate your positive work attitude.<br>我很感謝你積極的工作態度。 |
| 最後的工資支票會在兩個星期後發出。 | The last paycheque will be issued in 2 weeks. |
| 將會有遣散費。 | There'll be severance pay. |
| 未來不大可能再開設這職位。 | It's unlikely that the position will be reinstated in the future. |
| 這是通知信。 | Here is the notification letter. |
| 我們致力作出最佳解決方法。 | We're working on the best solutions. |
| 我們很享受與你一起工作。 | I have enjoyed working with you. |
| 我感謝你的協助。 | I've appreciated your help. |
| 你還有其他問題？ | Do you have further questions? |
| 我會解答你所有問題。 | You can get all your questions answered. |

## 相關生字

| | |
|---|---|
| Freebie | 免費禮物 |
| Exchange | 換貨 |
| Paycheque | 工資支票 |
| Severance pay | 遣散費 |
| Return | 退貨 |
| Repair | 修理 |
| Careless | 粗率 |
| Rude | 粗魯 |
| Sloppy | 馬虎 |
| Responsible | 負責任 |
| Angry | 憤怒 |
| Annoying | 令人煩惱 |
| Awful | 糟透 |
| Terrible | 糟糕 |
| Unpleasant | 不愉快 |
| Upset | 苦惱 |
| Snobby | 勢利的 |
| Snotty | 自大的 |

## 應付投訴

面對被別人投訴，自己難免會產生負面情緒。這個時候，更加要冷靜，沉着應付。無論如何，先讓對方覺得你願意擔起負責處理這個情況（in charge of the situation），起碼投訴人不會那麼反感，不會以為你想逃避被埋怨（skip the blame game）。若可以的話，先代表公司致歉，並表示同情理解（sympathetic）他們的感受，這樣他們才會聽你的解釋。提出的解決方法要清晰精簡（clear and concise），讓他們知道你會採取實質行動來改善產品或服務。

# Chapter 10

# 商務談判

# 上司指引（對下）

286.mp3

| | |
|---|---|
| 談判在哪裏舉行？ | When will the negotiation take place? |
| 你有得到甚麼關於對方的資料嗎？ | Did you get information about the opposing party? |
| 你有接觸甚麼人嗎？ | Have you approached anyone else? |
| 你有打聽關於他們公司的甚麼嗎？ | Did you hear anything about their company? |
| 會有其他可能的對手嗎？ | Would there be any other possible competitors? |
| 他們也會跟其他人談判嗎？ | Are they also negotiating with someone else?<br>作為上司，確保談判員做好了事前準備。 |
| 我委派阿健跟你一起合作。 | I'm assigning Ken to work with you. |
| 你們二人會是談判員。 | You both will be the negotiators. |
| 你認為你可以辦妥它嗎？ | Do you think you can take care of it? |
| 你有談判經驗。 | You're experienced in negotiating. |
| 你有足夠的談判經驗。 | You're got enough negotiation experience. |
| 你被期望帶領談判小組。 | You're expected to lead the negotiation team.<br>若不是單人匹馬去談判，找一個富有經驗和個性沉着的下屬帶領談判團。 |
| 為甚麼你認為這些是他們的期望？ | Why do you think these are their expectations? |

287.mp3

| | |
|---|---|
| 以你的意見，他們的期望是甚麼呢？ | In your opinion, what are their expectations? |
| 你有任何文件支持你的計算嗎？ | Do you have any documents to support your estimate?<br>Do you have any...... to support your estimate?<br>你有任何……支持你的計算嗎？<br>Do you have any proof to support your estimate?<br>你有任何證據支持你的計算嗎？<br>Do you have any data to support your estimate?<br>你有任何數據支持你的計算嗎？ |
| 你有支持你的數據嗎？ | What supporting data do you have? |
| 你的估計看來不錯。 | Your estimate looks good. |
| 你的估計有點過份樂觀。 | Your estimate may be a bit too optimistic. |
| 這有説服力。 | It's convincing. |
| 估計的價格應該減少 10%。 | The estimated rate should be reduced by 10%. |
| 你有甚麼假設？ | What assumptions did you make? |
| 告訴他們經濟仍然差勁。 | Tell them the economy is still getting bad. |
| 我們看不到下季市場會蓬勃。 | We don't see the market will be prospering again next season. |
| 他們應該把訂單增至 5,000 件。 | They should increase their order to 5,000 pieces. |

288.mp3

| | |
|---|---|
| 他們下訂的數量比我們預期少。 | Their order is smaller than the amount that we can accept. |
| 這不能填補勞工成本。 | It can't cover our labour cost. |
| 別讓他們延遲提議的日期。 | Don't let them delay the proposed date.<br>明確指出談判目標和底線。 |
| 請問你可否給我看看你怎樣得到這項分析？ | Can you please show me how you process the analysis? |
| 你會透露這些數字嗎？ | Will you reveal these numbers?<br>同 Will you disclose these numbers? |
| 別忽略成本減省。 | Don't overlook reduction in cost. |
| 他們會提出其他數字來分散你們的注意力。 | They distract you by quoting other figures. |
| 如果他們只同意首兩項條件，別妥協。 | Don't compromise if they only agree to the first two conditions. |
| 別表現猶疑。 | Do not show hesitation.<br>Do not show......<br>別表現……。<br>Do not show desperation.<br>別表現得如此渴望達成協議。<br>Do not show impatience.<br>別表現急於成事。 |
| 保持冷靜克制。 | Keep your cool. |
| 當他們的提議太離譜時，別猶疑拒絕。 | Do hesitate to say no when their offer is ridiculous. |

# 向上司保證（對上）

289.mp3

| | |
|---|---|
| 我已經看過他們更新了的網站。 | I've checked out their updated website. |
| 他們會有宣佈。 | They'll make an announcement. |
| 他們看來會改變方案。 | They seem to have a change in the scheme.<br>準備談判，必須好好準備打聽對方有甚麼消息。 |
| 但他們沒有通知我們。 | But they didn't inform us. |
| 我預備了建議書。 | I've prepared a proposal. |
| 我獲得關於他們目標的資料。 | I acquired information about their goals. |
| 我準備好了。 | I'm well prepared. |
| 我有信心。 | I'm confident. |
| 我會好好帶領談判團。 | I'll lead the team well.<br>盡量在上司面前表現自信。 |
| 我讓大衛先陳述我們的立場。 | I'll let David to state our position first. |
| 然後，我會要求對方提出一個數目。 | Then, I'll ask the opposite side to offer a number. |
| 我會跟談判團成員討論。 | I'll discuss with my team. |
| 我相信我們會達成談判協議。 | I believe we can reach the negotiated agreement. |

290.mp3 

| | |
|---|---|
| 他們很清楚認識我們的策略。 | They knew clearly about our strategies. |
| 我們是很好的團隊。 | We're a good team. |
| 他們其中一人經驗較少。 | One of them is less experienced. |
| 我給他更多訓練。 | I'll give him more training.<br>作為中層人員，除了要向上司負責，也要負責承擔訓練的責任。 |
| 我們想出計劃了。 | We've developed a plan. |
| 我會令他們覺得，他們要努力才能得到我們的讓步。 | I'll make them feel that they need to work hard to get a concession. |
| 我們一定不會在第一次議價中給予一切。 | We won't give everything in the first offer for sure. |
| 會徹底實行它。 | It will be thoroughly implemented. |
| 當然，如果他們改變招數，我會適度調整。 | Of course, I'll be adaptive if they changed their tactics. |
| 我已經説服他們，還有談判空間。 | I'll persuade them that there's room for negotiation.<br>I'll persuade them that there's......<br>我已經説服他們……。<br>I'll persuade them that they can't get a better offer.<br>我已經説服他們，他們無法得到更好的開價。<br>I'll persuade them that this is the only option.<br>我已經説服他們，這是唯一的選擇。 |

# 談判團團長召集開會（對下）

291.mp3

| | |
|---|---|
| 我希望這個會議，讓我們有更佳的議價位置。 | I hope this meeting can get us in a better bargaining position. |
| 這將會在我們的辦公室舉行。 | It will take place in our office. |
| 談判會議會有多久？ | How long will the negotiation meeting be? |
| 我們今天會決定我們到底要甚麼。 | We'll decide exactly what we want today.<br>We'll decide what...... today.<br>我們今天會決定……。<br>Today we'll decide what terms are beneficial.<br>我們今天會決定那些條款有利。<br>Today we'll decide what deadlines we can meet.<br>我們今天會決定我們可完成的限期。 |
| 讓我們商量基本的談判招數。 | Let's discuss basic negotiation tactics.<br>類 Let's discuss basic negotiation strategies.<br>讓我們商量基本的談判策略。 |
| 我們會採用進取的方式。 | We'll adopt an aggressive approach. |
| 我想鼓勵你們分享想法。 | I'd like to encourage you to share thoughts. |
| 你們清楚知道這個目標嗎？ | Are you sure about the goal? |
| 明白我們要求甚麼是極重要的。 | It's essential to know what we'll be asking for. |
| 我們要怎樣提交建議？ | How are we to present the proposal? |

| | |
|---|---|
| 我們有甚麼可交易？ | What do we have to trade? |
| 我們有甚麼另外的選擇？ | What alternative do we have? |
| 有隱藏的問題？ | Will there be any hidden issues? |
| 我們需要做甚麼市場調查來支持我們的根據？ | What market research do we need to do to back up our cause? |
| 我們的議價能力是多少？ | What is our bargaining power? |
| 我跟你們合作。 | I'll work with you. |
| 我們是那兩位談判員。 | We'll be the two negotiators. |
| 你要強硬。 | You'll be tough. |
| 我會遷就他們。 | I'll be accommodating.<br>類 I'll be adjusting.<br>我會調節。 |
| 你要嘗試使他們在條款上妥協。 | You'll try to get them to compromise on terms. |
| 我會警告他們，只要他們同意那些條款，談判才繼續下去。 | You may warn them to carry on only if they agree to the terms. |
| 讓他們知道交易不會繼續進行。 | Let them know that the proceedings of the deal won't carry on. |
| 我們會集中在一個問題上。 | We'll concentrate on an issue. |

# 團員發表意見（對上）

293.mp3

| | |
|---|---|
| 對手的反建議會可能有甚麼？ | What will our opponent's counter proposal likely include? |
| 我們可以怎樣回應他們的反建議？ | How can we respond to their counter proposal? |
| 會有甚麼可能的妥協？ | What possible compromises might there be? |
| 我們的 BATNA 是甚麼？ | What's our BATNA?<br>BATNA 是 the Best Alternative to Negotiation Agreement 縮寫。 |
| 這太苛求了。 | It's too demanding. |
| 我們可以好好拒絕這個要求嗎？ | How well can we refuse this request? |
| 他們會從這次談判中期望甚麼結果？ | What outcome will they be expecting from this negotiation? |
| 贏了這次談判對我們來說有甚麼後果？ | What are the consequences for us of winning this negotiation?<br>反 What are the consequences for us of losing this negotiation?<br>輸了這次談判對我們來說有甚麼後果？ |
| 這是我第一次做談判員。 | This is my first time being a negotiator. |
| 你可以給我們指示嗎？ | Can you give us more instructions? |
| 誰會提出第一次的開價？ | Who will offer the initial offer? |
| 我可以如何留意到他們心中的態度？ | How can I notice their mental attitude? |

294.mp3

| | |
|---|---|
| 如果他們堅持本來的開價會怎樣？ | What if they insist their original offer?<br>What if they......?<br>如果他們……會怎樣？<br>What if they don't make any concessions?<br>如果他們不讓步的話會怎樣？<br>What if they demand too much?<br>如果他們要求過份會怎樣？ |
| 你可以示範給我們看？ | Can you give us a demonstration? |
| 請示範你怎樣帶出這份析。 | Please demonstrate how you present the analysis. |
| 我們會採用甚麼談判作風？ | What negotiation style shall we adopt? |
| 我在公餘時間修讀過談判技巧的課程。 | I took a course in negotiation skill in my spare time. |
| 我學過談判的基本技巧。 | I've acquired the basics of negotiation skills.<br>同 I've acquired basic negotiation skills. |
| $4,000 是最差的情況局面嗎？ | Is $4,000 the worst case scenario? |
| 我們會接受這個數字？ | Shall we accept this number? |
| 我應該保持沉默多久？ | How long should I keep silent? |
| 對話停下來我會覺得不安。 | I feel uncomfortable when the conversation stops. |
| 我會重複陳述提議，而不會建議甚麼。 | I'll restate the offers rather than make suggestions. |

# 會後檢討（一般）

295.mp3

| | |
|---|---|
| 會議開始時，你有看到他們的關注點嗎？ | Did you see their concern in the beginning? |
| 在談判過程中，有新問題出現嗎？ | Were there any new problems that arose in the course of negotiation? |
| 你們有回應嗎？ | Do you have any feedback? |
| 誰是他們中間帶頭的呢？ | Who was the leader among them? |
| 他們的談判團團長很防備。 | Their team leader was defensive. |
| 我欣賞那位主要談判員。 | I appreciated the chief negotiator. |
| 那些談判員中有一位不徹底明白這個主題。 | One of the negotiators didn't understand the subject thoroughly. |
| 他們提出最後的數字你們認為如何呢？ | What do you think about the last number they offered? |
| 他們嘗試混淆我們。 | They tried to confuse us. |
| 他們沒有意圖妥協。 | They didn't intend to make compromise. |

They didn't intend to......
他們沒有意圖⋯⋯
They didn't intend to resolve the disputes.
他們沒有意圖解決爭論。
They didn't intend to accept our offer.
他們沒有意圖接納我們的開價。

296.mp3

| | |
|---|---|
| 你滿意我們這樣達成的交易？ | Are you satisfied how we closed the deal? |
| 你們滿意結果嗎？ | Are you satisfied with the outcome?<br>同 Are you satisfied with the result? |
| 這次交易好嗎？ | Was the deal good? |
| 我們不應該接受第三項選擇。 | We shouldn't have taken the third option. |
| 我們看來有點太激進了。 | We sounded a bit too aggressive. |
| 他們團體出現了分裂。 | There were cracks among them. |
| 我覺得出奇，他竟然透露出限期。 | To my surprise, he gave away a deadline.<br>類 To my surprise, he disclosed bottom line.<br>我覺得出奇，他竟然透露出自己的底牌。 |
| 我猜他們擔心現金流轉。 | I guess they are concerned about their cash flow. |
| 這是為甚麼他們不想要我們提出的最低價。 | That's why they didn't go for the lowest price we offered. |
| 我看不到他們的團結性。 | I didn't see teamwork among them. |
| 我們是成功的談判團。 | We're a successful negotiation team. |
| 我們的調查幫了我們很多。 | Our survey helped us a lot. |
| 結果不理想。 | The outcome isn't desirable. |
| 這是最差的情況局面。 | It was the worst case scenario. |

297.mp3

| | |
|---|---|
| 啊，交易終於完成！ | Gosh, the deal was finalized! |
| 贏得這份合約多好！ | It's so great to win the contract! |
| 謝天謝地，我們續約了。 | Thank god, we renewed the contract. |
| 我們下季可能需要跟進這項交易。 | We may need to follow up the deal next season. |
| 我們僵持不下。 | We were stuck at a deadlock. |
| 他們假裝漠視我們。 | They pretended to ignore us. |
| 他們不信任我們。 | They distrusted us. |
| 他們很少留心我們的論據。 | They paid little attention to our argument. |
| 我們要再談判了。 | We'll have to renegotiate again. |
| 他們轉換了談判員。 | They've changed the negotiator. |
| 從頭來過。 | It'll start all over again. |
| 我們不再讓步。 | We won't give in again. |
| 我要承認他們甚有策略。 | I have to admit that they are strategic. |
| 他們是很難應付的談判員。 | They were difficult negotiators. |
| 他們像敵人那樣應付我們。 | They behaved like an adversary. |

# 控制談判（對外）

298.mp3

| | |
|---|---|
| 謝謝你們同意今天會面。 | Thanks again for agreeing to meet today. |
| 謝謝參與這首次會議。 | Thank you for coming to this initial meeting. |
| 我感謝你們撥冗出席。 | I really appreciate you taking the time. |
| 請坐，來討論建議。 | Let's sit down and discuss the proposal. |
| 大家開始吧。 | Let's get started. |
| 我想儘快解決它。 | I'd like to resolve this as soon as possible. |
| 如果你有話要先説，請別客氣。 | If there's anything you'd like to say first, please be my guest.<br>先讓對方提出建議，方便自己應變。 |
| 這是我們最近的調查。 | Here's our recent survey. |
| 它證明了，我們的產品領導市場。 | It proved that our products are leading the market. |
| 我認為貨品的真實價值比你的提議少。 | I think the real value of the goods was worth less than your offer. |
| 這些產品已經在市場超過兩年了。 | These products have been on the market for more than 2 years. |
| 它的價值比問價更低。 | It was valued below the asking price. |
| 市場似乎衰退了。 | The market is likely to decline. |
| 我相信成本估計是準確的。 | I believe that the cost estimates are accurate. |

299.mp3

| | |
|---|---|
| 這是保守的估計。 | This is a conservative estimate. |
| 這項調查是謹慎檢討消費者的回應。 | This survey is to carefully examine the consumers' feedback. |
| 大公司相信我們的創新設計。 | Major companies trust us with our innovative designs. |

Major companies trust us with our......
大公司相信我們的……
Major companies trust us with our unbeatable price.
大公司相信我們的無以可比的價格。
Major companies trust us with our distribution.
大公司相信我們的分銷量。

| | |
|---|---|
| 它顯示消費者滿意我們的設計。 | It shows that the consumers are satisfied with our design. |
| 這些資料有力證明你們的顧客會繼續用我們的產品。 | It's strongly supporting data that your customers will keep using our products. |
| 你在上次會議也承認這一點。 | You also admit this point in the previous meeting. |
| 我們很高興提議不同的選擇。 | We're happy to suggest different options. |
| 請告訴我你的選項。 | Please tell me about your options. |
| 如果你有其他關注的問題，請告訴我們可以怎樣做。 | If you have any other concerns, please tell us what we can do. |
| 這些選擇是配合你們的需要。 | These options are to accommodate your needs. |

# 堅持原則（對外）

300.mp3

這是我們能夠提出的最低數目。
This is the lowest number that we can offer.

我們不能讓步。
We can't make any concessions.

我們已經開出最好的價錢。
We've offered the best price.

既有這一切有關因素，你知道這是最佳選擇。
Given all the factors involved, you know it's the best option.

其他公司可能提出稍低的數字，但你不會從他們那裏得到最好的售後服務。
Other firms may offer a slightly lower number but you can't get the best after-sale service from them.

別忘記我們的質量穩定。
Don't forget our quality is consistent.

我就是不能進一步妥協。
I just won't further compromise.

你們的要求聽起來不合理。
Your demands didn't sound legitimate.

我們只有 $5,000 預算。
We have only got $5,000 in our budget.

我已經提出最多的了。
I've given out the maximum.

這是一個問題。
That is a problem.

如果對方提了一個不能接受的建議，簡單指出這是你不想接受的「問題」。

我需要得到行政董事同意。
I need to have this agreed by the Executive Director.

301.mp3

| | |
|---|---|
| 如果他們同意這些條件，我們會達成交易嗎？ | If they agree to the conditions, do we have a deal? |
| 我們的經理不會考慮你提出的價錢。 | Our manager will not consider the price you've put forward. |
| 我的經理會拒絕這些條款。 | My manager will refuse the terms. |
| 我很難向經理説明這是對的。 | May be difficult for me to justify it to the manager. |
| 他不會讓我同意的。 | He won't let me agree. |
| 恐怕他的想法有些不同。 | I'm afraid he has something different in mind. |
| 我會跟他説，但我提議你同意作出妥協。 | I'll talk to him, but I'd suggest you to agree to a compromise. |
| 就數量方面，底線是多少？ | What is the bottom line on the amount? |
| 如果我知道你的底線，我可以跟他説，看看我能否為你爭取最大的利益。 | If I know your bottom line, I can talk to him and see if I can fight for your best interest.<br>若你不是最後決策人，就要令對方相信你會為他們着想，讓他們坦白告訴你他們的底線，這會增加你的優勢。 |
| 你要一定提出更好的建議。 | You'll have to do better than that. |

misleading 使人誤解　　unrealistic 不切實際

# 讓步軟化（對外）

302.mp3

| | |
|---|---|
| 如俗語説，你讓一步，反過來我也讓一步。 | As the saying goes, make concessions to get concessions in return. |
| 我願意放棄一些成本高的東西。 | I'm willing to give up something costly. |
| 我想讓步。 | I'd like to make a concession. |
| 別忽略我那麼多的犧牲。 | Don't ignore how much I'm sacrificing.<br>類 Don't ignore how much I've been giving.<br>別忽略我一直提出多少好處。 |
| 你可以把我的開價跟同類公司提出的比較。 | You may compare my offer with those made by similar firms. |
| 我的初步要求是認真和合理的。 | My initial demands are serious and reasonable. |
| 我本來的開價是合理的。 | My original offer was legitimate. |
| 我想縮窄鴻溝。 | I'd like to narrow the wide gap. |
| 我願意增加到最多$20,000。 | I'm willing to increase my offer by a maximum of $20,000. |
| 我樂於讓步。 | I'd be happy to concede. |
| 我們願意就這個問題妥協。 | We are willing to compromise on this issue. |

303.mp3

| | |
|---|---|
| 我認為，我們可以提出這些讓步，不過不會一次過全部退讓。 | I think we can offer all of these concessions, but not all at once. |
| 我們就這個價錢討價還價了好些小時。 | We've been haggling over the price for hours. |
| 嗯，我會提議另一個選擇。 | Well, I'd suggest an alternative. |
| 我要提出我們的一些要求。 | I'd suggest some of our demands. |
| 我預備妥協。 | I'm prepared to compromise. |
| 我們可以再談價錢。 | We're able to reopen the price issue. |
| 我認為雙方可以同意它。 | I think we can both agree to that. |
| 如果你提出扣 5%，我會購買更多服務。 | If you offer a 5% discount, we'd purchase more services. |
| 我們願意調整價錢來配合你的需要。 | We'd accommodate your needs by adjusting the price. |
| 這是一個公平的建議。 | That's a fair suggestion. |
| 我們處於更佳位置來改變建議的場地。 | We're in a better position to change the venue proposed. |
| 我們決定改變我們的立場。 | We've decided to change our position. |
| 我們想出一些雙贏的選擇。 | We came up with options for mutual gain. |

# 消極談判員這樣說……（對外）

304.mp3

| | |
|---|---|
| 市場價格決定一切。 | The market price determines everything. |
| 要求更多沒意義。 | It seems pointless to ask for more. |
| 跟他爭論沒有用。 | There's no point in arguing with them. |
| 他們取得更好的談判地位。 | They've got a better position.<br>類 They've got a dominating position.<br>他們取得支配地位。 |
| 他們在談判中處於優勢地位。 | They had an edge on the negotiation. |
| 在我看來，他們會控制整個討論。 | It seems to me that they'll control the discussion. |
| 我們的喊價可能太高了。 | Our bid is possibly too high.<br>There're so many competitors there......<br>有那麼多對手…… |
| 他可能會去找其他對手。 | He may go to other competitors. |
| 我們能夠預計他會拒絕我們的開價。 | We can predict that he'll refuse our offer. |
| 我們沒有甚麼特別的條件來説服他。 | We don't have anything particular to persuade him. |
| 我聽到其他競爭對手更有説服力。 | I've heard that other competitors are more persuasive. |
| 其他競爭對手比起我們，似乎是更好的談判員。 | Other competitors appear to be better negotiators than us. |

305.mp3

| | |
|---|---|
| 這是難以應付的情況。 | It's a difficult case.<br>類 It's a lousy case.<br>這是極壞的情況。 |
| 我們無法要求更多。 | We're not able to demand more. |
| 我們的要求太高了。 | Our demands are too high. |
| 我們是不是要求得太過份？ | Are we overly demanding? |
| 我們可以調整我們的要求嗎？ | Can we justify our demands? |
| 我發覺這會損害長期關係。 | I found that it may harm the long term relationship. |
| 恐怕這會破壞關係。 | I'm afraid that it'll spoil the relationship.<br>同 I'm afraid that it'll injure the relationship. |
| 這會危及關係嗎？ | Will it jeopardize the relationship? |
| 太多要求會令他們生氣。 | Too many demands will cause them to get mad.<br>Too many demands will cause them to......<br>太多要求會令他們……<br>Too many demands will cause them to terminate the negotiation.<br>太多要求會令他們終止談判。<br>Too many demands will cause them to refuse to continue.<br>太多要求會令他們拒絕繼續。 |
| 我們激進的方法會破壞一切。 | Our aggressive approach will ruin everything. |
| 沒有我們要求更好價格的空間。 | There's no more room that we may ask for a better price. |

# 粗率自大的談判員這樣說……（對外）

306.mp3

| | |
|---|---|
| 如果我透露限期，也沒有損害。 | It won't harm even if I disclose the deadline.<br>類 It doesn't matter even if I disclose the deadline.<br>如果我透露限期，也沒有相干。 |
| 嗯，我知道他們完全無法拒絕。 | Well, I know they won't be able to refuse at all. |
| 我們稍稍遲到不打緊。 | It doesn't matter if we're late a bit. |
| 我是最好的談判員。 | I'm the best negotiator. |
| 他們應該知道，我們處於優勢。 | They should know that we're in a much better position. |
| 我從來沒有輸過談判。 | I've never lost a negotiation. |
| 我總是贏的。 | I always win. |
| 在早些回合他們都沒有任何道理可言。 | They didn't make sense in the previous rounds. |
| 這顯示出，他們無可要求。 | It showed that they can't ask for more. |
| 我一定使他們同意。 | I must get them to agree. |
| 達成交易？完全沒問題。 | Make the deal? Not a problem at all. |
| 我是多麼有經驗，不用任何策略。 | I'm so experienced that I don't need any strategies. |
| 我要給他們看誰在話事。 | I'll show them who's in charge. |

| | |
|---|---|
| 我肯定已在控制一切。 | I can definitely control everything. |
| 我已經預期到他們每一個動作。 | I've predicted every move they'd make. |
| 他們只會重複同樣的説話。 | They'll just repeat the same thing. |
| 他們不會提出甚麼新的建議。 | They won't give anything new. |
| 我不會理會他們説甚麼。 | I'll ignore what they'll say. |
| 我會是那個圓滿完成這次磋商的人。 | I'll be the one who wraps up the discussion. |
| 他們其實不知道怎樣談判。 | They actually don't know how to negotiate. |
| 我會很快打敗他們。 | I'll knock them out fast. |
| 我認為這些數據完全不能幫助我們。 | I don't think the data can help us at all. |
| 成功的談判員自有正面的看法。 | Successful negotiators have a positive vision. |

knock out 打敗　　wrap up 圓滿完成

# 上司鼓勵（對下）

308.mp3

| | |
|---|---|
| 你只是需要更多經驗。 | You just need more experience. |
| 讓步好幾次是蠻平常。 | It's pretty normal to make concessions a couple times. |
| 談判是令雙方勝利的藝術。 | Negotiation is an art of making both parties win. |
| 你要求更多是沒有損害的。 | It doesn't harm when you ask for more. |
| 別向他們的提議讓步。 | Don't give in their proposal. |
| 對我來說，他們可以提出更好的價錢。 | To me, they can offer a better price. |
| 記住，你總是可以要求一些免費的東西。 | Remember, you may always ask for something for free. |
| 你將會知道他們不是那麼好的。 | You'll know that they're not that good. |
| 不，我不認為他們是更好的談判員。 | No, I don't think they are better negotiators. |
| 對，他們很有技巧。但我們擅於謀劃！ | Yes, they're skilful. But we're tactical! |
| 別擔心，我們的談判團是很出色的。 | Don't worry. Our negotiation team is excellent. |
| 我注意到你擔心商務關係的問題。 | I noticed your concern about the business relationship. |

309.mp3

| | |
|---|---|
| 但我們只想要協議。 | But we just want agreement. |
| 你只看消極的一面。 | You just see the negative side. |
| 這樣是沒有幫助的。 | It doesn't help. |
| 別把它當作人身攻擊。 | They won't take it personally. |
| 大家作為團隊一起克服障礙。 | Let's overcome the obstacles as a team. |
| 經歷談判過程需要忍耐。 | Be patient when going through negotiations. |
| 別期望我們會很快完成談判。 | Don't expect we may finish with things quickly. |
| 別那麼容易妥協。 | Don't compromise so easily. |
| 如果你立場不穩，你得不到應得的東西。 | If you don't stand firm, you wouldn't gain what you deserve. |
| 如果你表現軟化，他們不會讓步的。 | If you appear to be soft on people, they won't concede. |
| 別向他們表現出你會向壓力屈服。 | Don't show them that you're yield to pressure. |
| 談判本身是充滿壓力的。 | Negotiation is stressful itself. |
| 先戰勝恐懼吧。 | You conquer fear first. |
| 積極些，他不可能拒絕我們最後的喊價。 | Be positive. He may not be able to refuse our final bid. |

# 上司告誡（對下）

310.mp3

| | |
|---|---|
| 他們為了這場談判聘請了一位顧問。 | They've hired a consultant for the negotiation. |
| 我認識那個帶領談判團的人。 | I know the guy who led their team. |
| 他有談判經驗。 | He's experienced in negotiation. |
| 我聽講他們接觸了某些人。 | I heard that they've contacted someone else. |
| 我不同意你的觀點。 | I don't agree to your points. |
| 就事實來說，你不能支配整個過程。 | As a matter of fact, you won't be able to dominate the entire process. |
| 這是團隊工作。 | It's teamwork. |
| 你是談判團的一部分。 | You're a part of the team. |
| 作為團員，遵照計劃好的策略。 | As a team member, follow the strategy as planned. |
| 事前準備是談判過程的一部分。 | Preparation is part of the negotiation process. |
| 缺乏準備工夫只是證明你的慵懶。 | Lack of preparation just proves your laziness. |
| 你應該服從團長。 | You should be subordinate to the team leader. |
| 你應該學習聆聽。 | You should learn to listen. |

## 相關生字

| | |
|---|---|
| Bid | 喊價 |
| Bottom line | 底線 |
| Compromise | 妥協 |
| Concession | 讓步 |
| Concede | 讓步 |
| Negotiator | 談判員 |
| Opponent | 對手 |
| The opposite side | 對方 |
| The opposing party | 對手 |
| Condition | 條件 |
| Term | 條款 |
| Trade-off | 交換 |

## 談判技巧

談判技巧是一門高深的學問，因為你要事先做好準備，最好掌握到對方的短處和弱點，在對決時，才會得心應手。除此之外，必須了解我方的目標（goal）、利益（interests）、底線（bottom line）和最佳結果（the best outcome）。在解決問題（problem-solving）的大前提下，談判最理想的結果是雙方在離開談判桌時，都取得各自的好處（mutual gain）。談判技巧不僅要求談判員能言善辯，他們還得要積極聆聽（active listening），並有相當的草擬寫作（draft writing）技巧，因為達成協議後便要立即寫下談判內容，以準備合約文件。

# 自學商務英語：實況溝通123篇


編著

明朗兒

編輯

Kiyon Wong／Alvin

講讀

Christopher Musni

美術設計

Venus Lo

排版

劉葉青

出版者

萬里機構出版有限公司

香港鰂魚涌英皇道1065號東達中心1305室

電話：2564 7511

傳真：2565 5539

電郵：info@wanlibk.com

網址：http://www.wanlibk.com

http://www.facebook.com/wanlibk

發行者

香港聯合書刊物流有限公司

香港新界大埔汀麗路 36 號

中華商務印刷大廈 3 字樓

電話：2150 2100

傳真：2407 3062

電郵：info@suplogistics.com.hk

承印者

創藝印刷有限公司

出版日期

二零一八年八月第一次印刷





Published in Hong Kong

ISBN 978-962-14-6810-9